WITHDRAWN

LARGE PRINT LIN
LINDSEY, JOHANNA.
A HEART SO WILD /

A
Heart
So Wild

Also available in Large Print
by Johanna Lindsey:

Brave the Wild Wind
A Gentle Feuding
Love Only Once
Tender is the Storm
When Love Awaits

A
Heart
So Wild

Johanna Lindsey

G.K.HALL &CO.
Boston, Massachusetts
1987

For Dorene and Jerry, best friends,
best cousins, and for being there
always.

Published in Large Print by arrangement with
Avon Books.

British Commonwealth rights courtesy of
Transworld Publishers Limited.

G.K. Hall Large Print Book Series.

Set in 18pt Plantin.

Library of Congress Cataloging-in-Publication Data

Lindsey, Johanna.
  A heart so wild.

  (G.K. Hall large print book series)
  1. Large type books.   I. Title.
[PS3562.I5123H4   1987]   813'.54   87-8604
ISBN 0-8161-4301-3 (lg. print)

Chapter 1

Kansas, 1868

Elroy Brower slammed down his mug of beer in annoyance. The commotion across the saloon was distracting him from the luscious blonde sitting on his lap, and it was seldom Elroy got his hands on as tempting a creature as Big Sal. It was damned frustrating to keep getting interrupted.

Big Sal wiggled her hefty buttocks against Elroy's crotch, leaning forward to whisper in his ear. Her words, quite explicit, got the results she'd expected. She could feel his tool swelling.

"Whyn't you come on upstairs, honey, where we can be alone?" Big Sal suggested, voice purring.

Elroy grinned, visions of the hours ahead exciting him. He intended to keep Big Sal all to himself tonight. The whore he sometimes visited in Rockley, the town nearest his

1

farmstead, was old and skinny. Big Sal on the other hand, was a real handful. Elroy had already offered up a little prayer of thanks for having found her on this trip to Wichita.

The rancher's voice, raised in anger, caught Elroy's attention once more. He couldn't help but listen, not after what he'd seen just two days ago.

The rancher told everyone who would listen that his name was Bill Chapman. He'd come into the saloon a short time earlier and ordered drinks for one and all, which wasn't as generous as it sounded because there were only seven people there, and two of them were the saloon girls. Chapman had a ranch a little ways north and was looking for men who were as fed up as he was with the Indians who were terrorizing the area. What had caught Elroy's attention was the word "Indians."

Elroy had had no Indian trouble himself, not yet anyways. But he'd only come to Kansas two years ago. His small homestead was vulnerable, and he knew it—damn vulnerable. It was a mile from his nearest neighbor, and two miles from the town of Rockley. And there was only Elroy himself and young Peter, a hired man who helped with the harvest. Elroy's wife had died six months after they arrived in Kansas.

Elroy didn't like feeling vulnerable, not at all. A huge man, six feet four and barrellike, he was used to his size getting him through life without problems, except for the ones he started himself. No one wanted a taste of Elroy's meaty fists. At thirty-two, he was in excellent condition.

Now, though, Elroy found himself worried about the savages who roamed the plains, intent on driving out the decent, God-fearing folk who'd come to settle there.

They had no sense of fair play, those savages, no respect for even odds. Oh, the stories Elroy had heard were enough to give even him the quivers. And to think he had been warned he was settling damn close to what was designated Indian Territory—that huge area of barrenness between Kansas and Texas. His farm was, in fact, just thirty-five miles from the Kansas border. But it was good land, damn it, right between the Arkansas and Walnut rivers. What with the war over, Elroy had thought the army would keep the Indians confined to the lands allotted them.

Not so. The soldiers couldn't be everywhere. And the Indians had declared their own war on the settlers as soon as the Civil War broke out. The Civil War was over, but the Indians' war was just getting hot. They were more determined than ever not to give up the land they thought of as theirs.

Fear made Elroy listen carefully to Bill Chapman that night, despite his longing to retire upstairs with Big Sal.

Just two days ago, before he and Peter had come to Wichita, Elroy spotted a small band of Indians crossing the west corner of his land. It was the first group of hostiles he had ever seen, for there was no comparing this band of warriors with the tame Indians he'd seen on his travels West.

This particular group numbered eight, well armed and buckskinned, and they'd been moving south. Elroy was concerned enough to follow them, from a distance, of course, and he trailed them to their camp on the fork of the Arkansas and Ninnescah rivers. Ten tepees were erected along the east bank of the Arkansas, and at least another dozen savages, women and children included, had set up home there.

It was enough to turn Elroy's blood cold, knowing this band of either Kiowa or Comanche were camped only a few hours hard ride from his home. He warned his

4

neighbors of the Indians camped so close by, knowing the news would throw them into a panic.

When he arrived in Wichita, Elroy told his tale around town. He'd scared some people, and now Bill Chapman was stirring up interest among the regulars in the saloon. Three men declared they'd ride with Chapman and the six cowhands he'd brought with him. One of the regulars said he knew of two drifters in town who might be inclined to kill a few Injuns, and he left the saloon to go in search of them, see if they were game.

With three enthusiastic volunteers in hand and the chance of two more, Bill Chapman turned his blue eyes on Elroy, who had been listening quietly all this time.

"And what about you, friend?" the tall, narrow-framed rancher demanded. "Are you with us?"

Elroy pushed Big Sal off his lap but kept hold of her arm as he approached Chapman. "Shouldn't you be letting the army chase after Indians?" he asked cautiously.

The rancher laughed derisively. "So the army can slap their hands and escort them back to Indian Territory? That don't see justice done. The only way to insure a thieving Indian don't steal from you again is to kill him so he can't. This bunch of Kiowas slaughtered more'n fifteen of my herd and made off with a dozen prime horses just last week. They've cut into my pocket too many times over these last years. It's the last raid I'm standing for." He eyed Elroy keenly. "You with us?"

Cold dread edged down Elroy's spine. Fifteen head of cattle slaughtered! He had his only two oxen with him, but his other livestock on the farm could have been stolen or butchered in just the one day he'd been away. Without his livestock, he was wiped out. If those Kiowas paid him a visit, he was through.

Elroy fixed his hazel eyes firmly on Bill Chapman. "I saw eight warriors two days ago. I followed them. They've got a camp set up by a fork in the Arkansas River, about thirteen miles from my farm. That's about twenty-seven from here if you follow the river."

"Gawddamn, whyn't you say so!" Chapman cried. He looked thoughtful. "They might be the ones we're after. Yeah, they could've made it that far this soon. Them bastards can travel farther faster than any critter I know of. Were they Kiowas?"

6

Elroy shrugged. "They all look the same to me. But those braves weren't trailing any horses," he admitted. "There was a herd of horses at their camp, though. About forty."

"You gonna show me and my cowhands where they're camped?" asked Chapman.

Elroy frowned. "I got oxen with me to carry a plow back to my farm. I don't have a horse. I'd only slow you down."

"I'll rent you a horse," Chapman offered.

"But my plow—"

"I'll pay to store it while we're gone. You can come back for it, can't you?"

"When are you leaving?"

"First thing in the mornin'. If we ride like hell and if they've stayed put, we can reach their camp by mid-afternoon."

Elroy looked at Big Sal and grinned a huge grin. As long as Chapman wasn't fixing to leave now, Elroy wasn't giving up his night with Big Sal, nossir. But tomorrow . . .

"Count me in," he told the rancher. "And my hired hand, too."

Chapter 2

Fourteen hell-bent men rode out of Wichita the next morning. Young Peter, nineteen, was thoroughly excited. Nothing like this had ever happened to him before. He was thrilled for this chance. And he wasn't the only one, for some of the men simply enjoyed killing, and this was a perfect excuse.

Elroy didn't care much for any of these men. They weren't his kind of people. But all of them had been out West much longer than he had, which made him feel inferior. They all had one thing in common, at any rate. Each had his own reason for hating Indians.

Chapman's three regular hands gave their first names only—Tad, Carl, and Cincinnati. The three gunmen Chapman had hired were Leroy Curly, Dare Trask, and Wade Smith. One of the Wichita men was a traveling dentist with the unlikely name of Mr. Smiley. Elroy didn't understand why so many folks who came West felt the need to change their names, sometimes to suit their occupations, sometimes not. There was the ex-deputy between jobs who had wandered down to Wichita six months ago and was still between jobs. How did he support himself, Elroy wondered, but he knew better than to ask. The third Wichita man was a homesteader like Elroy who'd just happened into the saloon last night. The two drifters were brothers on their way to Texas, Little Joe Cottle and Big Joe.

With hard riding and the hope of picking up a few more men, Chapman led the men into Rockley by noon that day. But the detour gained them only one more man, Lars Handley's son, John. They found there was no hurry, however, because Big Joe Cottle, who'd ridden ahead with an extra mount, met them in Rockley and reported that the Kiowas were still camped on the riverbank.

They reached the Indian campsite in mid-afternoon. Elroy had never in his life ridden so hard. His backside was killing him. The horses were done in, too. He would never have ridden a horse of his own like that.

The trees and lush vegetation growing along the river gave Elroy and the others ample cover. They moved in close and watched the camp, and the roar of the river drowned out the little sounds they made.

It was a peaceful setting. Stately tepees spread out beneath the huge trees. Children tended the horses, and the women were gathered in a group, talking. One lone old man was playing with a baby.

It was hard to imagine that these were bloodthirsty savages, Elroy thought, and that the children would grow up to kill and steal. Why, the women were known to be even worse than the men at torturing captives, or so he'd heard. There was only one warrior visible, but that didn't mean anything. As Little Joe pointed out, there might be other warriors, all taking siestas the way Mexicans did.

"We should wait until tonight, when they're all asleep and unsuspectin'," Tad suggested. "Injuns don't like to fight at night. Somethin' 'bout their dyin' and their spirits bein' unable to find the happy huntin' grounds. A little surprise wouldn't hurt none."

"Seems to me we got surprise on our side right now," Mr. Smiley pointed out. "If those warriors are all napping anyway—"

"They might not even be around."

"Who says? They could be makin' weapons in them tepees, or humpin' their women." Leroy Curly chuckled.

"That'd be a mighty lot of women, then. There's only ten tepees, Curly."

"You recognize any of your horses over there, Mr. Chapman?" Elroy asked.

"Can't say as I do, but they're herded too close to get a good look at 'em all."

"Well, I know Kiowas when I see 'em."

"Don't think so, Tad," Cincinnati disagreed. "I believe they're Comanches."

"How would you know?"

"Same way you *think* you know Kiowas," Cincinnati replied. "I know Comanches when I see 'em."

Carl ignored them both, for Tad and Cincinnati could never agree on anything. "What's the difference? Injuns is Injuns, and this ain't no reservation, so it's sure as hell these aren't tame."

"I'm after the ones that raided—" Bill Chapman interjected.

"Sure you are, boss, but are you willin' to let this band go their merry way if they *ain't* the ones?"

"They could be the ones next year," Cincinnati pointed out as he inspected his gun.

"What the hell's goin' on?" Little Joe demanded. "You mean we blistered our butts all day and now you're thinkin' of turnin' back without killin' 'em? Bullshit!"

"Easy, little brother. I don't reckon that's

11

what Mr. Chapman was thinkin' at all. Was it, Mr. Chapman?"

"Not likely," the rancher said angrily. "Carl's right. It don't make much difference which band of savages we got here. We get rid of this band and others will think twice before they raid around here."

"Then what are we waitin' for?" Peter looked around eagerly.

"Just make sure you save the women for last." Wade Smith spoke for the first time. "I'm gonna have some. For my trouble, see?"

"Now you're talking." Dare Trask chuckled. "And here I thought this was gonna be just another *routine* job."

There was now a new element to the excitement running through the men as they moved back to collect their horses. Women! They hadn't thought of that. Ten minutes later the crack of rifles broke into the silence. When the last shot was fired there were four Indians left alive, three women and one young girl that Wade Smith had found too pretty to pass up. All four of the women were raped many times, then killed.

At sundown, fourteen men rode away. The ex-deputy was the only one of their casualties. As they removed his body from the scene, they felt that his death was a small enough sacrifice.

The camp was quiet after they left, all the screams born away on the wind. Only the roar of the river was heard. There was no one at the camp to mourn the dead Comanches, who were unrelated to the band of Kiowas who had raided Bill Chapman's ranch. There was no one to mourn the young girl who had caught Wade Smith's eye with her dark skin and blue eyes, eyes that gave away the trace of white blood somewhere in her background. None of her people heard her suffer before she died, for her mother had died before they finished raping the girl.

She had marked her tenth birthday that spring.

Chapter 3

"Courtney, you're slouching again. Ladies don't slouch. I swear, didn't they teach you anything in those expensive girls' schools?"

The chastised teenager glanced sideways at her new stepmother, started to say something, then changed her mind. What was the use? Sarah Whitcomb, now Sarah Harte, heard only what she wanted to hear and nothing else. Anyway, Sarah was no longer looking at Courtney, her interest now drawn by the farm just barely visible in the distance.

Courtney straightened her back anyway, felt the muscles around her neck scream in protest, and gritted her teeth. Why was she the only one to feel the lash of Sarah's scolding tongue? Sometimes the older woman's new personality amazed Courtney. Most times, though, Courtney just kept quiet, drawing into herself as she had learned to do to keep out the hurt. It was a rare thing these days when Courtney Harte drew on her old courage, only when she was overly tired and just didn't care anymore.

She hadn't always been a veritable mass of insecurities. She had been a precocious, outgoing child—friendly, mischievous. Her mother used to tease her, saying she had a bit of the devil in her. But her mother had died when Courtney was only six years old.

In the nine years since, Courtney had been sent off to one school after another, her father unable to cope with the demands of a child while he was so deeply in mourning. But apparently Edward Harte had liked the arrangement, for Courtney was allowed to come home only for a few weeks each summer. Even then, Edward never found time to spend with his only child. During most of the war years, he hadn't been at home at all.

At fifteen, Courtney had suffered being unwanted and unloved too long. She was no longer open and friendly. She had become a very private and cautious young girl, so sensitive to the way others treated her that she would withdraw at the slightest hint of disapproval. Her many strict teachers were responsible for some of the girl's awkward shyness, but most of it came from trying continually to regain her father's love.

Edward Harte was a doctor whose thriving practice in Chicago had kept him so busy he rarely found time for anything but his patients. He was a tall, graceful Southerner who had settled in Chicago after his marriage. Courtney thought there was no man handsomer or more dedicated than he. She worshiped her father and died a little every time he looked at her with those vacant eyes, the same honeyed brown as her own.

He had found no time for Courtney before the Civil War, and it was even worse after. The war had done something terrible to this man who ended up fighting against the home he'd come from because of his humanitarian beliefs. After he came home in '65, he had not resumed his practice. He became reclusive, locking himself away in his study, drinking to forget all the deaths he'd been unable to prevent. The Harte wealth had suffered.

If not for the letter from Edward's old mentor Dr. Amos asking Edward to take over his practice in Waco, Texas, Courtney's father would probably have drunk himself to death. Disillusioned Southerners were pouring into the West, looking for new lives, Dr. Amos wrote, and Edward decided to become one of those who chose hope over disillusionment.

This was going to be a new life for Courtney, too. There would be no more schools, no more living away from her father. She would have a chance now to make him see that she wasn't a burden, and that she loved him. It was going to be just the two of them, she told herself.

But when their train was delayed in Missouri, her father had gone and done the inconceivable. He had married their housekeeper of the last five years, Sarah Whitcomb. There had, it seemed, been some mention of the inpropriety of a thirty-year-old woman traveling with Dr. Harte.

Edward didn't love Sarah, and Sarah had eyes for Hayden Sorrel, one of the two men Edward had hired to escort them through the dangerous territory to Texas. The very day of the wedding, Sarah was transformed into a new person. Where she'd once been so kind to Courtney, she was now a veritable shrew—bossy, criticizing, unmindful of anyone's feelings. Courtney had given up trying to understand the change. She simply tried to keep out of Sarah's way. That wasn't easy when five people were traveling by wagon across the plains of Kansas.

Traveling along the Arkansas River since leaving Wichita that morning, they had left the river to see if they could find a homestead or town to spend the night. After all, sleeping under a roof was one of the things they would have to do without once they reached the two-hundred-mile stretch through Indian Territory.

Indian Territory. The name alone was enough to frighten Courtney. But Hayden Sorrel and the other fellow, called simply Dallas, said they had nothing to worry about as long as they took along some cattle to bribe the Indians with. Jesse Chisholm, a half-breed Cherokee, had discovered a comparatively flat route between San Antonio,

Texas, and Wichita. Chisholm used that route to haul merchandise in '66, and settlers had used it ever since to cross the plains. People were now calling it the Chisholm Trail. The first of the Texas cattle herds had reached Abilene over this route.

A livestock broker from Illinois, Joseph McCoy, was responsible for the herds coming through Kansas this year—McCoy and the Kansas Pacific Railroad, which had finally reached Abilene on its slow trek west. What with Abilene having ample water from the Smoky Hill River and good grazing land in the vicinity, as well as having Fort Riley nearby to protect folks, the Chisholm Trail was now the ideal route to bring the herds for shipping east.

The railroad had made a phenomenal difference to Abilene. Just last year the town had been no more than a dozen log dwellings. It had grown monstrously in just a year's time, and now there were a dozen saloons and other dens of vice to attract the cowhands who brought in the herds.

It would have been nice if the railroad had reached even farther, but it didn't yet, so Abilene was as far as the Hartes had been able to travel in relative comfort. They bought a wagon there to carry the few possessions from home, one of the chuck wagons, in fact, that had already traveled the Trail. Knowing that their mode of transportation had come safely through Indian Territory at least once was a little reassuring.

Courtney would much have preferred to return east and get to Texas a roundabout way. That had, in fact, been their original intention, to travel through the South and then enter Texas on its eastern border. But Sarah wanted to visit her folks in Kansas City before she settled as far away as Texas was. So when Edward heard about this cow trail that had been traveled safely and learned that it passed right by Waco—their destination—he was adamant about changing their route. After all, they were already in Kansas. So much time would be saved by traveling directly south. A secret truth was, he didn't want to travel through the South and see again the destruction wrought there, not if he could take this other route.

Dallas rode ahead to the farm they had sighted, then returned to inform them that they were welcome to spend the night in the barn. "It'll do, Doctor Harte," Dallas informed Edward. "No sense ridin' the extra mile out of our way to Rockley. It's an itty-bitty town anyhow. We can head back toward the river come mornin'."

Edward nodded, and Dallas fell into place beside the wagon. Courtney didn't like the man very much, or his friend Hayden, either. Hayden kept making eyes at Sarah. Dallas was much younger than Hayden, maybe twenty-three, so he wasn't interested in Sarah. He'd shown an interest in Courtney, though.

Dallas was good-looking in a rough sort of way, and Courtney would have been extremely flattered by his interest if she hadn't seen the way his eyes greedily took in every female they saw. She was smart enough not to let the novelty of a man paying attention to her go to her head. She knew she was only catching his eye because Dallas was a normal, healthy male, and she was the only female around young enough to suit his tastes.

Courtney knew she wasn't attractive, at least not enough to draw men's interest when other females were present. Oh, she had pretty hair and eyes, and her features were set up kind of nice if you saw beyond the fullness. But men didn't usually notice that. They would look at her short, chubby frame and then look no more.

Courtney hated the way she looked, but she often turned to food as a solace for unhappiness. A few years ago, she hadn't cared. When other children teased her about her weight, she just ate more. When she finally began to care about her appearance, she made an effort to lose weight and had succeeded. Now she was called chubby instead of fat.

One good thing had happened after her father's marriage, and that was his taking notice of Courtney. He began talking to her at length when they rode side by side in the wagon. She didn't actually credit the marriage with this. It was more likely the forced intimacy of the trail that did it. At any rate, she was beginning to think maybe it wasn't hopeless after all. Maybe he really was starting to love her again, the way he had before her mother died.

Edward pulled to a stop in front of a large barn. It still amazed Courtney, having lived in Chicago all her life, that people like this farmer who was coming out to greet them didn't mind living out in the middle of nowhere like this, with no neighbor in sight. Courtney liked being alone, but in a house surrounded by other houses, knowing there were people around. There was no security in this isolation, this wilderness where Indians still roamed.

The farmer was a huge man, at least two hundred and fifty pounds, with hazel eyes in his ruddy face. Smiling, he told Edward there was room to drive the wagon inside the barn. When that was accomplished, he helped Courtney down from the wagon.

"Aren't you the pretty one?" he said, then reached to give Sarah a hand. "But you need to put on a little weight, honey. You're a stick."

Courtney blushed three shades of red and ducked her head, praying Sarah hadn't heard. Was the man crazy? Here she'd spent two years trying to lose weight, and he was suggesting she was skinny.

Dallas came up behind her while she was trying to sort out her confusion. He whispered in her ear, "He's big enough to like big women, honey, so don't pay him no mind. In another year or so you'll be rid of that baby fat, and I'll wager you'll be the prettiest gal in north Texas."

If Dallas had seen her expression, he might have realized he wasn't paying her any compliment. Courtney was mortified. All this personal criticism from men was more than she could bear. She rushed out of the barn and ran behind it to the back. She stared out over the flat land that stretched for miles. Tears glistened in her golden brown eyes, making them look like pools of honey.

Too fat, too skinny—how could people be so cruel? Could there be any sincerity in two such opposing opinions? Or was she learning that men never told the truth? Courtney didn't know what to think anymore.

Chapter 4

Elroy Brower was at his most congenial. He'd never had so many people visiting his home since he'd built it. He hadn't gotten any work done yesterday, but he didn't mind. He didn't feel like heading back to Wichita for his plow, not with the hangover he'd woken up with the day before, but he didn't mind that, either. It did a man good to get drunk once in a while. He'd had lots of company, too, what with Bill Chapman and all the others bedding down in the barn night before last and breaking out whiskey flasks to celebrate their victory. Only the two Joes were absent, having ridden off directly south after the killing.

And then, yesterday, the doctor and his ladies and the doctor's cowhands had come by. Imagine that, ladies sitting down at his table for supper! And they were real ladies, too. He could tell that easily by their fancy traveling clothes and their manners. And their delicate white skin, of course. He'd even made the young one blush.

Elroy told himself he'd be perfectly happy if they wanted to stay a few days. His plow could wait. Chapman had paid to store it along with his oxen, and Elroy could fetch it when he had a mind to. But the doctor said they'd be heading out this morning. He had insisted on going hunting at the crack of dawn to replenish Elroy's table. Well, shoot, nothing wrong with that. A nice man, the doctor, with real class. He had noticed the three scratches running down Elroy's neck and offered to leave him some salve.

When the scratches were mentioned, Elroy got a little flustered. Not that he was ashamed, because he wasn't. But you didn't mention such things in front of ladies, things to do with sex, and what had happened at the Indian camp. But the doctor didn't ask how he had gotten the scratches, and Elroy said nothing about it.

The retaliation had been a thrilling experience. It also eased Elroy's mind about having Indians so close to his home. Hell, they were easy to kill—easy to rape, too. He didn't know why he'd been so worried about Indians in the first place. He'd felt only a second's hesitation when he saw that the little savage who scratched him wasn't pure Indian. Those eyes that couldn't belong to a pure Indian looked up at him with such loathing. But he raped her anyhow. He was too excited by all the killing not to. Elroy didn't even realize she was dead until he'd finished. He didn't feel any guilt over what had happened, just irritation because he couldn't stop thinking about those eyes.

Elroy decided the ladies were probably up and dressed, so he could head out to the barn in a few minutes and invite them in to breakfast. The doctor and Dallas ought to be back soon, too. The other hand, Sorrel, was shaving out back by the well and probably spinning more tall tales for Peter. That boy wouldn't be around much longer, Elroy feared. He was already talking about joining the 7th Cavalry so he could fight Indians. Elroy hoped he'd wait at least until after harvest.

Twenty yards from Elroy's log house was where his cornfield began. The tall stalks were swaying gently. If Elroy had noticed that as he went to the barn, he might have thought an animal was loose in the field, for there was no wind blowing, not even the slightest breeze. But he didn't notice. He was thinking that as soon as the Harte party departed, he'd head back to Wichita for his plow.

Courtney had been up for half an hour and was waiting for Sarah to finish her morning toilet. Sarah was pretty, and she always spent a great deal of time each morning making sure everyone would see just how pretty she was, fixing her hair just right, fooling with her powders and the lotion she had brought along that was supposed to prevent sunburn. It was Sarah's vanity that had them continuing this trip so late in the season that they'd be lucky to reach Waco before winter set in. Sarah had cajoled Edward into visiting her folks in Kansas City because she wanted to show off her husband, an important doctor, and let everyone in her hometown see how well she'd done for herself.

The farmer made a good deal of unnecessary noise outside the door before he stuck his head inside. "Bacon's done, ladies, and the eggs are ready to be whipped up if you'd care to come to the house for some break-fast."

"How kind of you to offer, Mr. Brower," Sarah said, smiling. "Has my husband returned yet?"

"No, ma'am, but I don't reckon he'll be much longer. There's plenty game around here this time of year."

The farmer left. Hearing him making noises against the door again, Courtney shook her head at his strangeness. She knew why he'd done it when he arrived, but why now?

And then the door was jerked open and Elroy Brower fell inside, clutching his thigh. A long, thin stick was stuck in it. Now, why would he . . .

"Jesus God, there *were* more of 'em!" Elroy groaned as he got to his feet, breaking off the arrow shaft as he did so.

"What's wrong, Mr. Brower?" Sarah demanded, coming toward him.

Elroy groaned again. "Indians. We're being attacked." Sarah and Courtney stood there staring at him, openmouthed, and Elroy said hoarsely, "Over there!" Pointing to what looked like a large feed box with a lid on it, he said, getting more agitated by the second, "I dug a hole for my wife for

27

just this reason. She was a big woman, so it should be big enough for both of you. Get in and *don't come out,* even if it gets quiet. I've got to get back to the house where I left my rifle."

And then he was gone. Neither Sarah nor Courtney wanted to believe him. This was not happening. It couldn't be.

Hearing a rifle shot, quickly followed by another, Sarah felt sick. "Get into that box, Courtney!" Sarah cried as she ran for the box. "Oh, God, this can't be happening, not now, not when everything's been going so well."

Courtney moved mechanically toward the low box and crawled in after Sarah. There was no bottom to the box. The hole had been dug two and a half feet into the ground, enough room for both to crouch down without their heads reaching the top of the box.

"Close the lid!" Sarah snapped, her gray eyes round with fear. Then, "We've got nothing to fear. They won't find us. They're just stupid savages. They won't even look in here. They—"

Sarah's words stopped as they heard a scream beyond the barn, a horrible scream filled with terrible pain. What followed was even worse: many sounds, animal sounds, getting louder by the second. And then there was a high-pitched howling just outside the barn door. Courtney snapped out of her trance and pulled the lid closed, enclosing them in blackness that was terrifying in itself.

"Sarah. Sarah!"

Courtney began to cry when she realized Sarah had fainted. Even with the warmth of the woman's body slumped next to her, she felt alone. She was going to die, and she didn't want to die. She knew she would die shamefully, would scream and plead and then die anyway. Everyone knew Indians had no mercy.

Oh, God, if I have to die, don't let me beg. Let me find the courage not to beg.

Edward Harte had heard the first shot and raced back to the farm, Dallas close behind him. But when they were near enough to see what was happening, the younger man turned tail and rode away. Dallas was not a hero.

Edward didn't know he rode the rest of the way alone, for all he could think about was his daughter and saving her. He approached from the side of the farm and saw four Indians surrounding the bodies of Pe-

29

ter, the young farmhand, and Hayden Sorrel. Edward's first shot scored, but immediately afterward an arrow was embedded in his shoulder. It had come from the front of the barn, and he fired in that direction.

It was his last shot. Two more arrows found him, and he fell from his horse. He didn't move again.

The eight Comanche braves had accomplished what they'd come for. They had followed the tracks of thirteen horses to this farm. They'd seen that only eleven horses had gone on from the farm. That left two men at the farm, two of the thirteen the warriors wanted. One of those two was already dead. The huge farmer was not.

The farmer had only one wound. He had been cut off from reaching his house, cut off from returning to the barn. Four braves played with him now, taunting him with their knives, while the other Comanches searched the house and barn.

Two Comanches entered the barn. One climbed into the wagon, tossing out its contents as he searched. The other scanned the building for hiding places. His eyes took in everything with deadly thoroughness.

His face revealed nothing of his thoughts, but he was filled with an awful, wrenching grief. He had gone into the Comanche camp yesterday and found the nightmare left behind by the white men. His entrance into the camp was his first visit to his people after three years' absence, and he had returned too late to save his mother and sister. Revenge would never make up for their suffering, but it would help to ease his own pain.

The footprints in the dirt caught his attention, and he walked slowly to the feed box. In his hand he gripped the short, razor-edged blade he used for skinning animals.

Courtney hadn't heard the two Indians enter the barn. Her heart was pounding so loudly she could barely hear all the noises out in the yard.

The cover of the feed box flew open, and Courtney barely had time to gasp before her hair was seized in brutal hands. She squeezed her eyes shut so she wouldn't see the death blow coming. She knew her throat was going to be cut, for he forced her head back, exposing her neck. Any second now, God, any second . . .

She wouldn't open her eyes, but he wanted her to be watching him when he killed her. The other woman was slumped over in the hole, passed out, but this one

31

was aware and trembling. But she wouldn't look at him, not even when he twisted her hair as hard as he could around his hand. He knew he was hurting her, but still she kept her eyes squeezed shut.

And then through the haze of rage, he began to look her over. He realized that she didn't fit in here. Her clothes were fine, neither calico nor faded cotton. Her skin was too white for a farmer's wife or child, nearly translucent, barely touched by the sun. Her hair was like silk against his fingers, not brown or blond, but a blending of the two. Looking at her carefully, he realized she couldn't be more than fourteen years old, perhaps a little more.

Slowly, he looked from her to the wagon and saw the many dresses Crooked Finger had tossed out. He let go of the girl's hair.

Courtney was too terrified to keep her eyes shut any longer. Too much time had passed and no blade had touched her throat. Once she was released, she didn't know what to think. But when she did open her eyes, she nearly swooned. Never had she seen a more frightening sight than the Indian.

His hair was long and black as pitch, worked into two braids. His bare chest was streaked with paint the color of watered blood. Paint of several colors divided his face into four parts, camouflaging his features. But his eyes, locked with hers, struck her strangely. Those eyes didn't seem to belong to him. They weren't at all threatening, not like the rest of him.

Courtney watched as he looked away from her then at her again. She dared to look at the rest of him, scrutinizing him. She got no farther than the hand holding the knife pointed at her.

He saw those catlike golden eyes widen at the sight of his knife, and then she fainted. He grunted as she collapsed beside the other woman. Stupid Eastern women. They hadn't even bothered to arm themselves.

He hesitated, sighing. With her rounded baby cheeks, she was too much like his sister. He couldn't kill her.

He quietly closed the lid on the feed box and walked away, signaling to Crooked Finger that they had wasted enough time.

Chapter 5

Elroy Brower cursed the fates that had seen fit to put him in Wichita the day Bill

Chapman rode through. He knew he was going to die. But when—when? He and his captors were miles away from his farm. They'd ridden north, following Chapman's tracks, and hadn't stopped until the sun was directly overhead.

It took nearly all of them to overcome Elroy once he realized what they were going to do to him. But in a moment, Elroy was staked out on the hot ground, spread-eagled, stripped, feeling the parts of his body that had never seen the sun slowly burn under the noon rays.

The goddamn savages sat around watching him sweat. One tapped a stick against the arrowhead embedded in his thigh, one tap every five seconds, and the pain shot through him in waves that didn't have time to recede before the next tap.

He knew what they wanted, had known since they indicated the three dead men on the farm. Patiently, they had made themselves understood, holding up two fingers, pointing to him and then at the three bodies. They knew two men who had participated in the Indian massacre were on the farm, and they knew he was one of them.

He tried to convince them he wasn't one of the ones they wanted. After all, there were two extra bodies, so how could they be sure? But they didn't believe him, and each time he didn't give them the answer they wanted, they cut him.

He'd had a half-dozen small wounds before he pointed to Peter's body. What did it matter? The boy was already dead and couldn't suffer anymore. But Elroy suffered, watching what they did to Peter's body. He puked all over himself when they castrated the corpse and stuffed the piece of flesh into Peter's mouth, then sewed the lips shut. The message would be clear to whoever found Peter's mutilated body. And only Elroy would know that it hadn't been done while Peter was still alive.

Would he be as lucky as Peter? He figured the only reason he was still alive was that they wanted him to take them to the others involved in the massacre. Yet, the longer they kept him alive, the more he would suffer. He could offer to tell them all he knew if they would put an end to it, but what good would that do if the bastards couldn't understand him? And, Jesus, he didn't know how to find most of the others. Would they believe that, though? Of course not.

One of the Comanches bent over him.

Elroy could see only a black shape because of the sun. He tried to raise his head, and for a moment he got a glimpse of the Indian's hands. The man was holding several arrows. Were they finally going to get this over with? But no. Almost gently, the Indian probed at one of Elroy's wounds. And then slowly, excruciatingly, an arrowhead was embedded inside the wound, not straight in but sideways, into the fatty muscle, and oh, God, they had put something on the arrowhead to make it burn. It was like a hot coal dropped on his skin and left there. Elroy gritted his teeth, refusing to scream. Nor did he scream when his other wounds were treated the same way. He held it in. He only had six wounds. He could stand that much. Then they would leave him alone for a while, letting his body absorb the pain.

Elroy tried to will the pain away. He thought of the ladies who had been unfortunate enough to stop at his farm. He was grateful he hadn't seen what had happened to them. And then, suddenly, he saw those haunting eyes again, looking up at him with loathing. Raping that Indian girl hadn't been worth this. Nothing could be worth this.

Finally, Elroy screamed. It didn't matter that the Indian had run out of wounds. He cut a new wound and embedded another arrowhead, and with that Elroy knew they wouldn't stop until his body was completely covered with arrows. He couldn't bear it anymore, knowing there would be no letup in the pain. He screamed and cursed and shouted, but he was cut again, and the burning turned to fire.

"Bastards! Goddamn bastards! I'll tell you what you want to know. I'll tell you anything!"

"Will you?"

Elroy stopped screaming, the pain forgotten for a split second. "You speak English?" he panted. "Oh, thank God!" Now there was hope. Now he could bargain.

"What is it you would tell me, farmer?"

The voice was soft, pleasant, confusing Elroy. "Let me go, and I'll give you the names of the men you want, every one of them. And I'll tell you where they're likely to be found," he gasped.

"You will tell us this anyway, farmer. It is not your life you may bargain for, but your death—a quick death."

Elroy had been straining forward with hope. Now he sagged back against the ground. He was defeated. All he could hope for was that it would be quick.

He told the Indian everything, every name, descriptions, and all the likely destinations he could think of. He answered every question thrown at him quickly and truthfully, ending with, "Now kill me."

"Like you killed our wives and mothers and sisters?"

The Indian who spoke such clear, precise English moved down to stand at his feet. Elroy could see him clearly now, his face, his eyes . . . Oh, Lord, they were *her* eyes, looking at him with the same blazing hatred. Then Elroy knew this man had no intention of letting him die quickly.

Elroy licked his lips. He didn't know where it came from, but he managed to say, "She was good. Not much meat on her, but she pleasured me real well. I was the last to have her. She died under me, with my—"

The howl came from deep in the warrior's soul, cutting off Elroy's taunt. One of the others tried to stop the young warrior but couldn't. The pain was minimal for Elroy, bringing to a crescendo all the rest of the pain. It was the shock of seeing the severed flesh he had been about to mention raised high in the Comanche's hand that killed him.

Three miles away, Courtney Harte stared dismally at the scattered contents of the wagon, ripped clothes, smashed china, food staples ruined. She couldn't cope with deciding what to salvage. She couldn't cope with anything right now, unlike Sarah, who was looking through their goods as if nothing much had happened.

To Courtney, just being alive was a shock. Worse, her father was gone.

Berny Bixler, Elroy Brower's closest neighbor, had seen the smoke from Elroy's fired house and come to investigate. He found the two dead bodies behind the house and Sarah and Courtney in the feed box. There was no sign of Dallas, Elroy Brower, or Edward Harte. But Courtney's father had been there because his horse was in the cornfield and there were spots of blood on it. Had Edward been wounded?

"Would've seen him if he'd got away and headed toward Rockley for help," Berny told them. "More like the Injuns took him and the other two away. Probably felt a couple of strong captives wouldn't hurt to have around till they can find another tribe to live with."

"What makes you say that, Mr. Bixler?" Sarah demanded. "I thought women were the ones usually taken captive."

"Beggin' your pardon, ma'am," Berny said. "But if an Injun looked at you and the youngun here, he'd figure you wouldn't last long on the move."

"On the move? You keep seeming to know what these Indians plan to do," Sarah snapped. "I don't see how you could know. Its just as likely they have a camp near here, isn't it?"

"Oh, they did, ma'am, they surely did. That's just it. This weren't no livestock raid. Lars Handley's boy John come tearin' into Rockley two nights ago, telling how he and Elroy and Peter joined up with some Wichita men to wipe out this band of Kiowas down south of here that was plannin' to attack Rockley. He claimed we wouldn't have no trouble now, 'cause they killed every last man, woman, and child. Well, looks like they missed a few. The bucks who struck here must've been out huntin' or somethin' and come back to find all their kin dead."

"Pure supposition, Mr. Bixler. Kiowas can't be the only Indians around here."

The farmer showed his annoyance enough to say, "John Handley also bragged about what he done in the Indian camp—somethin' I can't mention to ladies."

"Oh, for heaven's sake," Sarah said, sneering, "So they raped a few squaws. That doesn't mean—"

"You go on out there and take a look at Peter's body if you want to know what it means, lady," he said hotly. "But I wouldn't recommend it. What they done to that boy ain't pretty. Didn't touch that other fellow at all. His wound was clean. But I'm likely to have nightmares for a long time 'bout what they done to Peter. And I reckon we'll find Elroy somewhere hereabouts, done up just as ugly. It don't take a smart man to know they was only after them two and why. You'da been took if they was interested in women. No, it was revenge and nothin' else."

"You see if John Handley don't take off from this area real quick too, 'cause it ain't over. Them Injuns won't stop till they get every last one of the men they're after."

He stalked out of the barn, saying they'd better be quick about gathering their belongings 'cause he didn't have all day. He had been so sympathetic and kind to begin with, but Sarah had brought out the worst in him and now he was impatient to see them to Rockley and off his hands.

Elroy Brower's body was found a week later by soldiers who were searching for the marauding Indians. John Handley left Rockley for parts unknown, as predicted. His father never heard from him again. There was news from Wichita that a homesteader near there had been hit by Indians too, but that was the last story of Indian attacks heard in the area. Probably unrelated was the killing of a rancher named Bill Chapman farther north, though some said he was the man who had led the attack on the Indians. Chapman had been found brutally slain in his bed, and some said it was an Indian killing, some said not. The killer might have been one of the men who worked for Chapman, for many of his hired hands took off right after the killing.

No sign was found of Edward Harte or Dallas. Sarah Whitcomb Harte considered herself a widow. It was inconceivable that a wounded man could have survived as an Indian captive, especially a captive of Indians on the run.

Courtney was too numb to think at all beyond the possibility that her father was alive.

Sarah and Courtney were now stuck with each other, a most aggravating circumstance for both.

Chapter 6

"Well, there's another one, Charley. You reckon we'll have us another shoot-out?"

Charley spit a wad of tobacco into the spittoon by the porch rail before he eyed the stranger coming up the street. "Just might, Snub. There's a couple more in town right now. Just might at that."

The two old-timers leaned back in their chairs in front of Lars Handley's store. Handley's porch was the spot where they whiled away most of every day talking about whoever passed near to where they were sitting. From their spot they could see both ends of the only street in town.

"You reckon he come up on one of them trail-drives?" Snub wondered.

"Don't look the type to be pushin' cows," Charley replied. "That man's a gunfighter if I ever saw one."

"There's been many a gunfighter turned cowboy, and vici-versi."

"True."

Snub could see by Charley's expression that he was sticking to his first opinion and had agreed only to be agreeable. "I wonder how many he's killed?"

"I wouldn't ask him." Charley grunted. Then suddenly his eyes narrowed. "This one looks familiar. Ain't he been through here before?"

"I believe you're right, Charley. A couple a years ago, wasn't it?"

"More like three or four."

"Yeah. I remember. Came in late one night, checked into the hotel, but didn't stay. I remember you remarked on the vagaries of the young."

Charley nodded, pleased his remarks were weighty enough to be remembered. "Can't recall the name he put down at the hotel, though. Can you?"

"Foreign soundin', wasn't it?"

"Yeah, but that's all I remember. Now it's gonna nag me all day."

"Well, looks like he's goin' for the hotel again," Snub said as the stranger pulled up rein there. "Why don't we mosey on over and get a look-see at the desk book?"

"Not now, Snub," Charley replied testily. "Ackerman's missus will just shoo us out."

"Ah, don't be a pissypants, Charley. The witch probably ain't even out of bed yet. And Miss Courtney won't mind if we sit a spell in the lobby or take a peek at the book."

"Pissypants," Charley grumbled. "He's probably changed his name by now—like they all do—so my curiosity ain't gonna get satisfied anyhow. But if you wanna get yelled at by that shrew Harry married, then get up off your bee-hind and let's go."

A little smile tugged at Courtney's lips as she closed the door to the guest chamber she had just finished cleaning. She had found another newspaper. Rockley didn't have its own paper, and the only news she ever got from the outside world was from listening to the conversations of strangers passing through or from reading the rare newspaper left behind by hotel guests. That didn't happen often. Newspapers were as good as books if you lived in a town that didn't have its own paper. Most folks held on to theirs. Sarah had a collection of papers, but she never shared them, so Courtney always tried to find one first.

She hid the newspaper under the pile of dirty linens she had to wash and headed for the stairs, planning to slip the paper into her room downstairs before she tackled the laundry.

At the top of the stairs, Courtney slowed, taking notice of the stranger waiting below. Then she stopped altogether and did something she rarely did. She stared at a man. She even caught herself doing it and would have chided herself, except that she couldn't stop staring. For some reason, this man captured her interest like no one ever had.

The first thing she noticed was that he stood straight and tall. The second thing was his lean, hawkish profile. But the promise of his features being so very striking was what held her attention the most. He would be disturbingly handsome, she was sure of it, though all she could see was his left profile. And he was dark, from the black vest and pants to the bronze skin to the black hair that fell straight to just below his ears. Even the gray shirt and neckerchief were dark.

The man had not removed his wide-brimmed hat to come into the hotel, but at least he wasn't wearing any spurs. That was strange, for the saddlebags tossed over his shoulder suggested he had ridden into town,

46

and Courtney had never seen a man who didn't ride with spurs.

And then she noticed what she hadn't seen before because she'd been able to see only his left side. He wore double belts, which meant he undoubtedly had a gun strapped to his right thigh. That might not mean too much, for most men out West carried guns. But the guns, combined with the look of him, made her think he wasn't wearing a gun just for his own protection.

Courtney didn't like gunmen. She thought of them as overgrown bullies— which most of them, in fact, were. That breed of man believed they could do or say anything. Too few people had the courage to upbraid them, since you could get shot that way.

A person wouldn't think a small town like Rockley would see too many gunmen, but Rockley did. There had even been two gunfights in recent years. Cowboys passed through Rockley on their way to the wild cowtowns, Abilene, and recently Newton. Those cowtowns drew every type of riffraff, and next year Wichita would become a cowtown too, and it was just seventeen miles away, so Courtney couldn't see any letup in the steady stream of traffic.

Working in the only hotel in town, she couldn't avoid gunmen. One had nearly raped her, others had stolen kisses. She'd been fought over, pursued, and propositioned most shockingly. That was the main reason she wanted desperately to leave Rockley and why she wouldn't marry any of the Rockley men, not even if that would have gotten her out of the hotel, where she worked from morning to night as no more than a maid.

Having signed the register book, the stranger put down the pen. Courtney immediately turned and hurried back down the hall to the back stairs that led directly outside. It was inconvenient, going this way, but she didn't want to come in through the kitchen below, where she might run into Sarah and be scolded for dillydallying. No, she would have to go around the hotel and come in through the front lobby. But she would do that after the stranger had gone up to his room.

She wasn't sure why she didn't want him to see her, but she didn't. It certainly couldn't be because she was wearing her oldest dress and her hair was a mess. She didn't care what he thought of her. He would probably be staying only one night.

Most of the drifters did. And then she'd never see him again.

Courtney moved to the front, ducking under the dining-room windows on the side of the hotel so that she could peek around first and be sure he was gone. She edged her way to the front door, not even realizing she still had the bundle of dirty linen in her arms. She just wanted to get to her room, hide her newspaper, then get back to work.

Out in the street, Charley and Snub watched Courtney's antics. What the hell was she doing, peeking through the front door instead of just opening it, then suddenly slamming back against the wall, as if hiding. But then the door opened all the way and the stranger stepped outside, crossed the porch to the steps, and went to his horse. Watching the gunman, they didn't see Courtney dash into the hotel. Then Snub noticed she'd gone.

"What was that all about?"

Charley was watching the stranger lead his horse toward the stable. "What?"

"Sure looked like Miss Courtney was hidin' from that feller."

"Well, shoot, can't blame her none. Look what happened with that owlhoot Polecat Parker. Snuck into her room and scared the daylights outta her with his drunken pawin'. Don't know what mighta happened if Harry hadn't heard her scream and grabbed his shotgun. And then there was that dumb cowboy who tried to grab her right off the street and ride away with her. Sprained her ankle real bad, fallin' off his horse. And then—"

"We both know she's had her share of trouble since she's been here, Charley. She probably figures this one means trouble, too. So she's stayin' outta his way."

"Maybe. But did you ever see her leave the hotel before just to avoid a man?"

"Can't say as I have."

"Then maybe she's interested in this one."

"Gawddammit, Charley, that don't make sense."

"When did women ever make sense?" Charley chuckled.

"But . . . I thought she was gonna marry Reed Taylor."

"That's what her stepmamma'd like to see happen. But it ain't gonna happen—I heard it from Mattie Cates. Miss Courtney likes Reed about as much as she liked Polecat."

Inside the hotel, Courtney took a quick

look at the register book lying open on the desk before hurrying on to her room. His name was Chandos. That was all, just the single name.

Chapter 7

"Hurry, will you, Courtney? I don't have all day. And you promised you'd help me pick out material for my new dress."

Courtney looked over her shoulder at Mattie Cates, who was sitting on the over-turned washbarrel. She gave an unladylike snort. "If you're in such an all-fired hurry, then get over here and help me hang these sheets."

"Are you kiddin'? I've got my own wash to do as soon as I get home. And Pearce's pants are just as heavy as can be. My arms would never last if I started now. Don't know why I married such a big man, anyhow."

"Maybe because you love him?" Courtney grinned.

"Maybe." Mattie grinned back.

Mattie Cates was a contradictory mixture. The petite, blue-eyed blonde was usually friendly and outgoing, but she could be quiet and reserved, too. Seemingly independent, at times just as bossy as Sarah, she also had hidden uncertainties only her closest friends knew about. Courtney, of course, was a close friend.

Mattie firmly believed you got out of life what you put into it, that you could do anything you set your mind to doing, and she liked to say, "Do for yourself, for no one else will."

Mattie had demonstrated the truth of that philosophy by overcoming her own worrying nature and winning Pearce Cates two years ago, when he'd been one of the half-dozen men smitten with Courtney.

Mattie had never held Pearce's infatuation with Courtney against her friend. She'd been so pleased for Courtney when she'd changed from an ugly duckling into a beautiful swan, and she thought it hilarious when men who had barely noticed Courtney was alive suddenly fell all over themselves when they saw her.

Mattie sometimes thought of Courtney as her own creation. Not the beauty, of course, for that had come from growing several inches in the last two years and from working so hard that the last of her baby fat melted away. But Courtney wasn't as timid and nervous as she used to be, nor did she take everything heaped on her as if she were deserving of it. It had taken prodding and pushing and bullying, but Mattie liked to think she had put a little spunk into her friend.

Why, Courtney even stood up to Sarah now, not always, but certainly more than she used to. Even Mattie couldn't get away with bullying Courtney anymore. Courtney had come to realize how much courage she had.

Courtney set the empty laundry basket on the washtub next to Mattie. "Well, Miss Impatience, let's go."

Mattie cocked her head to the side. "Ain't you gonna change your dress or fix your hair or somethin'?"

Courtney pulled off the ribbon holding her long brown hair, retied it, and then smoothed down the rest. "There."

Mattie chuckled. "I guess you'll do. Your old dresses still look better'n my best calico."

Courtney's cheeks pinkened slightly, but she turned away so Mattie wouldn't see. She was still making do with the wardrobe she had owned four years ago when she first came to Rockley, even though she had outgrown it entirely and the colors were all the light pastels favored by younger girls. If her clothes hadn't been so big to begin with, she wouldn't have managed, but she had been able to take everything in to fit her much slimmer figure, and some of her gowns had had large enough hems to let down. Most had had to be lengthened, though, with scraps of material.

But Courtney's old clothes of silk and muslin, China crêpe and mohair, her finely laced collars, fichus, and basques, even her summer and winter wraps of superior velvet, were all out of place in Rockley. And Courtney had never liked to stand out in a crowd. Her looks made her noticeable as it was, and she was dismayed that her clothes only made things worse.

Rockley was a small town, having only recently acquired two saloons and a brothel. There was a marked lack of young marriageable women, and so Courtney found herself being courted seriously in the last two years.

When Richard, the young blacksmith, asked her to marry him, she was so surprised she nearly grabbed him and kissed him. An honest-to-God proposal of marriage, when she'd thought never to be asked! But the blacksmith merely wanted a wife.

He didn't love her. Too, she didn't love him, nor did she love Judd Baker or Billy or Pearce, all of whom wanted to marry her. And she certainly didn't love Reed Taylor, who was currently pursuing her. He took it for granted that he would win her.

"Did you ever hear of a Mr. Chandos, Mattie?"

Courtney blushed, wondering why the question had popped out. They were walking toward the front of the hotel, and Mattie replied thoughtfully, "Can't say as I have. Sounds like a name out of one of your history lessons, like those ancient knights you used to tell me about."

"Yes, it does have a certain classical ring to it, doesn't it?"

"Sounds kinda Spanish, too. Why'd you ask?"

"No reason." Courtney shrugged.

Mattie wasn't having any of that. "Come on, where'd you hear that name?"

"Oh, he checked into the hotel this morning. I just thought you might have heard of him before, that he might have a reputation."

"Another bad one, huh?"

"He did have that look."

"Well, if he's older, you could ask

55

Charley or Snub. They know all the fast guns with the worst reputations, and you know how they love to gossip."

"He's not that old, maybe twenty-five or -six, I guess."

"Then they prob'ly wouldn't know, but if you just wanna know how many men he's killed—"

"Mattie! I don't want to know any such thing."

"Well, but then what *do* you want to know?"

"Nothing, nothing at all."

"Well, God sakes, why'd you ask?" A moment later, she said, "Is that him?"

Courtney's pulse leaped, then returned to normal. Across the street, at Reed's saloon, leaning against a post, was one of two other gunmen recently come to town.

"No, that's Jim Ward," Courtney explained. "He came in yesterday with another man."

"Jim Ward? Now, that name does sound familiar. Wasn't that one of the names on those wanted posters Wild Bill sent down from Abilene last year?"

Courtney shrugged. "I never did understand why Marshal Hickok sent us those posters. We've never had a town marshal."

No one in Rockley wanted that job, which was why so many outlaws, or "owlhoots" as Charley called them, felt free to travel through Rockley. "It wouldn't matter if he is wanted. Who is there in Rockley to arrest him?"

"True," said Mattie, "but it helps knowin' who to stay clear of."

"I stay clear of *all* of them if I can." Courtney shivered.

"Well, naturally, but you know what I meant. If Harry had known Polecat Parker was wanted, he woulda shot him instead of just runnin' him out of town."

Courtney steeled herself against the mention of that name. "Don't remind me. Sarah was in a snit for months when she heard about the thousand-dollar reward that someone in Hays City collected on that vile man."

Mattie laughed. "Sarah is always in a snit about somethin'."

The two girls crossed the street, hoping to get out of the hot sun. It was nearing the end of summer, but Kansas didn't seem to know it. Courtney didn't get out in the sun often, except to hang out laundry, but even that was enough to give her a light golden tan each summer. It went very well with her honey gold eyes.

Lars Handley smiled at the girls as they entered his store. He was waiting on Berny Bixler, who acknowledged them as well. Four other customers milled around, no one in any particular hurry.

Just about anything you wanted could be found in Handley's store, provided it was of a practical nature. The only thing he didn't sell was meat, but Zing Hodges, an ex-buffalo hunter, had opened a meat market next door. In the front corner of Handley's, a man could get a shave or haircut, and if the need arose, a tooth pulled by Hector Evans. The barber rented this small corner of the store from Lars because he'd never made up his mind whether he wanted to stay in Rockley, and so he didn't want to spend the money to build his own shop.

Mattie pulled Courtney straightaway to the wall where the old wanted posters were hung.

"There, see?" Mattie beamed. "Three-hundred-dollar reward for Jim Ward, wanted for 'murder, armed robbery, and other numerous crimes in New Mexico.' "

Courtney studied the poster and its pencil sketch of a man that did in fact resemble the

Jim Ward staying at the hotel. "It says wanted dead or alive. Why do they do that, Mattie? It just gives all those bounty hunters a license to kill."

"They have to, or no one would bother huntin' criminals. You think someone is gonna go up against these hard cases if they know they can't kill 'em if they have to? There's always a fight, and if the bounty hunter or marshal or whoever isn't good enough, he's dead. He takes that chance. If he is good enough, then he gets his man and the reward—and that's one less criminal to bother decent folks. Would you rather no one tried?"

"No, I suppose not." Courtney sighed. She never had answers for Mattie's reasonable arguments. "It just seems so harsh."

"You're just too tenderhearted," Mattie said, "but you can't tell me you were sorry when Polecat Parker was killed."

"No."

"Well, they're all like that, Courtney. It's better for the rest of us if they're dead."

"I . . . guess so, Mattie."

Mattie grinned. "You're hopeless, Courtney Harte. You'd pity a snake."

Courtney shook her head. "A snake? I don't think so."

"Well, anyhow"—Mattie tapped the poster—"you'd think this fool would change his name, with so many of these posters around."

"Maybe I like my name the way it is."

The girls gasped and whirled around. Jim Ward stood right next to them, looking none too pleased. Of medium height and lanky, with close-set eyes over a hooked nose, he had a long, untrimmed mustache reaching clear to his jaw. He yanked the poster down, crumpling it and then stuffing it in his back pocket. He turned his cold gray eyes on Mattie, who was speechless for a change. Courtney managed to find her voice. "She didn't mean anything, Mr. Ward."

"Maybe I don't like bein' called a fool no time, no how."

"You gonna shoot me?" Mattie sneered, suddenly reckless.

Courtney could have pinched her black and blue. Her knees turned weak.

"That sounds like a right fine idea," Ward said hotly.

"Here now!" Lars Handley called out to them. "I don't want trouble in my store."

"Then stay where you are, old man," Ward ordered harshly, and Lars stopped where he was. "This here is between me and

Miss Bigmouth," Ward finished, and Lars eyed the rifle he kept under the counter. But he didn't reach for it.

No one else moved, either. It was deathly quiet. Charley and Snub had come in right after Ward did, and were sitting in the barber's section enjoying the show.

Hector, finished with his customer's shave, found his hands had began to tremble. The customer wiped his face clean, but he made no move to rise from the chair. Like the others, he quietly watched the drama unfolding.

Courtney was near to tears. My God, had she just moments before felt sorry for this man because someone would probably shoot him someday?

"Mattie?" She tried sounding calm. "Mattie, let's go."

"Uh-uh," Jim said, his hand snaking out to grab one of Mattie's braids. He jerked her face very close to his. "Bigmouth ain't leavin' until she apologizes. Then I'll tend to you, honey. Well?" he demanded of Mattie.

Courtney held her breath, seeing Mattie's blue eyes spitting sparks.

"I'm sorry," Mattie finally said quietly.

"Louder."

"I'm sorry!" the girl shouted furiously.

Chuckling, Jim Ward let her go.

But those close-set eyes lit on Courtney now. He smiled disagreeably.

"Now, why don't you and me go somewhere where we can get better acquainted, honey? I've had my eye on you since—"

"No!" Courtney blurted out.

"No?" His eyes narrowed. "You're tellin' me no?"

"I—I have to get back to the hotel, Mr. Ward."

"Uh-uh." His fingers moved up her arm, then clamped around it tightly. "I don't think you understood me, honey. I said we was gonna get better acquainted, so that's what we're gonna do."

"Please—don't," Courtney cried as he started dragging her out of the store. He paid no attention to her cries.

"Let go of her, Ward."

"What?" Jim stopped, looking around. Had he heard right?

"I don't repeat myself."

Jim continued to stand there with Courtney, looking around until he found the speaker.

"Two choices, Ward," the man said casually. "Draw or leave. But don't take up a lot of my time deciding."

Jim Ward released Courtney, freeing his right hand. He reached for his gun.

He was dead the next instant.

Chapter 8

Courtney willed herself to think of happy things. She remembered the first time she had ridden without a sidesaddle, how shocked she'd been but how delighted to find riding so much easier. The time Mattie taught her how to swim. The first time she'd told Sarah to shut up; the expression on Sarah's face.

It wasn't working. She could still see that man lying dead in Lars Handley's store. Courtney had never before seen a dead man. She hadn't witnessed other killings in Rockley. And she had not seen the bodies of young Peter and Hayden Sorrel on the Brower farm the day her life had changed so terribly, for Berny Bixler had covered the bodies before she could see them.

She had made such a fool of herself in the store, screaming her head off until Mattie managed to quiet her and get her back to the hotel. She was lying on her bed now, a cold compress over her eyes.

"Here now, I want you to drink this."

"Oh, Mattie, stop fussing over me."

"Someone has to, 'specially after the way Sarah lit into you," Mattie retorted, her blue eyes snapping indignantly. "The nerve of that woman, tryin' to blame you for what happened. Why, I'm to blame more'n anyone else."

Courtney lifted the compress to stare at Mattie. She couldn't bring herself to disagree. Mattie *had* made matters worse with her cockiness.

"I don't know what came over me," Mattie continued more softly. "But I'm real proud of you, Courtney. Two years ago you'da fainted dead away. But you stood right up to that bastard."

"I was scared to death, Mattie," Courtney cut in. "Weren't you scared at *all?*"

"'Course I was," the younger girl replied. "But when I get scared, I sass. Can't seem to help myself. Now drink this. It's my ma's cure-all, and'll have you feelin' good as new in no time."

"But I'm not sick, Mattie."

"Drink!"

Courtney drank the herbal concoction, then closed her eyes and lay back again. "Sarah *was* unfair, wasn't she?"

"'Course she was. If you ask me, she was just miffed 'cause she didn't recognize that owlhoot and didn't have a chance to sneak into his room and shoot him for that three-hundred-dollar reward."

"Sarah shoot someone?"

"Hey, I wouldn't put anythin' past that one," Mattie said, grinning. "I can just see her sneakin' down the hall in the dead of night with Harry's rifle—"

"Oh, stop, Mattie." Courtney giggled.

"That's better. You gotta laugh about things. And look at it this way, Court, you got the rest of the day off from your work."

"I would rather not think of it that way," Courtney said ruefully.

"Now, Courtney, you're not gonna blame yourself. You can't help it if men go all stupid when they're around you. And that bastard deserved what he got. You know damn well what he'da done to you if he'd managed to get you alone."

Courtney shivered. She did know. She had seen it in his eyes. And her pleas wouldn't have counted for beans.

"He really was a fool for thinkin' no one would stop him," Mattie went on. "Well, maybe not. Fact is, no one woulda stopped him if that stranger hadn't. And Ward was given a choice. He coulda just left, but he drew on that fella. His choice." After a pause, she went on. "You owe that stranger, Courtney. Wonder who he was."

"Mr. Chandos," Courtney said quietly.

"Damn!" Mattie exclaimed. "I shoulda known! God sakes, no wonder you were so curious about him. He's powerful good-lookin', isn't he?"

"I suppose."

"You *suppose?*" Mattie grinned. "That man saved your virtue, Courtney. You have to at least thank him 'fore he leaves in the mornin'."

"He's leaving?"

Mattie nodded. "I heard Charley and Snub talkin' about him in the lobby. He's takin' Ward's body over to Wichita for the reward."

Courtney was suddenly exhausted. "Shouldn't you be getting home, Mattie?"

"Yeah, I guess so. Pearce'll understand why I'm late after I tell him what happened, though. But you got to promise me you won't brood all evening."

"I won't brood, Mattie," Courtney replied softly. "It's just made me more determined than ever to get back East somehow.

66

Things like this don't happen there. This isn't civilization, Mattie."

Mattie smiled gently. "You had no luck findin' your aunt. All you finally found out was she really was dead, so you got no one back East, Courtney."

"I know. But I can get a job, even if it's just doing what I've been doing for the last four years. I don't care. But I don't feel safe here, Mattie. Harry doesn't protect me. He barely knows I'm alive. I need to feel safe, and if I can't with Harry and Sarah, then at least I need the security of a safe place to live."

"You've made up your mind to travel alone?"

"No," Courtney said dismally. "No, I still couldn't do that. But you know, Hector Evans has it in mind to leave here. Maybe after what happened today he'll be ready to go back East. I could offer to pay him to take me with him. I do have that money Sarah doesn't know about."

"Sure, you could pay Hector, but it'd be a pure waste of money, for he can't protect himself, let alone you. They're robbin' the trains in Missouri these days, you know that. You're likely to meet up with the James gang or somebody and lose what little money you have."

67

"Mattie!"

"Well, it's the truth."

"Then that's the chance I'll have to take."

"Well, if you're set on goin', at least pick someone who ain't a coward to escort you. Reed would probably take you if you asked him real nice."

"He would insist I marry him first."

"Well, you could do that," Mattie suggested. "Why not?"

"This is no teasing matter." Courtney frowned. "You know I don't even like Reed."

"All right." Mattie grinned. "Well, I better go, Court. We can talk this over some more tomorrow. But don't you dare think of usin' Hector. Why, he wouldn't do anything if some ornery cuss walked off with you. Fact is, you need someone like Chandos. You wouldn't catch him lettin' someone mess with you. Did you think about askin' him?"

"No! I couldn't," Courtney said with a shudder. "He's a killer."

"God sakes, Courtney, haven't you been listenin' to anything I've said? That's just the kind of man you need to escort you. If you're so all-fired worried about feelin' safe, well . . ."

After Mattie left, Courtney lay there quietly thinking about what she had said. No, Mattie was wrong. If she was going farther west, or south, or even north, then she might feel safer with someone like Mr. Chandos to escort her. But she was going east, back to the sanity of civilization. The railroad wasn't that far away, either. It would be easy traveling. She just needed someone to travel with so she wouldn't be so alone.

But Mattie was right about one thing. She did owe Mr. Chandos the courtesy of a thank-you.

It took Courtney another hour to get up the courage to seek her rescuer out.

She hoped not to find him in his room. It was one of her jobs to supply fresh water and towels in the evening, but because it was dinnertime, she hoped Mr. Chandos would be in the dining room. Then she'd be able to tell Mattie truthfully that she had tried to thank him but hadn't been able to find him. No, she was already feeling guilty. She *should* thank him, she knew, but to come face-to-face with that alarming man! However, if he wasn't in his room, she could leave him a note.

She knocked on his door twice, holding

her breath. She listened carefully, then tried the doorknob. It was locked. Well, so much for that. There were no duplicate keys to the rooms, for Harry firmly believed that if a guest locked his room, it was because he didn't want anyone to go in. True. But the other fact was, with the kind of guests they had, you were likely to get shot for entering a room without being asked in.

Courtney let her breath out, relieved. This man was dangerous, the kind of man she always took pains to avoid.

Yet she was, in some strange way, disappointed not to find him in. When she'd heard him tell Jim Ward to get his hand off her, she'd stopped being afraid. This gunfighter had made her feel safe. She hadn't felt that way since her father's death.

Courtney turned away, intending to write a note that she would leave for him at the desk. But suddenly she heard the door open. She turned around again and froze, for he had his gun in his hand.

"Sorry," he said, and tucked the gun into his pants. He opened his door wider and stepped back. "Come on in."

"No, I—I couldn't."

"That water's not for me?"

"Oh! Yes—yes, of course. I'm sorry—I— I'll just put these on your washstand."

Courtney's face was burning as she hurried over to the washstand and set the water and towels down. She felt exactly the way she sounded, like a nervous twit. Oh, what must he think of her? First her hysterics in Handley's store after the shooting, and now this idiotic babbling.

It took all of Courtney's courage just to turn around and face him. She found him leaning against the doorframe, arms crossed over his chest, his tall frame blocking her only exit, whether intentionally or not. Unlike her, there wasn't any tension in him. In fact, he exuded a careless self-assurance that made her feel even sillier.

He was staring at her with those beautiful sky blue eyes that seemed to strip her right to the core, bringing to light all her weaknesses. Of course, he revealed nothing about himself, no curiosity, no interest, not even a hint that he found her a little attractive. He made all her old self-consciousness return, and she found herself getting angry.

Get it over with, Courtney, and get the hell away from him before he destroys every bit of the self-confidence you've gained over the years.

"Mr. Chandos—"

"No mister. Just Chandos."

She hadn't noticed it before, but his voice had a deep, soothing timbre.

Flustered at being thrown off track, she wondered what she'd been about to say.

"You're scared," he said bluntly. "Why?"

"No, no I'm not, really I'm not." *Don't ramble, Courtney!* "I—I wanted to thank you. For what you did today."

"For killing a man?"

"No! Not that!" Oh, God, why did he have to be so difficult? "I mean—I suppose that couldn't be helped. But you—you saved me—I mean, he wouldn't listen, and—and you stopped him—and—"

"Lady, you'd better get out of here before you fall apart."

God, he saw right through her! Mortified, Courtney watched as he unwound and moved out of the doorway. She rushed past him.

She wouldn't have stopped, either, except that her shame over handling everything so badly overcame her mortification. She turned back. He was still staring at her with those incredible light blue eyes. But this time, his eyes soothed her, easing her fear and leaving her feeling strangely calm. She didn't understand it, but she was glad for it.

"I am grateful," she said plainly.

"Don't be. I'll be paid for my trouble."

"But you didn't know he was a wanted man."

"Didn't I?"

He *had* been in the store. He might have overheard Mattie and her talking. Still . . .

"Whatever your reason, mister, you helped me out," Courtney insisted. "And whether you want it or not, you have my thanks."

"Have it your way," he said. His voice held dismissal.

Courtney nodded stiffly and walked away, picking up speed before she reached the stairs. She felt him staring after her. Thank God he would be gone tomorrow. The man totally unnerved her.

Chapter 9

When Reed Taylor called on Courtney that evening, she refused to see him. This earned her a sharp scolding from Sarah, but she didn't care.

Sarah liked Reed. Courtney understood

why. They were two of a kind, those two, both domineering and hard to get along with. And both had decided she should marry Reed. It didn't seem to matter what Courtney thought.

Yes, Sarah was all for her marrying Reed. Her favorite parting shot at the end of every tirade these days was, "I want you married and off my hands! I've supported you long enough!"

This was a joke. Courtney more than earned her keep. In fact, all Sarah provided the girl with was room and board. She had never given Courtney one penny for all the work she did, not even to buy personal essentials. Courtney had had to earn money by sewing for the Misses Coffman in her spare time. She'd had to, for she couldn't let Sarah know she had five hundred dollars hidden in her room.

That money had come from selling the few items of furniture that weren't wanted by the new owners of their house before Courtney and her father and Sarah left Chicago. Sarah didn't know the money had been given to Courtney or that Courtney hadn't turned it over to her father. Edward was too preoccupied to ask for it, and in the upheaval of leaving, Courtney had forgotten about it. She left it tucked away in the bottom of her trunk, and there it stayed, even through the Indian attack.

She didn't know why she hadn't mentioned the money when Sarah wailed that they were penniless, that Edward should never have kept all his money on his person, but Courtney was glad now that she'd kept silent.

She supposed she would have brought the money forward if there had been a great need, but there hadn't been. Sarah quickly got them both jobs at the hotel, and not more than three months later, Sarah married Harry Ackerman, who owned the place. He wasn't as good a catch as Edward had been, but he had prospects.

The marriage did nothing good for Courtney. She stopped receiving wages for her work, and Sarah settled into the role of giving orders and doing nothing.

Courtney wasn't deceived as to why Sarah was anxious to have Courtney out of her life. Folks had started to refer to her as "old Sarah" because they thought of Courtney as her daughter. No matter how often Sarah pointed out that Courtney was nineteen and would be twenty before the year was out, people still saw them as mother and daughter. Sarah was only thirty-four, and that assumption was intolerable.

What had started Sarah nagging constantly about Courtney getting married was that she'd talked Harry into moving to fast-growing Wichita. Their new hotel was already under construction. That was the place to make money, according to Reed, who was also making the move. His new Wichita saloon and gambling hall would be finished before the '73 droving season began.

Sarah didn't care whether Courtney moved to Wichita, just so long as she was no longer living with Sarah and Harry.

Courtney looked on the move with trepidation. Wichita would be ten times worse than Rockley for attracting unsavory elements. She didn't want to make the move with Sarah, and she certainly wouldn't marry Reed. She had, therefore, no options worth considering—until today's plan began forming.

She had always wanted to return East, and now she didn't want to stay in Rockley anymore and was afraid of living in Wichita under the careless protection of Harry.

Courtney tossed and turned, unable to sleep. Finally she lit the candle beside her bed and fetched the newspaper she had hidden in her bureau. She'd been looking forward to it all day. To her disappointment, it wasn't an Eastern paper, just a weekly out of Fort Worth, Texas, and eight months old at that. Still, it was a newspaper, even if it was worn and faded.

She spread the paper out on her bed and read the first few articles but skipped the one about a shoot-out. That reminded her too much of Mr. Chandos and dead Jim Ward.

Her mind shied away from Ward but stayed with Chandos, no matter how hard she tried not to think about him. She had to admit he appealed to her and had from the moment she laid eyes on him. He wasn't the first man ever to attract her, but no one had ever disturbed her so thoroughly. Reed Taylor attracted her when he first came to town, but not after she got to know him.

With Chandos, the difference was that she knew who he was, what he was, yet she still found his appeal overwhelming.

He was lean and hard from head to foot, from his face to his flat, tapering waist to the tightly compact muscles of those long legs. The span of his shoulders would be too wide on a shorter man but was perfect for his tall frame. His face was deeply tanned, the skin unmarred except for a tiny scar high on his left cheek. But it was his mouth and eyes that combined to make his face so disturbingly handsome. The lips were straight, with just enough fullness to make them incredibly sensual. And the eyes, his most striking feature because they were so light next to his dark skin, were truly beautiful, with thick black lashes to frame them. Yet he was undeniably masculine.

Being near him, Courtney had been more aware of her femininity than ever before—which explained why she'd acted like such a ninny.

Courtney sighed. Her eyes gradually focused again on the newspaper, and the picture she had been staring at without seeing. And then her heart accelerated as she stared, disbelieving, at the picture. Was it possible? No—yes!

Quickly, she read the article that accompanied the fuzzy photograph, the first photograph she'd ever seen in a newspaper. The article was about the apprehension of one Henry McGinnis, known cattle rustler in McLennan County, Texas, who'd been caught red-handed by rancher Fletcher Straton. Straton's men had brought McGinnis into the nearest town, Waco. There were no other names mentioned except the name of the marshal and the cowboys who had turned the prisoner over to him. The picture showed the rustler being led down the main street of Waco, and the townspeople gathered to watch. The photographer had focused on McGinnis, and the onlookers behind him were not clear. But one of the men in the crowd looked exactly like Edward Harte.

Courtney threw her robe around her and grabbed the newspaper and the candle. She ran to Sarah and Harry's room, around the corner from hers. Her pounding on the door elicited a curse, but she burst inside. Harry groaned when he saw that it was only Courtney. Sarah glowered.

"Do you have any idea what time—"

"Sarah!" Courtney cried. "My father is *alive*."

"What?" the two cried at once.

Harry gave Sarah a sidelong look. "Does that mean we aren't married, Sarah?"

"It means no such thing!" Sarah snapped. "Courtney Harte, how dare you—"

"Sarah, look," Courtney interrupted, sitting on the bed to show her the photograph. "You can't tell me that's not my father."

Sarah stared at the picture for a good while. Then her features relaxed. "You can go back to sleep, Harry. The girl's imagination has run away with her. Couldn't you have waited until a decent hour, Courtney, before you started this nonsense?"

"It's not nonsense. That's my father! And the picture was taken in Waco, which proves—"

"Nothing," Sarah scoffed. "So there is a man in Waco who vaguely resembles Edward—and I said *vaguely*. The picture isn't clear, and the man's features are blurred. Just because there's some resemblance, that doesn't make him Edward. Edward is dead, Courtney. Everyone agrees he couldn't possibly have survived captivity."

"Everyone but me!" Courtney said angrily. How dared Sarah disregard such evidence? "I never believed he was dead. He could have escaped. He could—"

"Fool! Then where has he been for four years? In Waco? Why did he never try to find us?" Sarah gave a sigh. "Edward is dead, Courtney. Nothing has changed. Now go to bed."

"I'm going to Waco."

"You're what?" It took a moment, but

80

Sarah began to laugh. "Of course you are. If you want to get yourself killed wandering off by yourself, by all means do so." And then, abrasively, "Get out of here and let me sleep!"

Courtney started to say more, then changed her mind. She left the room quietly.

She didn't go back to her room. She wasn't imagining things. No one was going to tell her that wasn't her father in the picture. He was alive. She felt it instinctively, had always felt it. He had gone on to Waco—why, she did not know. Why he hadn't tried to find her she couldn't say, either. But she was going to find him.

To hell with Sarah. She scoffed for the simple reason that she didn't want Edward to be alive. She had found herself a husband who was going to make her rich and who suited her better than Edward had.

Courtney left the living quarters at the back of the hotel and entered the lobby. A candle burned at the desk, but there was no sign of young Tom who worked at the desk through the night in case some drifter came in. Without a desk clerk, a man might wake everyone to get a room. It had been known to happen.

81

Courtney gave little thought to Tom or to being seen in her robe and nightgown. With her candle in her hand and the precious newspaper tucked under her arm, she mounted the stairs to the guests' chambers.

She knew exactly what she was going to do. It was the boldest thing she had ever done in her life. If she thought about it, she wouldn't do it, so she didn't think about it. She didn't hesitate even for a second before knocking on the door, though she had sense enough to knock quietly. What time was it? She didn't know, but she didn't want to wake anyone else, just Chandos.

She was knocking for the third time when the door flew open and she was jerked roughly inside. Her mouth was covered by a tight hand, and her back was pressed against the rocklike chest. Her candle fell, and with the closing of the door, the room was pitched into total darkness.

"No one ever tell you you can get killed waking a man in the middle of the night? Someone half-asleep wouldn't have taken the time to notice you're a woman."

He released her, and Courtney nearly crumbled to the floor.

"I'm sorry," she began. "I—I had to see you. And I was afraid to wait until morning—afraid I might miss you. You are leaving in the morning, aren't you?"

She fell silent as a match flared. He picked up her candle—how on earth had he seen it in the dark?—and it came to life again. He set it on the small chest of drawers, and she saw that beside the chest were his saddlebags and saddle. She wondered if he had bothered to unpack and put away his things at all. She doubted it. He struck her as a man who would be ready to leave at a moment's notice.

She had been in this room hundreds of times to clean it, but tonight she was seeing it differently. The large woven rug had been rolled up and set out of the way against the wall. Why? And why had the rug by the bed been kicked under the bed? The towels and water she had brought earlier had been used, the towels hung over the washstand bar to dry. The single window was closed, the curtains drawn, and she imagined the window was locked. The cast-iron stove in the center of the room was cold. The straight-backed wooden chair beside it was hung with a clean blue shirt, the black vest and neckerchief he had worn earlier, and one belt. The gunbelt hung by the bed, its holster empty. His black boots were on the floor.

The sight of his rumpled bed mortified her, started her backing up toward the door. She had woken a man from his sleep. How could she have done something so thoroughly improper?

"I'm sorry," she apologized. "I shouldn't have disturbed you."

"But you did. So you're not leaving until I know why."

That sounded like a threat, and as it registered, she realized that he was bare-chested, wearing only pants, incompletely fastened, revealing an indecent amount of navel. She noted the wide mat of dark hair that stretched between his nipples and formed a T with the straight line of hair that ran down the center of his belly, disappearing into his pants. She also noted the short, wicked-looking knife stuck through one of his belt loops. His gun was probably tucked into the back of his pants.

No, he wouldn't have taken any chances before opening the door. Men lived by a different set of rules in the West, she knew, and men like this one never relaxed their guard.

"Lady?"

She cringed. There was no impatience in his voice, but she knew he must be fed up with her.

Hesitantly, she met his eyes. They were as unrevealing as they always were.

"I—I had hoped you might help me."

As she had thought, his gun was on him. He reached behind him for it and moved to the bed, returning it to the holster. Then he sat down on the bed, staring at her thoughtfully. It was too much for Courtney, the rumpled bed, the half-dressed man. Her cheeks began to burn.

"You in some kind of trouble?"

"No."

"Then what?"

"Will you take me to Texas?"

She said it in a rush, before she could change her mind. And she was glad.

There was a brief pause before he said, "You're loco, right?"

She blushed. "No. I assure you I am serious. I have to go to Texas. I have reason to believe my father is there, in Waco."

"I know Waco. There's more than four hundred miles between here and there—half of it straight through Indian lands. You didn't know that, did you?"

"I knew it."

"But you weren't thinking of going that way?"

"It's the quickest route, isn't it? That's the route I would have traveled four years ago with my father if— Well, never mind. I know the dangers. That's why I'm asking you to escort me."

"Why me?"

She had to think for a moment before the obvious answer came to her. "There is no one else here I can ask. Well, there is one man, but his price would be too high. And you proved today that you're more than capable of protecting me. I have every confidence that you would get me to Waco safely." She stopped, wondering whether to say the other thing. "Well, there is one other reason, strange as it may sound. You seem somehow . . . familiar to me."

"I never forget a face, lady."

"Oh, I'm not saying we've met. I would certainly remember if we had. I think it's your eyes." If she told him how his eyes had soothed her, he really would think she was loco. She still didn't understand it, so didn't mention it. Instead she said, "Maybe as a child I trusted someone with eyes like yours, I don't know. But I do know for some reason you make me feel safe. And honestly,

I haven't felt safe, really safe, since I . . . I've been apart from my father."

He made no comment. He got up, crossed to the door, and opened it. "I'm not taking you to Texas."

Her heart sank. She had worried only about asking him, not over his refusal. "But—but I'll pay you."

"I'm not for hire."

"But—you're taking a *dead* man to Wichita for money."

He looked amused. "I would have passed through Wichita anyway on the way to Newton."

"Oh," she said. "I didn't realize you planned to stay in Kansas."

"I don't."

"Then—"

"The answer is no. I'm not a nursemaid."

"I'm not completely helpless," Courtney began hotly, but his dubious gaze stopped her. "I'll find someone else to take me," she said stoutly.

"I wouldn't suggest it. You'll get killed."

That was too close to what Sarah had said, and Courtney's anger rose. "I regret disturbing you, *Mister* Chandos," she said sharply and deliberately before marching stiffly out of his room.

Chapter 10

Twenty-five miles north of Wichita, Newton was becoming Abilene's successor as the cattle-shipping center of Kansas. Built on the bawdy pattern of its predecessor, the town would likely enjoy only one season, since Wichita was already gearing up to claim the next season.

South of the railroad tracks, in the section called Hide Park, was where all the dance halls, saloons, and bordellos were. Cowboys from the cattle outfits were always in town, and the hell-raising went on around the clock. Gunfire was common. Fistfights, begun at the slightest provocation, were equally common.

This was standard during the droving season, for cowboys were paid off at the end of the trail, and most of them spent their earnings in a matter of days.

As Chandos rode through Hide Park, he noted that these cowboys were no different. Some would head back to Texas once their pockets were empty, some would drift on to other towns. One heading south might even stop off in Rockley and be enticed by Courtney Harte to take her to Texas.

Chandos rarely let on what he was thinking, but just then he came damn close to scowling. The thought of young Courtney Harte alone on the prairie with one of these women-hungry cowboys was not a comforting one. He liked even less the fact that he cared. Stupid Eastern woman. She hadn't learned a thing in the four years since he'd held her life in his hands. She still had no instinct for survival.

Chandos stopped in front of Tuttle's Saloon but didn't dismount. He reached into his vest pocket and drew out the small ball of hair he had carried with him these four years, the long strands he had found stuck in his hand after he'd twisted Courtney's hair.

He hadn't known her name then, but he'd found out soon after, when he went to Rockley to find out what had happened to his cateyes. Cateyes was how he thought of her, even after he learned her name. And Chandos had thought of her often over the years.

He'd never pictured her as she was now, of course. Her image in his mind had been of the frightened girl not much older than his sister had been when she died. The image had changed now, for the foolish girl had become a beautiful woman—one who was just as foolish as ever, maybe more so. He could easily imagine her raped and killed because of her stubborn determination to get to Texas, and he knew his imaginings were based in reality.

Chandos dismounted, tethering his piebald pinto in front of Tuttle's. He stared at the ball of hair in his hand for a few seconds more. Then, disgusted, he tossed it away and watched as the breeze took it skittering a few feet down the dirt street.

He went into the saloon and saw that though it was only midday, there were at least twenty people scattered around the bar and tables. There were even a couple of low-cleavaged ladies. A professional gambler had a game going at one of the tables, and the town marshal sat at the other end of the room, drinking with six buddies, making as much noise as the rest of the drinkers. Three cowboys were having a friendly argument over the two whores. Two dangerous-looking hombres were quietly nursing drinks at a corner table.

"Dare Trask been in yet?" Chandos asked the bartender as he ordered a drink.

"Don't ring a bell, mister. Hey, Will, you know a Dare Trask?" the man called to one of his regulars.

"Can't say as I do," Will replied.

"He used to ride with Wade Smith and Leroy Curly," Chandos supplied.

"Smith I know. Heard he was shacked up with some woman down in Paris, Texas. The other two?" The man shrugged.

Chandos downed a whiskey. That was something, at least, even if it was only a rumor. In fact, it was by asking some innocent questions in a saloon that Chandos had heard that Trask was headed for Newton. He'd heard nothing about Smith for two years, however, not since he learned the man was wanted in San Antonio for murder. Chandos had trailed Leroy Curly to a small town in New Mexico, and hadn't even needed to provoke a fight. Curly was a born troublemaker. He delighted in showing off his fast gun, and he picked the fight with Chandos that got him killed.

Chandos wouldn't be able to recognize Dare Trask, for he had only a sketchy description of brown hair and brown eyes, a short man in his late twenties. That fit two of the cowboys and one of the gunmen at the corner table. But Dare Trask had one notable feature. He was missing a finger on his left hand.

Chandos ordered a second whiskey.

"Trask comes in, tell him Chandos is looking for him."

"Chandos? Sure thing, mister. You a friend?"

"No."

That said it all. Nothing riled a gunman more than hearing someone he didn't know was looking for him. Chandos had found the sometimes-cowboy, more-times-drifter Cincinnati with that same challenge. He hoped it would draw out Trask, who had managed to continually elude him these last four years, just as Smith had.

Just to be thorough, Chandos turned his scrutiny on the three men who came close to Trask's description. Everyone's fingers were intact.

"What the hell you lookin' at, mister?" said the cowboy who now sat alone at his table, his two friends having just gotten up, with the whores, to go upstairs. He had obviously lost the argument and so was forced to wait until one of the whores returned. He wasn't happy about it.

Chandos ignored him. When a man was itching for a fight, very little could be done to calm him down.

The cowboy got up and grabbed

Chandos's shoulder, whirling him around. "Sonofabitch, I asked you a ques—"

Chandos gave him a hard kick to the crotch, and the fellow went down, landing hard on his knees and clutching his injured area, his face sickly pale. As the cowboy fell, Chandos drew his gun.

Another man might have fired, but Chandos did not kill for the sake of killing. He merely aimed the gun, prepared to shoot if he had to.

Town Marshal McCluskie, who had gotten to his feet at the start of trouble, made no move to interfere. He was not in the same league as his predecessor, who had tried to tame Newton. For a brief moment the stranger's blue eyes looked at the marshal. The message was clear. He was not a man to trifle with. Besides, you didn't confront a stranger who already had his gun drawn.

The other two cowboys inched forward from the stairs to collect their friend, hands outstretched in a conciliatory gesture. "Easy, mister. Bucky's got an empty basket when it comes to sense. He's not tied too tight, but he won't be causin' any more trouble."

"Like hell I—"

The cowboy jabbed an elbow in Bucky's

side as he hauled him to his feet. "Dumb shit! Shut your trap while you still got one. You're lucky he didn't blow your head off!"

"I'll be in town a few more hours," Chandos told them, "if your friend wants to resume."

"No sir! We'll just take Bucky back to camp, and if he still ain't got no sense, then we'll beat some into him. You won't be seein' him again."

That was questionable, but Chandos let it pass. He would just have to be on his guard until he left Newton.

The moment Chandos's gun slipped back into its holster, the noise in the room picked up again. The marshal sat down with a relieved sigh, and the card game continued. Altercations of this type weren't even worth discussing. It took some bloodshed to stir excitement in Newton.

Chandos left Tuttle's saloon a few minutes later. He still had the other saloons to cover in his search for Trask, as well as the dance halls and bordellos. The latter might just claim some of his time too, for he hadn't been with a woman since before leaving Texas, and his unexpected run-ins with Courtney Harte in her goddamn nightgown hadn't helped.

As he thought of her, he saw the ball of hair in the dirt a few yards from where he had tossed it. As he watched, a light breeze rolled it back toward him. It stopped a few inches from his feet. His impulse was to step on it before it blew away again. Chandos picked it up and put it back in his vest pocket.

Chapter 11

While the good folks were off to church that Sunday morning, Reed Taylor was sitting in his parlor–office, one of the two rooms he kept for himself above his saloon. He had a chair pulled up to the window and a stack of dime novels beside the chair.

He was a fanatic for tales of high adventure. Ned Buntline had once been his favorite writer, but tales about Buffalo Bill by Bill's friend Prentiss Ingraham had taken the top spot recently. Reed loved Buffalo Bill's own novels, too, but his all-time favorite was still *Seth Jones, or The Captive of the Frontier*, by Edward Sylvester Ellis. That one was Beadle and Adams's first dime novel to feature a Wild West background.

Reed was thoroughly engrossed in his

fifth reading of *Bowie Knife Ben, The Little Hunter of the Nor'west* by Oll Coomes when Ellie May sauntered out of his bedroom, purposely distracting him with a loud yawn. But that was the extent of his distraction. Her scantily clad body held no interest for him that morning because he had used it so well the night before.

"You shoulda woke me, sugar," Ellie May said throatily as she came up behind Reed, draping her arms around his neck. "I thought we was gonna spend the whole day in bed."

"You thought wrong," Reed murmured absently. "Now run along to your own room—that's a good girl."

He patted her hand, not even bothering to look up at her. Ellie May's mouth screwed up in vexation. She was a pretty girl, had a fine figure, and she liked men, liked them extremely well. So did Dora for that matter, the other girl who worked with her in Reed's saloon. But Reed wouldn't let them service any of the customers. He had even hired a particularly mean gunman who was passing through town last year to enforce his rule that there be no hanky-panky. Gus Maxwell did as he'd been ordered.

Reed considered both girls his own private stock, and could be mighty unpleasant if he was kept waiting when he was in the mood to take one of them to bed. Problem was he didn't take either to bed often enough because he divided his attentions between the two. Ellie May and Dora, once friends, were now mutually hostile because Reed was the only man available to the two of them.

Ellie May almost wished Courtney Harte would marry Reed. Maybe then he'd let her and Dora leave, as they both wanted to do. He'd threatened them not to leave, and neither was willing to see what he would do. He said he was going to take them with him to Wichita, so maybe it would be different there, Ellie May hoped. At least there would be a marshal they could complain to if things didn't change. Here in Rockley, no one would believe Reed was a bully, for he ran a clean, decent saloon and was respected.

"You know what your problem is, Reed?" Ellie May was dissatisfied enough to say. "You only got three things that really interest you—money, them stupid dime novels, and that fancy miss across the street. I'm surprised you didn't walk Miss Goody-Goody to church so's you could finagle an invite to lunch. 'Course, it'd shock the reverend if you was to show up in church. Poor man might just keel right over."

Her sarcasm was wasted. Reed wasn't even listening. Ellie May turned away angrily. The open window caught her eye and, down the street, the lady in question. Ellie May smiled, her eyes gleaming wickedly.

"Well now, I wonder who's the fella walking Miss Courtney home from church?" she drawled.

Reed was out of his chair instantly, shoving Ellie May away from the window so he could get a good view. Then he yanked the curtains together and turned to glare at Ellie May.

"I ought to slap you silly!" he said furiously. "You know Pearce Cates when you see him!"

"Oh, was that Pearce?" she asked innocently.

"Get out!"

"Sure thing, sugar."

She smiled smugly. It had been worth Reed's anger to see him upset, even for only a few moments. He was so used to getting everything he wanted that he fell apart if it looked like things weren't going his way. Courtney Harte was one of the things Reed wanted, and although she hadn't tumbled right into his arms, he had no doubt that, in the end, she would. He already thought of her as his. Ellie May hoped the little lady would stick to her guns, though. It would do Reed Taylor good to be humbled for once.

"Courtney!"

She stopped, groaning when she saw Reed Taylor crossing the street toward her. Of all the luck. Another few yards and she'd have been safely inside the hotel.

Mattie and Pearce stopped too, but with a long-suffering look, Courtney nodded them on, then waited for Reed to reach her. He did quickly. In fact, she noted, he must have rushed out of his saloon the moment he saw her, for he'd come out without his coat or hat, most unusual for a man who prided himself on dressing impeccably at all times.

His grooming wasn't up to par, either. His blond hair was mussed, and he hadn't yet shaved. His disheveled state made him no less handsome, however. Courtney doubted anything could detract from Reed's appearance. The combination of dark green eyes, aquiline nose, and engaging dimples was lethal. And he was a big man, tall and thick-set—strong. She always thought of strength when she saw Reed. He was a winner, a very successful man. Yes, strong.

Courtney sometimes wondered if she wasn't crazy to let his faults determine her feelings about him. But they did. He was the most bullishly stubborn, hardheaded man she had ever met. She just didn't like him. That didn't show in the gaze she turned on him, though, for Courtney was far too well brought up for that.

"Morning, Reed."

He came right to the point. "You haven't received me since that trouble in Handley's store."

"No, I haven't."

"Were you that upset?"

"Well, of course I was."

And she had been. But the other fact was that she was preoccupied with finding someone to take her to Texas. She was packed and ready to go. And Berny Bixler had a wagon and a sturdy horse for sale. She lacked only an escort.

But the trouble in Handley's served as an excuse to put Reed off. A simple "I don't want to see you" just didn't work with Reed.

"I couldn't believe it when Gus told me. I didn't get back from Wichita until that night," Reed told her. "It's damned fortunate that Chandler fellow was there."

"Chandos," Courtney corrected softly.

"What? Yes, well, whatever. I meant to thank him for coming to your assistance, but he took off too early the next morning—which is probably just as well. The man was too quick to draw his gun at the slightest provocation."

Courtney knew what he was referring to. After being up half the night, she had slept late that following morning, thus missing the second shoot-out. It seemed Jim Ward's friend had challenged Chandos in front of the hotel. According to old Charley, the fellow hadn't stood a chance against Chandos's lightning-quick draw. But the gunman's wound was to his gun hand. Chandos hadn't killed him. After that, Chandos tied the man up, collected Jim Ward's corpse, and rode out of Rockley with the dead man and the live one in tow.

"It was not your place to thank the man on my behalf anyway, Reed," Courtney said. "I tried to thank him myself, but he didn't want thanks."

"I just wish I could have been there to help you, honey," Reed replied warmly. Then, in the next breath, and with equal

101

enthusiasm, he said, "But my trip was successful. I was able to secure a prime location over in Buffalo City. The fellow who told me about it was right. Thanks to the railroad, another town has sprung up practically overnight, this one around that old whiskey peddlers' camp. They've already rechristened it Dodge City, after the commander of the nearby garrison."

"Another cowtown in the making?" Courtney remarked dryly, no longer amazed by Reed's single-minded self-centeredness. "Then you'll be moving there instead of Wichita?"

"No, I'll find someone to run the Dodge saloon for me. Wichita will still be the home base, as I planned."

"How enterprising of you. Why not keep your place here in Rockley too, instead of tearing it down?"

"I've considered that. If you think it's a good idea—"

"Don't, Reed," Courtney cut in quickly. Good grief, the man's hide was so thick, sarcasm didn't penetrate. "Whatever you decide has nothing to do with me."

"Of course it does."

"No, it does not," she said firmly, then

added, "You might as well know, I've decided to leave Rockley."

"Leave? What do you mean? Of course, you've wanted to return East, and I can't blame you. The only reason I put down stakes in Rockley was because of you. But there's nothing for you back East, honey. Sarah's told me—"

"I don't care what Sarah has told you." Courtney's voice rose against his patronizing attitude. "And where I go is none of your concern."

"Of course it is."

God sakes, he made her want to scream. But it had always been like this. He could never take no for an answer. Her frank refusal to marry him had simply been ignored. How did a person get through to such a man?

"Reed, I have to leave. Mattie and Pearce are waiting for me at home."

"They can wait," he said, frowning. "Listen to me, Courtney. About this notion of yours about leaving. I simply can't allow you—"

"You can't *allow!*" she gasped.

"Now, I didn't mean it quite that way." He tried to pacify her. Lord, she was something when her eyes lit up like that. It

103

happened so rarely, but when it did, she aroused him like no woman ever had. "It's just that I'm pulling up stakes in about two weeks, and I thought we could get married first."

"No."

"Honey, it's a damned long ride between here and Wichita just to continue courting."

"Good."

His frown grew more pronounced. "You have never given me one good reason why you won't marry me. Oh, I know, you say you don't love me—"

"Oh, you've heard me say that much?"

"Honey, you'll learn to love me," he assured her, his dimples appearing. "I'll grow on you."

"I don't *want* you to grow on me, Reed, I—"

She suffered through his unexpected kiss without any undignified struggles. It wasn't distasteful. Reed knew an awful lot about kissing. But the only thing he stirred in her was exasperation. How she would have liked to slap him for his boldness. But the scene they were causing was bad enough without compounding it.

When he released her, she stepped back. "Good day, Reed."

"We *will* marry, Courtney," he said as she walked past him.

Courtney didn't acknowledge those words, which had sounded like a threat. Perhaps she ought to put off leaving until after Reed moved to Wichita. She didn't really think he would try to stop her, but where Reed was concerned, a person just never knew.

She was so preoccupied that she nearly ran into the gunman. In fact, he reached out to stop her from colliding with him. He was standing in the entrance of the hotel, blocking the doorway. Why hadn't she noticed him? God sakes, had he seen her kissing Reed? His eyes gave away nothing of his thoughts, as usual.

The blush crept embarrassingly into her cheeks anyway. She glanced to the side to see if Reed was still watching her, but he had gone back to his saloon.

"I—I never thought to see you—" she began, stopping when he flipped a wad of paper at her.

"Can you fill that in an hour?"

She opened the crumpled paper and briefly scanned the contents. Her heart skipped a beat. It was a list of supplies, a detailed list.

Slowly, her eyes rose to his. "Does this mean you've changed your mind?"

He stared at her for several long moments. She was so easy to read, hope and excitement in her catlike eyes.

"One hour, lady, or I ride out alone," was all he said.

Chapter 12

Mattie knocked only once before opening the door. "So he came back?"

Courtney glanced over her shoulder. "What? Oh, Mattie, I forgot about you and Pearce waiting. I'm sorry. But don't just stand there, come in and help me!"

"Help you with what?"

"What's it look like?" Courtney said impatiently.

The younger girl's eyes widened as she took in the sight of the room in utter shambles. Clothes were scattered everywhere, petticoats and gowns draped over the chair, the bed, the bureau, everywhere.

"You want me to help you mess up your room?"

"Silly. I can't take my trunk because there's no mention of a wagon on the list, just a horse with all the trappings. Here, see?" Courtney handed the list over.

Mattie's eyes widened. "So he's going to take you to Texas? But I thought you said—"

"He changed his mind. He's a man of few words, Mattie. He just handed me the list and asked if I could fill it in an hour. Oh! Come on, I don't have much time. I still have to go to Handley's for the saddlebags and supplies and buy a horse, and—"

"Courtney! I can't believe you're willin' to travel all the way to Texas without a wagon. You'll have no privacy. You'll have to sleep on the ground."

"I'll have a bedroll," Courtney said cheerfully. "See, there's a bedroll on the list."

"Courtney!"

"Well, I don't have much choice, do I? And look at all the time we'll save without a wagon to slow us down. I'll get to Waco much sooner than I thought."

"Court, you've never even ridden a horse for one entire day, much less weeks. You're gonna be so sore—"

"Mattie, I'll manage, really. And I don't have time to argue. If I'm not ready, he'll leave without me."

"Let him. God sakes, Courtney, that

man's in too much of an all-fired hurry. He's gonna race you across the plains. Your blisters will have blisters. In two days you'll wish you were dead and beg him to bring you back. Wait for someone else to take you."

"No," Courtney said, her chin set firmly. "Others coming through Rockley might say yes, but will I trust them? I trust Chandos. You said yourself that he's perfect for the job. And there's something else, Mattie. I have the feeling Reed might try to stop me."

"He wouldn't dare," Mattie said indignantly.

"Yes, he would dare. And not many men would stand up to Reed."

"And you think Chandos would? Yes, I guess he would, all right. But—"

"Mattie, I have to get to Waco. Chandos is the best man to get me there. It's as simple as that. Now, are you going to help me? I'm running out of time."

"All right." Mattie sighed. "Let's see what's on this list—are you going to buy pants and shirts? He has those on here."

Busy sorting through her gowns, Courtney shook her head. "I'm sure he only put that on the list because I can't ride in a dress. But I have that mohair skirt that I altered for riding, so that'll be fine."

"You're sure that's his reason? Maybe he wants you to look like a man. You forget the country you'll be traveling through."

"Don't start on the dangers, Mattie! I'm scared enough."

"Maybe you better buy at least one pair of pants just to be safe."

"I suppose I could, but Mr. Handley's going to think I'm crazy. And I don't have enough time for all that."

Mattie stared at the carpetbag Courtney was stuffing two gowns into. "I know he says to bring only a few clothes, Court, but you can get one more dress in there. Why not? You're gonna need an extra sack for all the food anyway, and you've still got the saddlebags. You're gonna be cramped on your horse, but there's no way around that."

"Oh! Mattie? You know horses better than I do, and he says I need a good horse. Could you buy the horse for me?"

"There's not much to choose from over at the stable. If there was time, well, we've got a beauty out at our place."

"There's no time, Mattie. He said an hour and he meant an hour."

"I'll see what I can do," Mattie grumbled.

"Then I'll meet you in front of Handley's. Does Sarah know yet?"

Courtney handed over some of her stash of bills, grinning at her friend. "Are you serious? If she knew, she'd be in here giving me her long list of dire predictions."

"Why don't you leave without tellin' her? You'd save yourself a sore ear."

"I can't, Mattie. After all, she *has* taken care of me these last years."

"Taken care!" Mattie cried indignantly. "Worked you to the bone, you mean!"

Courtney smiled at Mattie's outspokenness. She had picked up some outlandish sayings from her friend over the years, things she herself sometimes said without thinking. At least she no longer blushed at the outrageous things Mattie said, like she used to do.

Realizing how long it might be before she saw Mattie again, Courtney said, "I'm going to miss you, Mattie. And I want you to have anything you wish from what I have to leave behind."

Mattie's eyes widened. "You mean . . . all these pretty dresses?"

"I'd rather you had them than Sarah."

"Well, shoot, I don't know what to say. I mean—I'll miss you, too."

She ran out of the room before she started crying. No sense in that. Court was determined to go.

Tears misted in Courtney's eyes too as she hurriedly finished packing and dressed in her riding outfit.

Before she left the hotel, she ran into Sarah. She had wanted to save her good-byes until the last minute, after she'd finished buying the other things she would need, but that was not to be.

"So you didn't let go of that fool notion about going to Waco?" was Sarah's response.

"No, Sarah," Courtney said softly.

"Little fool. If you die out there on the prairie, I'll be damned if I'll mourn you."

"I'm not going alone, Sarah."

"What? Who's going with you?"

"His name is Chandos, and he's the one who—"

"I know who he is!" Sarah hissed. Then, unexpectedly, she began to laugh. "Oh, I see. All that ridiculous nonsense about your father was just an excuse so you could run off with that gunslinger. I always knew you were a tramp."

Courtney's eyes flashed angrily. "You knew no such thing, Sarah. But believe whatever you like. After all, if my father really is alive, that makes you an adulteress—doesn't it?"

In the brief moment that Sarah was rendered speechless, Courtney walked out of the hotel. She was afraid that Sarah might follow her, but she didn't.

There was no sign of Chandos in the street, or of his horse, so Courtney still had a few minutes before the deadline. Quickly she bought what she needed. She was able, too, to say good-bye to a few of the folks who had been kind to her, because Lars Handley, Charley and Snub, and the Coffman sisters were all in Handley's store.

Mattie came in before she was done. "He's waitin', Courtney."

She looked out the window. Chandos was there, mounted on his horse. She felt a little tingle of fear race along her spine. She barely knew this man, yet she was going away alone with him.

"He brought along an extra horse," Mattie continued, subdued. "It's all saddled and ready. He did it—even picked out the saddle. Guess he figured you wouldn't find a good mount here. I bought old Nelly for you, though. Got her real cheap." Mattie handed over what was left of Courtney's money. "She's nothin' to ride, but she'll make a good packhorse, so you won't be cramped riding."

"Then don't sound so unhappy."

"Do I?" Mattie became defensive. "You're leaving . . . Oh, that's not all. I don't know. Chandos, he shook me up, I guess, the way he just took over at the stable, and without sayin' anything. You're right, he is a man of few words. And he—he scares the shit out of me."

"Mattie!"

"Well, he does. What makes you so sure you can trust him, Court?"

"I just trust him, that's all. You're forgetting he already saved me once, from that terrible Jim Ward. Now he's willing to help me again."

"I know, I know. But I can't figure out *why*."

"It doesn't matter. I need him, Mattie. Now, come on and help me tie everything to old Nelly."

When the two girls came out of the store, Chandos made no acknowledgment. He didn't even dismount to help them secure Courtney's bags to the packhorse. Courtney hurried, not so much because of him as because she didn't want Reed to see what she was doing. She sent nervous glances down the street toward his saloon, hoping she and Chandos would be able to leave before there was a scene.

After the two friends embraced for the last time and Courtney mounted, Chandos said, "You get everything on the list?"

"Yes."

"I suppose it's too late now to ask if you know how to ride?"

He said it so dryly that Courtney laughed. "I can ride."

"Then let's ride, lady."

Picking up old Nelly's reins, he headed south. Courtney had no time to do anything more than return Mattie's wave.

They reached the end of Rockley almost instantly, and with a heartfelt sigh, Courtney said good-bye to that chapter of her life.

It didn't take long for her to get used to staring at Chandos's back. He simply wouldn't ride beside her. She tried to catch up to him a few times, but he always managed to stay a good length ahead of her, no farther than that but not close enough to talk. Yet he was always aware of what she was doing. He never looked back, but each time her horse lagged, Chandos slowed. He kept the exact same distance between them all the time. This reassured her.

It shouldn't have. A few moments later Chandos stopped to dismount, then walked purposefully toward her. She looked at him curiously. It was only nearing sunset, and she hadn't thought they would make camp so early.

Then she felt a twinge of alarm, for his face was set, his eyes coldly determined.

Without a word, he reached up and dragged her off her mount. With a startled cry, she fell into him, her boots slamming against his shins. He didn't flinch. An arm snaked tightly around her waist, his other hand shot out and clenched her buttocks.

"Chandos, please!" she cried out, shocked and horrified. "What are you doing?"

He said nothing. His eyes were blue ice, and they said all she needed to know.

"*Why?*"

"Why not?"

Oh, God, she couldn't believe this was happening. "I trusted you!"

"I guess you shouldn't have," he said coldly, wrapping both arms around her tightly.

Courtney began to cry. "Please. You're hurting me."

"You're going to hurt a lot more if you don't do exactly as I say, lady. Now put your arms around me."

He displayed no anger at all. He didn't raise his voice even a little. Courtney would have preferred fury to this cold determination.

Staring into his frigid eyes, she did as he said, afraid not to. Her heart was beating a terrified tempo. God help her, how could she have been so terribly wrong about him?

"That's better," he said evenly. And then he slipped one hand free and, in a single motion, ripped the front of her blouse open.

Courtney screamed, knowing it was useless but unable to stop it. That accomplished one thing however. Chandos pushed her away from him as she screamed, and she landed on her backside, sprawled at his feet. Hastily, she pulled her blouse together.

She had trusted Chandos to protect her, and she felt utterly betrayed. She looked up at him, and her eyes told him just how she felt.

She shivered. He looked so merciless standing there, his feet braced apart, so strong and so handsome, but so cruel.

"I don't think you've grasped your situation yet, otherwise you wouldn't tempt my anger by screaming."

"I—I have."

"Then spell it out for me. Now."

"You're going to rape me."

"And?"

"And—and I can't stop you."

"And?"

"I—I don't know what else there is for me to say."

"There's a hell of a lot more, lady. Rape is the least of your worries. You've put yourself at my mercy. That was stupid, because now I can do any goddamn thing I want with you. Do I make myself clear? I can slit your throat and leave you where your bones will never be found by anything human."

Courtney was trembling violently. She hadn't understood any of this when she should have, and now it was too late.

When she didn't stop shaking, Chandos bent over and slapped her. She promptly burst into a loud torrent of tears, and he swore. Perhaps he *was* being too hard on her, but she had needed the lesson.

He had been prepared to do more than just frighten her, if more was what it took.

But that wasn't necessary. She frightened easily enough.

He put a hand over her mouth to silence her. "You can stop crying. I'm not going to hurt you now."

He could see she didn't believe him, and he sighed. He'd done a better job than he meant to.

"Listen to me, cateyes," he said, his voice deliberately gentle. "Pain is remembered. That's why I used it. I don't want you to forget what you learned today. Another man would have raped you, robbed you, then probably killed you to hide his crime. You can't put your life in the hands of a stranger, not in this part of the country, not ever. I tried to tell you that, but you wouldn't listen to me. There are too many dangerous men riding this trail."

She had stopped crying and he took his hand away from her mouth. He watched her run her small, pink tongue over her lips. Then he stood up and turned his back on her.

"We might as well make camp here for the night," he said without looking at her again. "In the morning, I'll take you back to Rockley."

Chapter 13

Courtney lay there watching the stars for several hours. Then she turned over and stared at the dying fire. It was nearing midnight, she guessed, not knowing for certain.

She had calmed down. Chandos hadn't touched her again, hadn't even come near her except to hand her a plate of food. He hadn't spoken either, but he undoubtedly figured he didn't need to say any more.

The bastard! What right did he have to appoint himself her teacher? What right to raise her hopes so high, then destroy them? Still, she didn't quite have the nerve to risk provoking him by telling him what she thought of his "lesson."

The tears began, tears born of misery. They were silent tears for the most part, with only a few sniffles and an occasional ragged breath to give her away. But that was enough. Chandos heard.

He had not been sleeping. He had his own troubled thoughts keeping him awake. Not the same thoughts, for he felt no remorse over what he'd done. His intentions had been good, even if the execution had been a bit drastic. Better the girl suffer a fright now than end up in some unmarked grave on the prairie later on. Talking wouldn't have done any good, he knew that, because she wouldn't have listened.

Trouble was, he hadn't expected her pain to have such an effect on him. It was almost the same as that other time, when he'd held her life in his hands. Some protective instinct had risen in him, and he wanted only to comfort her, soothe her. Knowing she was crying was ripping away at him. He couldn't stand it.

His first thought was to take off until she settled down, but he knew damn well that she would think he was leaving her, and he didn't want to frighten her any more. Damn her! Women's tears had never bothered him before. What was so different about these tears?

Soundlessly, Chandos got up and crossed the space between them. He dropped down beside the girl without warning, and she gasped as he wrapped his arms around her, pulling her gently into the curve of his body, her back pressed to his front.

"Easy, little cat. Relax. I won't hurt you."

She was stiff as a board. She didn't trust

him. Well, he could hardly blame her for that, could he?

"I'm only going to hold you, nothing else," he said in a soothing voice. "So you can stop crying."

She turned around just enough that she could see him. Chandos was stung by the sight of her wet face. Her eyes were like great wounds.

"You've ruined everything!" she said pitifully.

"I know I have," he found himself saying. Anything to placate her.

"I'll never find my father now!"

"Sure you will. You'll just have to find another way to get to him."

"How? You made me spend so much of my money on supplies that I can't afford to get to Waco now. I bought clothes I'll never wear, a horse that's so old Mr. Sieber will never take her back, and a useless gun that cost even more than the horse!"

"A gun is never useless," Chandos said patiently. "If you'd been wearing yours today, you could've stopped me before I ever got near you."

"I didn't know you were going to attack me!" she retorted indignantly.

"No, I suppose you didn't," he said reasonably. "But you should have. You have to be prepared for anything out here."

"I am now."

She cocked the gun she'd hidden beneath her blanket. His expression didn't change.

"Very good, lady. You're learning. But your timing will have to improve." His hand slipped beneath her blanket to grasp the gun barrel and pull the gun from her grip. "Next time make sure you're facing your target first, especially if you're so close to it."

"What's the difference?" She sighed forlornly. "I couldn't have shot you anyway."

"With enough provocation, you can shoot anything. Now stop crying, will you? I'll pay you back the money."

"Thank you very much," she said tightly, not in the least pacified. "But that isn't going to help much. No matter how I get to Texas, I still can't travel alone. You've proved to me that I can't trust anyone. So where does that leave me?"

"You shouldn't have to go to your father anyway. He should come to you. Write to him."

"Do you know how long it would take a letter to get to Waco? *I* could get there faster."

"I could take a letter for you."

"You're going to Waco?"

"I wasn't going that far, but I can."

"You won't," she said disagreeably. "Once you leave here, you won't bother."

"I said I would, and if I said I would, then I will."

"But what if my father isn't there?" she ventured. "How will I know?" Her eyes pleaded with him, but he gave no sign that he understood.

"I'll probably come back this way sometime."

"Sometime? I'm supposed to wait for *sometime?*"

"What the hell do you want from me, lady? I have other things to do than run errands for you."

"I want you to take me to Waco! You said you would."

"I never said I would. I told you to fill a supply list. You drew the conclusion you wanted to draw."

He hadn't raised his voice at all, but she knew he had lost patience with her. Even so, she couldn't let it go.

"I don't see why you can't take me. You're going to Texas anyway."

"You haven't learned a thing, have you?"

123

His voice was cold now. "I—I have," she said nervously.

"Uh-uh. Otherwise you wouldn't still be willing to travel with me."

Courtney looked away, embarrassed. He was right, of course. She shouldn't even be speaking to him.

"I know why you did what you did," she said in a small voice. "I can't say I appreciate it, but I don't think you meant to hurt me."

"You don't know that at all," he said flatly.

Courtney tensed as suddenly his arms tightened around her.

Breathlessly she said, "Would you—would you really have . . . ?"

"Listen to me, lady." Chandos cut her off sharply. "You don't know what I'm capable of. So don't try to guess."

"Are you trying to frighten me again?"

He sat up. "Look," he said curtly. "All I wanted was for you to stop crying. You have. Now let's both try to get some sleep."

"Why not?" she said resentfully. "My problems aren't any concern of yours. Forget I asked for your help. In fact, just forget everything."

Chandos stood up. Her flippancy didn't

bother him. She was a woman, and he supposed complaining made her feel better. But her next words stopped him cold.

"I've got one option. Reed Taylor will take me to Waco. Of course, that means I'll have to marry him, but what else can I do? I'm used to things not turning out the way I want them to, so what's the difference?"

She had turned back onto her side, facing away from him, and was talking to herself, not to him. Sonofabitch! He didn't know whether to ignore her or beat some sense into her.

"Lady?"

"What?" she snapped.

Chandos smiled. Maybe she had some spunk after all.

"You should have told me you were willing to use your body to get to Waco."

"What?" She swung around so fast her blanket fell away. "I would never—"

"Didn't I just hear you say you would marry that fellow?"

"That's got nothing to do with—with what *you* said," she retorted.

"Doesn't it? Do you think you can marry a man without sharing his bed?"

Hot color rushed into Courtney's cheeks.

She hadn't thought about it at all, had only been talking to make herself feel better.

"It's really none of your business what I do after you take me back to Rockley," she said defensively.

He approached, towering over her. "If you're selling your virginity, I might be interested."

She was speechless. Was he doing this just to shock her?

"I was speaking of marriage," Courtney said, her voice quavering. "Were you?"

"No."

"Then we have nothing further to discuss," she said firmly and turned away.

Chandos watched as she reached behind her for her blanket and pulled it up to her chin.

He turned away for a moment and looked up at the black starry sky, thinking he must be crazy.

He took a deep breath and said it anyway. "I'll take you to Texas."

There was a shocked silence. Then she said, "Your price has become too high."

"No extra price, lady, just what you're willing to pay me."

After everything, he was changing his

mind yet again! She was too vexed to say anything except, "No, thank you."

"Suit yourself," he answered casually, then walked away.

She was proud of herself for refusing. Who did he think he was, playing with her life?

For a long time there was only the sound of the crackling fire. And then she said in a whisper, "Chandos?"

"Yes?"

"I've reconsidered. I accept your offer."

"Then get to sleep, lady. We'll be leaving early."

Chapter 14

The strong smell of coffee woke Courtney. For a moment she lay there, feeling the morning sun on her face. She had never slept under the open sky before, and she found it very pleasant to wake up to the gentle caress of the morning sun. Her bed-roll was quite comfortable, too, spread out on the thick grass. Maybe she wouldn't miss having a wagon along after all.

When she moved, she had second thoughts. God sakes, her body was sore all over. And then she remembered Mattie's warning. They had ridden nearly six hours yesterday. It wasn't hard riding, and they'd covered only fifteen or twenty miles, no more. But to sit that long in a saddle wasn't what Courtney was used to. Her muscles were making their grievances known.

She turned over, wincing. It was worse than she'd thought. And then her eyes fell on her companion and all thoughts of discomfort were forgotten.

Chandos was shaving. He stood about three yards away, where the horses were tethered. A shaving mug with brush in it was set on the ground at his feet. A mirror was hooked onto his saddle, which was already cinched to his horse. The mirror didn't meet his height but was angled so that he could look down into it.

She had watched her father shaving often, but it was not the same as watching Chandos. He wore no shirt, only pants and boots, and the gunbelt that clung to his hips, slanting down to where the holster was strapped to his right thigh.

She watched as he raised his arm to scrape the lather from his face. She watched his muscles bunch and move, her gaze drawn irresistibly to the straight, hard lines of him.

His bare skin was dark and smooth and fascinating.

"Easy, Surefoot."

His horse took a step away from him, and she was amazed by how soothing and gentle Chandos's voice could be. He said something else in a language she didn't recognize. And then Courtney gasped as she heard, "You'd better help yourself to some coffee, lady. We're not going to be here much longer."

Pink rose to her cheeks. Did he know she'd been watching him? How on earth did he even know she was awake?

Courtney sat up slowly, feeling once again the soreness of her muscles. She felt like groaning, but she didn't dare let Chandos know she was hurting. They had ridden only one day. If he thought she couldn't take it, he might change his mind again.

"Was that Spanish you were speaking?" she asked conversationally.

"No."

"Mattie thought perhaps you might be Spanish. Is your name Spanish?"

"No."

Courtney made a face. God sakes, what a sourpuss he was. Couldn't he be pleasant for once? She tried again.

"If you're not Spanish, what are you?"

"Coffee's getting cold, lady."

So much for a civil conversation, she thought. And then her attention focused on the coffee. She was hungry!

"Is there any food, Chandos?"

Finally, he looked at her. Her hair had come unbound while she slept and spilled over her left side, covering most of her plaid shirt. He remembered twisting his fingers in that hair. She was looking at him now with heavy-lidded eyes that were even more slanted than usual. She was tired from crying and from being awake half the night. He knew damn well she had no idea how utterly seductive she looked.

"There's biscuits by the fire," he said curtly.

"Is that all?"

"I usually eat light in the morning. You should have eaten last night."

"I wouldn't have been able to keep it down. I was so—" She stopped herself. *Don't mention yesterday, Courtney.* "Biscuits will be fine, thank you."

Chandos turned back to finish shaving. He must be loco, he told himself. There was no other excuse for taking a woman—*this woman*—through more than four hundred miles of wilderness. A goddamn virgin! She didn't even know any better than to stare at him, thinking he wasn't aware of her. But the moment her eyes touched him, he'd known. He had felt those eyes as surely as if it had been her hands instead of her eyes, caressing his body.

He didn't like what she made him feel. But he would take her to Waco. He would take her because otherwise he would never be able to forget her beautiful tearstained face, her cat eyes filled with despair. He had no desire to carry that image with him the rest of his life, as he had carried these last four years the image of that frightened girl who reminded him of his dead sister.

To his chagrin, she had been linked with him from the day he first saw her, linked through what he had suffered and what she was about to suffer. When he spared her life, she became a part of his.

She didn't know this. There was no reason for her to know.

It had been a mistake to visit Rockley in order to see whether she was still there. It had been an even worse mistake to go back to save her from her foolishness. She was not his responsibility. He wanted only to be free of this affinity, to sever the link that bound them. Instead, he was taking her to Waco. Yes, he definitely was loco.

"Chandos?"

He wiped the remaining lather from his face, grabbed the shirt hanging on the saddle horn, then turned to look at her while he slipped it on. She was sitting next to the fire, so very ladylike. She held a tin cup in one hand and the remains of a leftover biscuit in the other. On her face was a stain of hot color, and she wouldn't meet his eyes. She looked around at the flat expanse of land all around them, devoid of brush or trees. He guessed her dilemma instantly and waited to see what she meant to do about it.

Her eyes flitted to his, then away again. "I—I seem to have a . . . what I mean . . . oh, never mind."

His eyes lit with laughter. She was incredible. She would rather suffer than mention what she doubtless considered an unmentionable subject.

He sauntered over to the fire and hunkered down next to her. "You ought to do something with this," he said, flipping a lock of her hair over her shoulder.

Courtney found herself staring at his bronzed chest, the black mat of hair. He really shouldn't have come near her with his shirt open. Still, she supposed she would have to get used to his lack of propriety if she was going to travel with a man who totally disregarded such things.

"All right," she said demurely. She pulled the pins she'd collected from her bedroll out of her pocket and quickly twisted the long length of honey brown hair into a knot, securing it at her nape. Chandos studied her intently while she kept her eyes averted from his. He was going to have to keep his distance from her.

"I'm going to ride out," he said abruptly. When her eyes darted to his, alarmed, he added, "Don't be long, or you'll have trouble catching up."

He gathered up the coffee pot and his tin cup, kicked out the fire, and then rode off. Courtney sighed audibly with relief. Now she would have a few minutes of privacy to answer nature's call.

And then, quickly, came the realization that Chandos had known what her problem was. How utterly mortifying. Well, she was just going to have to squelch her delicate sensibilities and adjust to traveling with a man.

She wasted no time, worried that she

might not be able to catch up with Chandos. As soon as she could, she lit out after him.

She needn't have worried. He had put about a quarter mile between them, but no more. He sat facing west, and didn't even bother to look back as she approached. When she pulled to a halt beside him, he glanced at her.

He handed her a strip of jerky. "Gnaw on that. It ought to hold you until we stop at midday."

So he knew she was ravenous. Those two biscuits hadn't satisfied her hunger, not when she hadn't eaten since yesterday morning.

"Thank you," she said softly, keeping her eyes lowered.

But Chandos made no move to ride on. He was staring at her. Finally she was forced to look up. She found those beautiful blue eyes as inscrutable as ever.

"This is your last chance to turn back, lady. You know that, don't you?"

"I don't want to turn back."

"Do you really know what you're letting yourself in for? You won't find anything even remotely civilized out there. And I told you, I'm no nursemaid. Don't expect me to do anything for you that you can do for yourself."

She nodded slowly. "I will take care of myself. I ask only that you protect me if the need arises." Then she added hesitantly, "You will do that, won't you?"

"As well as I can."

She sighed as he looked away from her to return the pack of dried jerky to his saddlebag. At least that was settled. Now if only he would stop acting as if she had forced him into this, they might get along. At least he could stop calling her "lady," which sounded more like a derogatory remark than a title of respect.

"I do have a name, Chandos," she ventured. "It's—"

"I know what it is." He cut her off, prodding his horse forward and into a canter.

She stared after him, stung.

Chapter 15

Courtney saw the Indian for the first time just before they crossed the Arkansas River at midday. Chandos had ridden west toward the river that morning, following it south until he found a place shallow enough for crossing.

Courtney was nearly blinded from staring so long at the river while it reflected the midday sun. In her condition, it was hard to focus on the shadows along the bank where trees and vegetation grew. So the movement she saw in the brush might have been anything, really. The man with the long black braids might have been an illusion.

When she told Chandos she thought she'd seen an Indian on the other side of the river they were preparing to cross, he shrugged it off.

"If it was, it was. Don't worry about it."

Then he grabbed hold of her reins and old Nelly's reins, dragging them all into the river. She forgot about the Indian then, worrying instead about staying in the saddle as freezing water lapped first at her feet, then at her thighs, and then at her hips. The skewbald mare bucked and dipped as it tried to keep its footing in the swift current.

At long last, when they'd crossed the river and her mohair riding skirt and petticoat were stretched over a bush to dry and she had donned the unaccustomed pants, Courtney made friends with the little mare that had brought her safely across the river.

Her mare and Chandos's gelding, Surefoot, were called pintos. They were beautiful blue-eyed animals, nearly identical in markings except that Surefoot was patched in black and white, while the mare was brown and white.

Pintos, Courtney knew, were favorites of the Indians. Their endurance, their stamina for long-distance travel, was why, she supposed.

Courtney had never owned her own horse before, except for Nelly, and she wanted to name the mare.

She moved out from behind the bushes, where she'd been lingering with the horses as long as she could, putting off making an appearance in her pants.

There had been no time to try them on at the store, and she'd simply looked them over and assumed they would fit. She'd been wrong. They didn't fit at all. They were boys' pants, not men's pants, and if she hadn't been starving, she'd have stayed behind the bushes.

She saw Chandos down by the river's edge, filling their canteens, but forgot him when their cooking lunch caught her eye. A stew bubbled in a skillet over the small driftwood fire. She found the spoon and bent over to stir it, the aroma making her mouth water.

"Sonofabitch!"

Courtney dropped the spoon with a cry of surprise. She straightened slowly, turning around to look at Chandos. He stood a few feet from her, the two canteens dangling from one hand while his other hand was spread across his forehead as if to ward off pain. But when he lowered his hand and his eyes locked with hers, Courtney knew he wasn't in pain.

"Chandos?"

He didn't answer. His gaze moved slowly to her pants, moving over the curves outlined so starkly by the skintight material. She knew they were too tight, but Chandos made her feel as if she were wearing nothing at all.

Her face was burning. "You needn't look like that. I didn't want to buy them in the first place, but Mattie said you might want me to look like a man for disguise, so I did. How was I to know they wouldn't fit well? I'm not exactly in the habit of buying men's apparel, you know. And there was no time to try them on because you *did* only give me an hour to—"

"Shut up, woman!" He cut her off. "I

don't give a goddamn why you're wearing them, just get them off and put your skirt back on."

"But you *told* me to buy them!" Courtney protested in vexation.

"Pants and shirt, I told you. That doesn't mean . . . if you've got no more sense than to flaunt that tight little ass in front of me—"

"How dare you—" she gasped.

"Don't try me, lady," he growled. "Just get your skirt back on."

"It's not dry yet."

"I don't care if it's sopping wet. Put it on—now!"

"Fine!" She turned in a huff, adding angrily, "Don't blame me if I catch cold and you have to—"

Grabbing her shoulder, he swung her back around so swiftly that she fell into his arms. It must have surprised him as much as it did her, Courtney thought afterward, for why else would he grip her buttocks and then continue to hold on even after she'd steadied herself?

Courtney had had enough of his high-handedness. "Well?" she demanded sharply. "I thought you wanted me to change?"

His voice was low and husky, soothing,

yet strangely disturbing. "You don't understand at all, do you, cateyes?"

Nervously, she asked, "Do—do you think you might let go of me now?"

He didn't, and for a split second his eyes were as confused as hers. She felt breathless all of a sudden.

"In the future, lady," he finally murmured, "I suggest you try as well as you can not to surprise me this way. You can wear your pants, since, as you pointed out, I insisted you bring them along. If I can't control my . . . disapproval, well, that's my difficulty, not yours."

She supposed that was an apology for his strange behavior. And she certainly would try not to surprise him again if it made him so irrational.

"If you don't mind then, I would rather eat first and let my skirt dry a bit more. Is that all right?"

He nodded, and Courtney went to fetch the plates from the packhorse.

About an hour after they moved on, still following reasonably close to the river, though far enough away to avoid the thick foliage that grew along the banks, Courtney saw the Indian again. Was he the same one? How could she know? But she had no illusions this time that she was indeed seeing an Indian. He was astride a pinto very much like the one she was riding, just sitting there on the small hill, west of them, watching her and Chandos.

She moved her mount close to Chandos. "Do you see him?"

"Yeah."

"What does he want?"

"Nothing from us."

"Then why is he there? Watching us?" she demanded.

He finally turned and looked at her. "Settle down, lady. He's not the last Indian you're going to see in the next few weeks. Don't worry about him."

"Don't—?"

"Don't," he said firmly.

Courtney clamped her mouth shut. God sakes, he was infuriating. But she wasn't so nervous about the Indian, not as long as Chandos was unconcerned.

Before long, they were well beyond the Indian, and she looked back to see that he hadn't followed but was still sitting on that little hill.

Still, as the afternoon wore on, Courtney began remembering all the Indian attacks she had ever heard or read about—including the one she'd been in. She supposed some attacks were the justifiable result of the massacre George Custer and his 7th Cavalry had perpetrated against a friendly band of Cheyennes. That massacre had happened later the same year she lost her father, and Custer had only recently, in fact, been acquitted for that massacre due to a lack of evidence.

She sighed. The white men killed. Indians sought revenge. Then the white men sought revenge for that, and the Indians retaliated again—couldn't it ever stop?

It didn't seem like it would, not anytime soon. And with Indian tribes spread from Mexico to the Canadian border, every place was affected.

A year ago, ten wagons were set upon in northern Texas by a hundred and fifty Kiowas and Comanches. The wagons had been freighting grain from Weatherford to Fort Griffin, and although the wagonmaster managed to corral the wagons and offer resistance so that some of his men could get away, those who didn't escape were all found dead and mutilated.

The Kiowa chief Set-Tain-te, better known as Satanta, was said to have led that attack. This colorful chief was easily identifiable because he often wore the plumed brass helmet and epauletted jacket of a U.S. army general.

Courtney could remember Mattie laughing at the Indian chief's display of humor following his raid against Fort Larned. After stealing most of the regimental herd, he actually sent a message to the commanding officer complaining of the inferior quality of the stolen horses and requesting that better mounts be available for his next visit!

Courtney was sure that was one Indian she wouldn't be meeting on the trail, for Satanta was now in the Texas State Penitentiary, though there was a rumor that he might be paroled. There were other notable, colorful chiefs, like the half-breed Quannah Parker, who had recently become leader of a band of Comanches. And there were other war parties, even from supposedly tamed reservation Indians.

Yes, there was a very real danger in this journey. Could one man really protect her?

She supposed they would just have to pray for safety and hope their horses were dependable. If she dwelled on the possibilities, she wouldn't be able to go on. No, better to adopt Chandos's attitude.

She only hoped he was right to be so calm.

Chapter 16

Chandos waited until he was certain Courtney was asleep. Then he rose, grabbing only his boots and gun, and soundlessly moved away from their campsite. He walked in the direction away from the river. The night was dark, and all was in shadow.

He didn't go far before Leaping Wolf found him, falling into step beside Chandos. They walked on without words until they were far enough away that their voices wouldn't carry on the wind.

"Is she your woman?"

Chandos stopped, staring ahead. His woman? That had a nice sound to it, really. But there had never been a woman he'd called his, or wanted to. There was never time for that. The only woman he returned to time and again was the passionate Calida Alvarez. But Calida belonged to many men.

"No, she is not my woman," he said at last.

Leaping Wolf did not miss the sound of regret. "Why not?"

There were many reasons, Chandos knew, but he gave only the obvious one.

"She isn't the kind to follow blindly—and I am not meant to quit what isn't finished."

"But she is with you."

White teeth flashed in the black night as Chandos chuckled. "You are not usually so curious, my friend. Would you think me insane if I told you she is stronger than I, or rather, more persistent?"

"What power does she wield?"

"Tears—goddamn tears."

"Ah, I remember the power of tears very well."

Chandos knew Leaping Wolf was thinking of his dead wife. It never failed. In a word or a look, Leaping Wolf could bring it all back to Chandos in vivid detail.

Although his path now led from the blood of those he had loved, Chandos tried to forget what had happened. Not so Leaping Wolf. The Comanche brave lived daily with the memory. It was his sustenance and his reason for living.

The nightmare wouldn't be over for either of them until the last of the fifteen butchers was finally dead. Only then would Chandos stop hearing screams in his sleep, stop seeing Leaping Wolf, his closest friend, tears streaming down his cheeks as he fell to the ground near his dead wife, staring blindly at his two-month-old son lying a few feet away. A tiny baby with its throat slit!

Sometimes when the images haunted him, Chandos lost touch with his surroundings, and then he would cry inside himself again, as he had done the day he arrived home and found the nightmare. The tears wouldn't flow freely for him as they had for Leaping Wolf, and as they had for his stepfather, who had covered his wife's legs, stained with the blood of repeated rapes, and closed her eyes, those beautiful blue eyes filled with the pain and horror of her death. Woman of the Sky-Eyes Chandos's mother was called.

Maybe someday the tears would flow. Then he could stop hearing her screams. Perhaps then she could finally sleep in peace. But he didn't think the image of White Wing would ever fade. His little half-sister, who he had adored and who had worshiped him. It was the butchery of that sweet, loving child that seared his soul—the broken arms, the teeth marks, the twisted, bloody body. The rape of his mother was not beyond understanding. She had been a beautiful woman. But the rape of White Wing was an abomination beyond imagining.

Only two of the fifteen white men responsible for the horror were still alive. Leaping Wolf and the five braves who rode with Chandos had found and executed most of the killers within that first year. Chandos's stepfather had gone after the two Cottle brothers and was later found dead by their bodies. It was only when the bastards had taken to hiding in towns where a small group of Indians couldn't get to them that Chandos had cut his hair like a white man and strapped on his guns so that he could enter those towns and flush the men out.

The cowboys known only as Tad and Carl had left town when they heard Chandos was looking for them. They ran right into Leaping Wolf's arms. Later on, Cincinnati had faced Chandos, and Curly had, too. Both of them were dead.

It was Wade Smith Chandos wanted most, Wade Smith who kept eluding him, just as Trask kept eluding him.

John Handley had volunteered more information than the fat farmer had before he died, actually putting names to deeds. It was Trask who had killed Leaping Wolf's young wife, and the Comanche would not rest until he was dead, just as Chandos couldn't stop his quest until Smith was found. If Chandos couldn't give Trask to Leaping Wolf, he would kill him himself, for his friend. But it was Wade Smith who had tortured White Wing before cutting her throat, so Chandos wanted Smith for himself.

The Indian friends all rode together when they could. They had gone to Arizona together, where Chandos found Curly. They'd ridden through Texas more than once, following leads, and into New Mexico—even as far north as Nebraska. Chandos was one of them when they rode, but then he was Chandos again when he had to leave them behind at the approach of towns. They had come up with him from Texas this last time, and he would have returned with them if it hadn't been for Courtney.

"He was not in Newton," Chandos said quietly.

"And now?"

"I have heard Smith is holed up in Paris, Texas."

There was the briefest pause.

"And the woman?"

"She is going to Texas, too."

"So. I do not think you will want our company on this crossing."

Chandos grinned. "I don't think she would understand, no. She was skittish enough today when she saw you. I'll have a hysterical woman to deal with if she sees the others."

"Then know we are near if you need us," Leaping Wolf offered. And he slipped away as quietly as he had come.

Chandos stood there for a long while looking up at the black night sky, feeling empty. He would feel that way until the last butcher was dead. Only then would his dead loved ones sleep and stop screaming in his dreams.

Suddenly, chilled to the core of his being, he heard his name being screamed. This was no dream. Chandos felt a depth of fear he hadn't felt since that terrible day when he'd arrived home at the camp.

He ran, running like the wind until he reached her.

"What's wrong? What?"

Courtney collapsed against him, clinging tightly to his bare chest.

"I'm sorry," she babbled, her face hidden against his shoulder. "I woke up and you weren't there. I didn't mean to scream— really I didn't—but I thought you'd left me here. I—I was so frightened, Chandos. You wouldn't really leave me, would you?"

His hand had twisted in her hair, pulling her head back. He kissed her, hard. His lips, those lips she thought so very sensual, were moving on hers, and not softly, either. There was nothing soft about his kiss or the way he was holding her.

After a moment something began mingling with her stunned confusion. That funny feeling again in the pit of her belly, that feeling she had felt before.

When it dawned on her that she was the one prolonging the kiss because she was holding on to him so tightly, she thought of letting go, pulling back, but she didn't do it. Ending the kiss was the last thing she wanted to do.

But all good things eventually come to an end. Chandos finally released his hold on her, then even went so far as to set her at arm's length, which caused her to lose her hold on him.

Meeting the intensity of his sky blue eyes, Courtney was bemused. It was a bit late to wonder about her own behavior, but she certainly wondered about his. Unwittingly, she raised her hand and touched her lips.

"Why—why did you do that?"

It was all Chandos could do to keep a little distance between them, yet she had to ask why! Well, what did he expect from a virgin? She asked why? Those soft, ripe breasts burning into his chest. Those silky bare arms clinging to him. Nothing but a thin chemise and petticoat to shield him from her warmth. Why? Good Lord!

"Chandos?" she persisted.

He didn't know what he might have done just then if he hadn't caught sight of Leaping Wolf behind her. His friend had apparently heard her scream and had come to help. How much had he seen? Too much, said the knowing grin he flashed at Chandos before he turned to leave.

Chandos gave a deep sigh. "Forget it," he told her. "It just seemed the best way to shut you up."

"Oh."

Damn her, did she have to sound so disappointed? Didn't she know how close she was to finding herself flat on her back? No, she didn't know, he reminded himself. She had no idea what she was doing to him.

He stalked to the fire, angrily tossing another piece of wood onto it. "Go back to sleep, lady," he said, his back to her.

"Where were you?"

"There was a noise that needed investigating. It was nothing. But you should have checked to see if my horse was gone before you jumped to conclusions. Next time, remember that."

Courtney groaned inwardly. What a complete fool she had made of herself. No wonder he sounded so put out. He must be thinking he was stuck with a hysterical female who would mean nothing but trouble to him.

"It won't happen again—" Courtney began, falling silent when Chandos rasped out one of the foreign words he often used when he was upset. He whipped around then and headed for his horse. "Where are you going?"

"As long as I'm wide awake, I'm going to take a bath." He pulled a towel and bar of soap from his saddlebag.

"Chandos, I—"

"Go to sleep!"

Courtney wrapped herself in her bedroll again, her own temper shooting upward as he stalked to the river. She had only wanted to apologize. He didn't have to bite her head off. And then her eyes fell on the neat pile of clothes next to her bedroll—her clothes. Hot color flooded her cheeks. She hadn't even realized . . . oh, no! She had thrown herself into his arms while she was wearing nothing more than her underthings! How could she?

Courtney didn't know whether to cry in shame or laugh at the absurd picture she must have presented to Chandos. Well, it was nothing to laugh about. No wonder he had behaved as he had. He was probably more embarrassed than she was, if such a thing was possible.

Courtney sighed and turned over to face the fire and the river beyond. She couldn't hear Chandos or see him, but she knew he was down there. She wished she had the nerve to bathe in the river as he did, instead of only rinsing off, fully clothed, as she had done earlier. It would probably do wonders for her sore muscles.

She was still wide awake when Chandos returned to camp. She pretended to be asleep, however, afraid that he might not have cooled off enough yet to talk to her. But she watched him through the thick fringe of her lashes, not altogether surprised that she wanted to.

He reminded her of a sleek animal, the way he moved with such lithe grace. There was definitely something predatory about him, not in the habitual sense, but in the way he seemed master of his surroundings, able and certain to overcome any challenge, a very comforting thought.

She followed him with her eyes as he tossed his towel over a shrub to dry and returned the soap to his saddlebag. He then hunkered down by the fire to poke a stick at it. She wondered why he didn't even glance her way to see if she was asleep or not, but then he did, and she became quite breathless, for he didn't look away. He was staring at her just as she was staring at him, only he didn't know she was. Or did he?

What was he thinking as he looked at her? Probably that she was an inconvenience he could do without. Whatever it was, she was better off not knowing.

When he finally stood up and turned toward his bedroll, she felt almost bereft with the sudden loss of his interest, when her own was still so strong. She even noticed that his back was still wet from his bath, at least in the valley between his shoulder blades, and she had an overwhelming urge to smooth the skin dry with her bare hand.

Oh, God Sakes, Courtney, go to sleep!

Chapter 17

"Good morning! The coffee's ready, and I've kept your food warm."

Chandos groaned at the cheerful sound of her voice. What the hell was she doing up before him? Then he remembered that he'd hardly slept at all last night, thanks to her.

He shot her a level look.

"Do you want to eat now?"

"No!" he barked.

"Well, God sakes, you don't have to bite my head off!"

"God sakes?" he echoed, then began to laugh. He couldn't help it, it seemed so funny.

Courtney stared at him in complete wonder. She had never seen him laugh before, never even seen him smile. She was amazed. The rigid lines of his face relaxed, and he was so much more handsome, devastatingly handsome, in fact.

"I'm sorry," he said finally. "But I thought it was only Westerners who were fond of getting their point across with as few words as possible."

Courtney smiled. "I'm afraid my friend Mattie was a bad influence with her ofttimes abbreviated speech, but—"

"'Ofttimes'?" He cut her short. "My, you do go from one extreme to the other, don't you?" he said, laughing.

Courtney was fast losing her humorous mood. Now he was making fun of her.

"The food, sir," she reminded him curtly.

"You don't remember my telling you that I don't eat in the morning?" he said softly.

"I remember your words precisely. You said you eat *light* in the morning, not that you don't eat at all. So I made you two corncakes, no more, no less, a very light breakfast to be sure. But I wish to point out that if you would eat more substantially in the mornings, we might forgo stopping for lunch, which is a waste of good daylight. We would make better time, possibly gaining—"

"If you'd stop running off at the mouth, lady, I'd tell you that we stopped at midday yesterday for your sake, not mine. Without you along, I'd be covering this distance in half the time. But if you think your backside is up to it—"

"Please!" Courtney gasped. "I'm sorry. I only thought . . . no, obviously I didn't think at all. And actually . . . I'm not up to spending any more time in the saddle than we have been, at least not yet." She blushed. "And I appreciate your considering my—" She faltered, blushing furiously now.

"I'll take those corncakes," he said gently.

Courtney rushed to serve him. Once again she had made a fool of herself. And he was so right, she hadn't even thought of her sore body and what a few extra hours in the saddle each day might do to it. As it was, she wasn't suffering nearly as badly as Mattie had predicted, but that was due entirely to Chandos's thoughtfulness, she realized.

When she handed Chandos his coffee, she asked, "When will we cross into Indian Territory?"

Casually, he said, "About two hours before we made camp last night."

"Oh!" she gasped. "Already?"

It certainly didn't look any different than the Kansas soil they had left behind. What had she expected, Indian villages? As far as the eye could see there wasn't another living soul, just flat terrain, the only trees those along the riverbanks. Yet this land had been allotted to the Indians, and they *were* there, somewhere.

"Don't worry, lady."

She glanced back at him with a nervous smile. Was her fear so obvious?

"Won't you call me Courtney?" she asked suddenly.

"That's your civilized name. It has nothing to do with out here."

She felt chagrined again. "I suppose Chandos isn't your real name, then?"

"No." She took it for granted that he would say no more, as usual, but this time he surprised her. "It's the name my sister used to call me, before she could pronounce my name."

What name could possibly sound like Chandos, Courtney wondered, simultaneously glad to know something about him. So he had a sister?

Then he seemed to be speaking more to himself than to her.

"It's the name I'll use until I've finished what I must do so my sister can stop crying and sleep in peace."

Courtney went strangely cold all of a sudden. "That is quite cryptic. I don't suppose you would care to explain what it means?"

He seemed to shake himself. His eyes, so brightly blue, held her entranced for a long moment before he said, "You wouldn't want to know."

She wanted to say that she did, in fact, want to know—not just know about what

158

he'd said, but know everything about him. But she held her tongue.

She left him to finish his coffee, and tackled the job of saddling her horse. She knew it would take her twice as long as it took Chandos.

When she fetched her bedroll to secure it behind the saddle, she said, "Does the mare have a name, Chandos?"

He was getting ready to shave and didn't glance at her. "No."

"Could I—?"

"Call her whatever you like, cateyes."

Courtney savored the irony of that as she hurried back to the horse. Call it whatever she liked—just as *he* called *her* whatever he liked? He knew she didn't like being called "lady," but "cateyes"? Well, she preferred it to "lady." And the way he said it, why, it sounded somehow more intimate even than her own name.

She moved to the fire to clean up and put away the utensils. As she worked, she found herself peeking again at Chandos while he shaved. His back was to her, and her eyes moved slowly, caressingly, over the long, hard length of him.

It was a very nice body, as male bodies went. *God sakes, Courtney, that's putting it mildly*. *Superb* was more like it. She imagined a sculptor might carve Chandos just as he was if he wanted an enviable creation.

As she gathered up the cooking utensils to take them down to the river, Courtney sighed. She had finally admitted the truth to herself, and she wasn't really surprised. She admired Chandos's body.

"'Desire' would be a better word than 'admire,'" she mumbled to herself as she hurried down the slope.

She blushed. Was it true? Was that why she felt so funny when she looked at him, or when he touched her, and especially when he kissed her? What, she asked herself, did she really know about desire? Thanks to Mattie, who had often been explicit about her feelings for her husband, Courtney knew more than she might have.

"I can't keep my hands off him," Mattie would say, and Courtney realized she might say the same about her feelings for Chandos. The urge to touch him was certainly there, to trail her fingers over that firm, tight skin, to explore what was unknown.

How was she supposed to push aside these feelings? She couldn't avoid Chandos. On the other hand, he'd shown very little interest in her. She knew he didn't desire her as a woman, not at all. Why, he didn't even like her. That left Courtney alone with her imaginings.

Last night's kiss kept floating to the top of her mind. She was no novice to kissing: kisses from her beaus in Rockley, Reed's possessive kisses. But she couldn't remember ever enjoying a kiss so much, and she wondered intensely what it would be like to be kissed by Chandos if he really *meant* to kiss her. Shockingly, she actually found herself wondering how this man would make love. Primitively? Savagely, as he lived? Or would he be gentle? Maybe a little of both?

"How much washing does one pan need?"

Courtney started and dropped the pan in the water, then had to leap after it as the current caught it. She swung around, pan in hand, ready to upbraid Chandos for sneaking up on her like that, but her eyes lit on those incredibly sensual lips and she groaned instead and quickly looked away.

"I'm afraid I was—daydreaming," she offered guiltily, praying he wouldn't guess what she'd been thinking about.

"Save it for when we ride, will you? It's past time we lit out."

He walked away, leaving her fuming over his curtness. *That* was reality, she told herself harshly. He was a gunman, ruthless, hard, savage. Utterly disagreeable. He was no dream-lover.

Chapter 18

The difference became noticeable when they left off following the meandering Arkansas River. Gone were the currents of cool air that flowed with the river, so helpful in blowing away annoying insects. Gone too was the shade of trees. But the river was moving southeast now, and Chandos took them southwest, telling her that they would meet up with the Arkansas again later that day, where it snaked sharply westward again. They would cross a fork in the river that evening.

Courtney suffered with the heat. It was the first week in September, but there was no falling off of temperature to announce the end of summer. It was extremely humid. Sweat poured from her temples and brow, down her back and underarms, between her breasts, soaking her thick skirt between her legs. She lost so much moisture, in fact, that

Chandos added salt to her drinking water, much to her annoyance.

They reached the sandstone hills region by late afternoon, an area of low, flat hills extending across the eastern part of Indian Territory until it eventually blended in with the Arbuckle Mountains on the southern border. Rising four hundred feet in some areas, the hills were heavily forested with blackjack and oak, and rich in game.

While Courtney was wringing the water out of her skirt from their second river crossing, Chandos told her he was going out after their dinner. He expected camp to be set up by the time he returned. Courtney got out no more than two words of protest before he was gone. She sat down then and stared angrily after his departing figure.

It was a test. She knew it and resented it. But she did it, seeing to her pinto and Nelly, gathering wood as she had seen Chandos do. Some of it wasn't quite dry, and the fire smoked terribly. She got the beans started— oh, how many cans of beans were in her supply sack—and decided she would never want to see another bean when this trip was over. She even made some sourdough bread.

She was extremely proud of herself when she was done. It had taken only a little over an hour, and most of that time had been devoted to the horses. It was only when she sat down to await Chandos's return that she remembered her wet skirt, realizing this would be a good time to wash it and her underclothes. And as long as Chandos wasn't in camp, she could take a nice, long bath.

Her spirits soared instantly, and she was no longer annoyed with Chandos for leaving her alone. The light was still good, with a dusky pink sky overhead, and she had her Colt revolver, even if she was clumsy with it.

She quickly gathered soap and towel and a change of clothes. The bank was rocky with stones and boulders. One boulder had fortuitously fallen right in the path of the current, which stemmed the worst of it, giving her a few square feet of gentle water to bathe in.

She sat in the shallows and washed her clothes first, tossing them up onto the rocks. Next she washed her matted hair, and then her underclothes, which she refused to remove. She soaped them down on her body. She scrubbed her body with a vengeance, getting rid of dust and sweat. The water was invigoratingly cold, delightful after the sweltering ride. She was happy there in her sheltered place. Unable to see over the rocks, she felt delightfully isolated.

The sky was just beginning to streak with vivid red and violet when she came out of the water to gather her wet clothes. She got no farther than the water's edge. Four horses were spread out along the bank, blocking her way back to camp. Four horses and four riders.

They weren't Indians. That was Courtney's first thought. But that didn't stop alarm bells from going off in her head. They sat there, all four staring at her in a way that made her skin crawl. The men were wet from the legs down, which meant that they had recently crossed the water. If only she had seen them crossing, or heard them approach.

"Where's your man?"

The one who spoke was a study in browns, hair and eyes, jacket, pants, boots, hat, even his shirt was light brown. He was young, in his late twenties, she guessed. They were all young, and she recalled the adage that all gunmen die young. These were gunmen. They had that look she had come to recognize, the look that said they made their own rules and wore guns to enforce those rules.

"I asked you a question." The man's voice was raspy.

Courtney hadn't moved an inch. She couldn't. She was frozen. But she had to get hold of herself.

"My escort will return any moment now."

Two of them laughed. Why? The one in brown didn't laugh. His face remained impassive.

"That doesn't answer my question. Where is he?" he repeated.

"He went hunting."

"How long?"

"Over an hour."

"Ain't heard no shots, Dare," said a red-haired youth. "Looks like we got a long wait."

"That suits me just fine," said a huge, black-haired fellow with a scraggly beard. " 'Cause I can think of a way to make the time pass real quick."

There was more laughter. "There'll be none of that, not now anyway," said the brown-clad man. "Bring her up to their camp, Romero," he ordered softly.

The man who dismounted and approached her looked as Mexican as his name sounded, except that he had the greenest eyes she'd ever seen. He was only a few inches over her height, but his body was wiry and encased entirely in black, with silver conchas shining blood-red in the sunset. His face was swarthy and as darkly serious as Chandos's usually was. This one was dangerous, perhaps more dangerous than the others.

When he reached her and took hold of her arm, Courtney found the courage to shake the hand off. "Now, just a minute—"

"Do not, *bella*." His warning was sharp. "Make no trouble, *por favor*."

"But I don't—"

"*¡Cállate!*" he hissed.

Instinctively, Courtney knew he was telling her to keep her voice down, or something to that effect. It was almost as though he were trying to protect her. The others were already climbing the hill. She began to tremble, as much from the river breeze against her dripping wet body as from the man standing beside her, his green eyes cold.

He took her arm again, but again she shook it off. "You can at least let me dry off and change."

"To those wet clothes?"

"No, to those." She pointed toward the

bush at the top of the bank where she had left her other clothes.

"*Sí*, but quickly, *por favor.*"

Courtney was so nervous when she reached for her towel with the gun under it that the gun slipped out of her fingers, dropping loudly on the rocks. The man beside her gave an exasperated sigh and reached down to get it. She groaned as he stuck it into his belt.

Ashamed, for she knew Chandos would have something to say about such stupidity, she hurried up the hill.

Romero followed her up the hill and stood near her, giving her no privacy at all. There was no question of removing her wet underthings to don the dry ones she had laid out, so she simply put on the dry dress over them. The dress quickly became wet.

"You will catch cold, *bella*," Romera noted as she stepped out from behind the bush.

Since that was his fault, she snapped, "I don't have much choice, do I?"

"*Sí*, you always have a choice."

The very idea! Thinking she would strip naked with him right there. "No. I don't," Courtney insisted emphatically.

He shrugged. "Very well. Come."

He didn't try to take her arm again, but extended his arm toward the camp, indicating that she should lead the way. She quickly gathered up her things and did, and a few moments later they entered the small clearing where she had set up camp.

The other three men were sitting by her campfire, eating her beans and bread and drinking her coffee. Courtney was outraged, but she was also all the more frightened by what this meant.

"That didn't take long." The black-haired giant chuckled. "Didn't I tell you, Johnny Red, 'bout his quick draw?"

The insult went right over Courtney's head, but the Mexican hissed, "¡*Imbécil*! She is a lady."

"When I shit pink, she's a lady," the giant said, sneering. "Bring her on over and set her down right here."

Courtney blushed scarlet, seeing him pat his crotch. She turned wide, imploring eyes on the Mexican, but he shrugged.

"It is up to you, *bella*."

"No!"

Romero shrugged his narrow shoulders again, but this time it was for the giant's benefit. "You see, Hanchett? She does not want to know you better."

"I don't give a friggin' damn what she wants, Romero!" Hanchett snarled, getting to his feet.

The Mexican took a step forward, putting himself in front of Courtney as he turned to Dare. "Should you not tell your *amigo* the woman is all you have to bring Chandos out into the open? Chandos has his horse, so he does not need to return to camp—except for her. For myself, if my woman was used, however unwillingly, I would not want her back. I would simply ride on."

Courtney was appalled by his callousness. What kind of a man . . . ? She watched Dare for his answer, as he was obviously in charge.

"Romero's right, Hanchett," Dare said finally, and Courtney let out a sigh that was, unfortunately, premature. "Wait until I have the bastard and know what the hell his game is."

"You—you know Chandos?" Courtney whispered in an aside to the Mexican.

"No."

"But they do?"

"No," he said again and explained, "Chandos looked for Dare, then did not stay around to find him. Dare does not like this."

"You mean, you've been following us?"

"*Sí,*" he answered. "We were more than a day behind you, with little hope of catching up so soon, but he surprised us by traveling slowly."

Courtney knew it was her fault Chandos had not made better time, her fault these men had caught up with him.

She ventured softly, "After he comes and your friend has his answers, what then?"

Romero's dark eyes didn't even flicker. "Dare will kill him."

"But why?" Courtney gasped.

"Dare is angry to waste this time tracking him. The way he searched for Dare in Newton was a challenge that cannot be ignored. But we had ridden to Abilene and did not return until the day after your man left town."

"He's not my man. He's taking me to Texas, that's all. I hardly even know him, but—"

He waved aside her explanation. "The reason you ride with him does not matter, *bella.*"

"*But,*" she continued emphatically. "How can you calmly tell me your friend is going to kill him? You don't kill a man for the silly reason you just gave me."

"Dare does."

"And you won't stop him?"

"It is nothing to me. But if you worry for yourself, don't. You will not be left alone here. We return to Kansas, and you will ride with us."

"That doesn't make me feel any better, sir!"

"It should, *bella*. The alternative is for you to die, too." Courtney lost her color, and then he shocked her even more. "You have time to consider whether you will fight. But think well, for they will have you either way. And what matters one man or four?"

"*Four?* You, too?"

"You are *bella* and I am a man," he said simply.

Courtney shook her head, disbelieving. "But you—you prevented Hanchett from— from—"

"He is *estúpido*, that one. He would have you now and distract us all, giving Chandos the advantage."

"He has the advantage now," she pointed out deliberately, hoping to shake his confidence. "You four are circled in light, while he has the darkness to conceal him."

"*Sí*, but we have you."

Her moment of bravado fled.

Her mind raced toward some way to help Chandos. An idea seized her and she said, "I've been such a nuisance to Chandos that I'm sure he'd just as soon be rid of me. So you really are wasting your time here."

"Nice try, missy, but I ain't buying," Dare overheard and replied.

Courtney stared at the fire. It probably was true. Chandos would surely sense danger here. Why should he walk in and face these men just because she was there? The odds would be four against one. Would he risk his life for her?

She didn't want Chandos to die. But, Lord, she didn't want to be raped, either.

"We heard he's a half-breed. That right?"

It took Courtney a moment to realize Hanchett was speaking to her. It took a moment longer to grasp his question. They really didn't know anything about Chandos, did they? Neither did she, but they didn't know that.

She gave the scraggly bearded giant a level look and said unemotionally, "If you mean is he half Indian, no, he isn't. He's actually three quarters Comanche. Is there a name for that?"

Courtney was amazed that she had managed to unsettle the big man with her lie. He looked away from her, out into the surrounding darkness. One of their horses stepped on a twig just then and he started.

"You got some nerve, lady, beddin' down with a half-breed." Johnny Red was trying to get back at her with the slur and it worked.

Courtney's eyes flashed. "I'm only going to say this once more! Chandos is not my—my—lover! He's a ruthless savage. But when I saw him kill Jim Ward, a vicious outlaw, well, I knew he was exactly the man I needed to escort me to Texas."

"Shit! Old Jim's dead?" Hanchett demanded.

Courtney sighed. She wasn't surprised that they knew the outlaw Ward. They were outlaws themselves.

"Yes. Chandos killed him," she replied. "He's a bounty hunter. Could that be why he was inquiring after you?" she asked Dare.

He shook his head slowly, unperturbed. "I ain't wanted by the law, missy. I make sure I don't leave no witnesses to *my* crimes."

Hanchett and Johnny Red laughed. Courtney had lost her advantage and sought to regain it.

"Well, I'm sure you're ruthless and despicable and so forth, so you have a lot in common with Chandos. He isn't nice at all. Why, do you know he tried to frighten me by telling me how many scalps he'd taken? I won't tell you the number. *I* didn't believe it, so why should you? He told me he'd ridden for several years with that vengeful Satanta, too. But I ask you, how could he have killed those seventeen wanted men for the bounties, as he claims? He isn't *that* old. How could he possibly have done so much killing in so short a time? Impossible, I tell you—as I told him."

"Shut up, woman," Dare rasped, furious now.

"Why? Did you hear something?" Courtney said innocently. "It's probably Chandos. He should have been back long before now. But he won't come forward, you know. Why should he when he can just pick you off—"

"Johnny Red, stuff something in her goddamn mouth!" Dare snarled.

The shot was fired as the boy reached for her. It caught him in the left shoulder, propelling him away from her. The others leaped to their feet, including Courtney, who was suddenly terrified again.

Johnny Red was squirming on the ground, screaming that his bone was shattered. Courtney hardly heard him for the ringing in her ears, but she knew she had to warn Chandos.

"They mean to kill you, Chandos!"

She stopped as Dare's hand reached to slap her. His hand didn't touch her, however, because a bullet struck his elbow, paralyzing his arm. He dropped his gun. When Hanchett saw what happened to Dare, he turned his drawn gun on her. It was shot right out of his hand. Courtney's ears continued ringing as she stared around in utter amazement.

"Fools!" Romero shouted. "He protects the woman! Leave her alone!" Then he called out to Chandos, "*Señor,* no more shooting, *por favor*. You see, I put my gun away."

This he did, then spread his arms wide. He was taking quite a chance that Chandos wouldn't shoot him, helpless as he was.

The ploy seemed to work, for Chandos didn't fire again. All was utterly still outside the circle of fire. Close to the fire, Johnny Red groaned and Hanchett made gasping sounds as he held his bleeding hand.

Courtney wasn't nearly so frightened anymore, though her limbs still trembled. Chandos had done it. He had gotten the upper hand.

Why didn't he just tell them all to get on their horses and leave? Why didn't he speak?

Romero came slowly around the fire to help Dare bandage his arm. "Be sensible, *amigo*," Courtney heard Romero whisper. "He could have killed us all in a matter of seconds. Instead, he only wounded us. Ask your questions of him and then let us go. You no longer have the advantage."

"I still have her," Dare hissed, looking at Courtney.

She stared back at him. "I don't think so, mister. I could walk out of here now, and you wouldn't dare stop me. Wherever he is out there, he has all of you covered."

How much pleasure she derived from watching the man's eyes burn with anger because it was true. But as if Dare couldn't accept the facts, he took a step toward her. Another shot rang out, this bullet smashing into Dare's thigh, the pain bringing him down with a scream.

Romero grabbed Dare's shoulders and held on to him. "No more! You will have us all riddled with holes if you do not desist!"

"Good advice."

"Chandos!" Courtney cried delightedly, turning in the direction of his voice.

As she began to focus on the darkness outside the clearing, she had the greatest urge to run and throw herself at him, but she didn't dare distract him. He stood on the edge of the clearing, his gun leveled at the outlaws, his hat shadowing his eyes so that no one could tell who he was watching. He looked hard and uncompromising. To Courtney, he looked wonderful.

"You are Chandos?" Romero stood up, keeping his arms extended away from his body. "You make much over nothing, *señor*. You were looking for my friend here. He accommodates you by coming to you. He only wanted to know why you hunted him."

"That's a lie!" Courtney retorted, pointing a damning finger at Dare. "He meant to kill you after he had his answers. That one told me so." She nodded at Romero. "He also told me what would happen after you were dead, they would—would—"

"You still having trouble with the word, lady?" Chandos said. How could he joke at a time like this, she wondered.

"Well, they would have!" she snapped.

"Oh, I've no doubt of that, love,"

Chandos replied. "And while you're still so full of indignation, why don't you gather up their guns for me?"

It took her a moment to move, she was so surprised at what he had called her. But as she leaned over to pick up the first gun, she realized he wanted the men to believe she was his woman.

Careful not to step in front of any of the men, and thereby block Chandos's view, she scooped up Dare's and Hanchett's guns from the ground. Johnny Red's was still in his holster. Romero handed her his, and then she snatched her own gun from his belt, giving him a triumphant look as she did so.

"Do not be vengeful, *bella*," he told her softly. "You will remember that I helped you?"

"Certainly," she replied. "As I will remember the reason you gave for helping me. Shall I tell Chandos all of it and let him judge whether you helped me or not?"

She moved away without giving him a chance to answer. She disliked him in particular, for he had played on her fear, frightening her terribly, then giving her hope, then dashing that hope. They were all despicable, but he was crueler than the others.

She moved along the outer edges of the clearing until she was beside Chandos, dropping the guns behind him. She kept her own gun. "I know you'd probably rather not be overwhelmed by my gratitude right now," she said softly, pressing close to his back. She gave him a quick hug. "But I have to tell you how glad I am you came back when you did."

"You're all wet," he muttered.

"I was taking a bath when they showed up."

"In your clothes?"

"In my underclothes, of course."

"Of course." He chuckled.

And then he amazed Courtney—and amazed the others as well—by saying to them quietly, "Take off . . . while you still can."

He was letting them go!

Chapter 19

It wasn't a full moon, but it was bright enough to cast a silvery glow on the wide tributary that fed into the Arkansas River. It was bright enough that Courtney could see clearly the men who were forced to cross the water.

She stood on the bank next to Chandos and watched the horses floundering. The swift-moving current parted Hanchett from his horse. With his injured hand, she had doubted he would make it across. But he did, surprisingly, as did his horse, and she and Chandos stood there watching Hanchett and the other two men as they headed north, back toward Kansas. They watched until the men were out of sight.

Then, as if everything were perfectly normal, as if Dare Trask weren't strung up to a tree within sight of the fire, Chandos proceeded to skin the two squirrels he had caught. He had apparently caught them with his bare hands, for they bore no wounds and he hadn't fired a single shot while he was hunting. He put them over the fire to roast, then opened another can of beans and brewed more coffee. Courtney sat there staring at Dare Trask, feeling sick.

Chandos had announced that Trask wasn't leaving with the others. He had called Trask by his whole name, indicating that he knew him, or knew of him. Then he forced Romero to bind Trask's hands and feet together, incredibly, with Trask's own shirt and pants. He sent Courtney after the rope on his saddle, and she nearly got lost trying to find Surefoot where Chandos had left him.

She brought both the pinto and the rope to Chandos, and stood there as Chandos directed Romero to tie the rope to Trask's bound wrists, warning that if it wasn't tight enough, Trask would probably break both legs in the fall. What he meant became obvious when Chandos dragged Trask to the nearest tree, using only one hand, for his other hand was holding his gun. He hoisted Trask several feet into the air, securing the rope around the tree trunk.

"Are you going to kill him?" Romero asked.

"No," Chandos replied. "But he's going to suffer a little bit for what he did here."

"He did nothing to you, *señor*."

"True. It's what he would have done to the lady that I object to. No one touches her but me, you understand."

Romero looked at Courtney, wondering whether she had lied to him about her relationship with Chandos. Then he looked back at Chandos.

"I think this has to do not only with the

woman, but with why you were looking for my *amigo, sí?*"

Chandos didn't answer. He brought forward the men's horses, removing the rifles sheathed on two of the horses before he handed the beasts over to their riders. He tossed their rifles and handguns into the river a bit later.

Well, they were gone now, and Dare Trask was still dangled from the tree, a handkerchief stuck in his mouth now because he had started shouting for his men to come back for him and Chandos had gotten tired of listening to it. Stretched as he was, Courtney knew he must be in terrible pain. His wounds continued bleeding, even the one that had been hastily bandaged.

She supposed he deserved this, and more, but she had no stomach to watch. She knew she would have felt differently if he had succeeded in raping her, or if Chandos were dead. But, nevertheless, she couldn't enjoy Trask's suffering.

Did Chandos? She couldn't tell. His expression was, as always, inscrutable. He prepared their food and ate his supper with an air of indifference. Still, he watched Trask the whole time.

When she tried to talk to Chandos, he told

her to keep quiet, that he needed to listen in case the others decided to come back. She did as she was told.

Then he told her to get everything packed up and to saddle her horses. They were leaving, and she was delighted. But when she was ready, and had led the horses forward, including his and Trask's, Chandos seemed to have changed his mind. The fire wasn't out. In fact, he was banking it to last. Nor had he moved Trask.

Chandos turned and looked at her with such a serious expression that her stomach leaped in apprehension.

"You're not thinking of—of—you are!" She didn't know how she fathomed what he was thinking, but she did. "You want me to leave without you, don't you?"

Taking her hand, he pulled her to the far edge of the clearing. "Don't upset yourself unnecessarily, lady. I want you to ride out ahead of me is all. Walk the horses slowly south. I'll catch up with you in a few minutes."

He was back to calling her lady. And he was dead serious. She couldn't believe it.

"You're going to kill him, aren't you?" she demanded.

"No."

"Then you're going to torture him!"

"Woman," he said, "where's that calm that had you talking circles around four desperadoes?"

"You're sending me out where there are Indians and you expect me to be calm? Your shots were probably heard. There's probably a dozen . . . a hundred savages swarming around out there right now."

"Do you really think I'd let you walk into danger?"

He said it so softly she was brought up short.

"I'm sorry," she said, shamefaced. "It's just that I'm such a coward."

"You're braver than you think, lady. Now go on, and I'll catch up in a few minutes. I've got some things to say to Trask that you shouldn't hear."

Chapter 20

Brown hair, brown eyes, those could belong to anyone, but the missing two fingers identified the man as Dare Trask. Chandos stood in front of his enemy, trying to control himself, trying to keep the memories at bay so they wouldn't interfere. Dare Trask had

185

raped his mother. He hadn't killed her, but he had defiled her. He was the last man living who had done so.

Dare Trask was also one of three men who had raped Leaping Wolf's wife. And it was Trask's knife that had plunged into the young woman's belly when he was finished with her—not a clean thrust, but one intended to make her suffer more before she died.

For that alone Trask deserved to die, and for the rest he deserved to die slowly. And he would, today or tomorrow, possibly even the day after. But Chandos wouldn't be there to see it. Nor did he want to see it. After four years, the desire for vengeance had pretty much gone out of him—except where Wade Smith was concerned. Wade Smith would die by Chandos's hand. But with Trask, well, it had become a matter of finishing what he had sworn to do. Beyond that, Chandos didn't care.

Trask wouldn't know why he was going to die unless Chandos explained. And Chandos wanted Trask to understand everything, to realize that his brutal outrages had caught up with him.

Chandos pulled the gag out of Trask's mouth, then stepped back several feet and

186

looked up at him. Trask spit at Chandos to show his contempt. There was no fear in the man's eyes.

"Breed," Dare rasped. "I know you ain't gonna kill me. I heard you tell your woman that."

"You sure that's what you heard?"

Some of the belligerence went out of Trask. "What the hell do you want? I didn't touch the goddamn woman. You got no call to—"

"This has nothing to do with the woman, Trask."

"So Romero was right? Then what'd you use her as an excuse for?"

"Your friends don't need to know what's between you and me. They'll merely think I'm a jealous man, that's all. They'll wonder why they never see you again, but they'll never know what really happened here."

"Like hell! They'll be back, and soon! They ain't gonna just leave me here."

Chandos shook his head slowly. "I'll make you the last wager of your life, Trask. I'll bet your friends have already seen signs of Indians in the area, and at this very moment they're riding like hell for the border."

"Liar," Trask blustered. "We didn't see no—you seen signs?"

"I didn't have to. I know they're near. We usually travel together. But this time, because of the woman, they're keeping a distance. Indians frighten her, you see."

"She travels with you," Trask pointed out.

Chandos nodded without offering any explanation.

"I know what you're trying to do, breed," his adversary said. "Dare Trask don't frighten that easy. We're too close to the border for there to be Indians hereabouts anyhow."

Chandos shrugged. "It's not something I have to prove to you, Trask. When they find you, you'll know it. I'm leaving you for them as a gift, you might say."

"A gift?" Trask shouted, showing the fear he was beginning to feel. "If you want to kill me, do it—or aren't you man enough?"

But Chandos wouldn't be goaded, and he was tired of talking to the vermin. "It's not that I don't want to kill you, Trask," he said softly, stepping closer. "Look at me. Look at my eyes. You've seen these eyes before, Trask, though they weren't mine. Or have you raped so many women that you can't

remember the woman I'm referring to?"
When Trask gasped, Chandos added coldly,
"So you *do* remember."

"That was four goddamn years ago!"

"Did you think, because so much time
had passed, you had escaped Comanche
vengeance? Don't you know what happened
to the others who were with you that day?"

Trask did know. He paled. He had believed it was over, that the savages who had
searched out the others had taken their fill of
vengeance. Not so.

Trask fought wildly at his bonds, but they
were tight. Chandos could smell his fear
now, and the eyes that beseeched him were
filled with knowledge of his death.

Satisfied, Chandos turned away and
mounted his horse. He caught the reins of
Trask's roan and called to Trask, "You
know my reason for wanting you dead,
Trask. But remember also the young
Comanche woman who suffered first your
rape and then a cruel, slow death."

"She was nothing but a goddamn Indian!"

Chandos's pangs of conscience were silenced by that. "She was a beautiful, gentle
woman, a mother whose baby also died that
day, and a wife whose husband still mourns

her. She had never hurt a soul in her whole life. She was all that was good and kind. And you killed her. So I am giving you to her husband. He wants you, and I don't."

Chandos rode away, his mind closed to Trask's screaming for Chandos to come back and kill him. Chandos heard, instead, the screams of women and children, raped, tortured, slaughtered. They were nearby, just as the warriors were, though he couldn't see them. But he could feel them watching, and he knew they understood.

After a little while, Chandos caught sight of Courtney in the distance, and the spectres faded away. She banished the past. She was balm for his soul, this sweet innocent woman in the midst of a cruel world.

She had stopped in the middle of a flat plain, and she and her mare were cloaked in a mantle of silver moonlight. He quickened his pace.

As he approached, she burst into tears. Chandos smiled. It wasn't like her to hold her feelings in, but she had done so tonight, admirably. She'd been calm and courageous when she needed to be. Now that she was safe, she cried.

He swept her off her horse and onto his, holding her tightly in front of him. She snuggled against him, continuing to cry, and he held her, glad she was crying the fear out of her. When she was done, he gently tilted her face to his and kissed her.

It didn't take Courtney long to realize that this kiss was entirely intentional. A giddy rush rose up so quickly inside her that she became frightened of it and pushed herself away from Chandos.

She stared up at him breathlessly. His composure sparked her temper.

"You can't say you meant to shut me up this time."

"Are you going to ask me why I kissed you?" he said with a sigh.

"I was—"

"Don't, little cat, because if I tell you, we're going to end up bedding down right here, and come morning you won't be the innocent you are now."

Courtney gasped. "I—I didn't think you found me—attractive."

He grunted. There were no words of assurance that he did, no declaration, just a grunt. What the devil did he mean?

"I think you'd better set me back on my horse, Chandos," she said hesitantly.

"Is that the 'proper' thing to do at this point?"

Every fiber of her being wanted to stay right where she was, but his sarcasm got to her. "Yes," she said primly, "It is."

She landed in her saddle with a jolt, and barely had time to gather her reins before her horse started following Chandos's horse.

She was in a veritable daze for the whole ride. Chandos wanted her!

Chapter 21

Chandos wanted her! It was her first thought the next morning, when she woke up in the same euphoric daze. But then later, it hit her like a bucket of cold water. The truth was oh, so obvious! What a daydreaming little fool she was. Of course he wanted her. She was the only woman out there, and he was a man. From what she was able to understand, men took whatever was available. It wasn't that he *really* wanted her. He had shown his indifference to her from the start. It was only that he was tempted, as men were tempted to lust without really caring for the woman in question.

"You going to kill that blanket, or what?"

Courtney swung around. "What?"

"You've been staring at it as if you meant to murder it."

"I—oh, I had a bad dream."

"That's not surprising, all things considered."

He was hunkered down by the fire, a tin of coffee in his hand. He was shaved and dressed, and was already wearing his wide-brimmed riding hat. He was ready to go, but had apparently let her sleep as long as she wished. How had he known she needed sleep so badly?

"If you're not in too much of a hurry, would you mind pouring me some coffee?" she asked, getting up to fold her blanket. And then she realized that she was still wearing the clothes she'd been wearing last night. "God sakes, I must have been out of my mind," she mumbled as she felt the dress, still damp in places.

"Belated shock, probably," Chandos offered.

"Shock?" Her eyes impaled him. "But *you* knew! Why didn't you remind me?"

"I did. You thanked me very much and promptly lay down and went to sleep."

Courtney looked away. She must have seemed like a fool, going to sleep in wet clothes. And all because Chandos had wanted her for a few moments! How could she have been such an idiot?

"I'll—have to change," she said and hurried away.

But that wasn't the end of it. She had packed so quickly last night that she had unthinkingly stuck her wet clothes in her carpetbag with the others, and now everything was damp.

She glanced at Chandos over her shoulder, then looked back at her bag.

"Chandos, I—I—"

"It can't be that bad, cateyes."

She peeked at him again over her shoulder, then said in a rush, "I don't have anything to wear."

"Nothing?"

"Nothing. I—I packed some wet clothes and—and forgot to take them out to dry."

"Drying will have to wait until tonight. What about those pants? How wet are they?" He came toward her and glanced at the bag.

"They're not wet. I stuck them in my saddlebag."

"Well, then they'll have to do."

"But I thought—"

"Can't be helped. Wait. I'll get you one of my shirts."

She was amazed. He didn't seem angry at all. A moment later he tossed her a cream-colored shirt of the softest buckskin she had ever felt. The only problem was that it didn't button. It laced up the front, and she didn't have a dry chemise to wear under it.

"Don't frown, cateyes, because that will have to do. All the rest of my things need washing."

"I didn't mean . . . I would be happy to wash your clothes for you."

"No," he replied curtly. "I take care of my own gear."

Now he was angry. Of all the—oh! Courtney fetched her pants and stalked off into the bushes. Infuriating man. She had only offered to help. You'd think she was angling to be his—wife or something, the way he'd reacted.

Five minutes later, Courtney stomped back to the campsite to pack up her bedroll. Her color was high, the result of temper and self-consciousness. Chandos's shirt hung well past her hips, so she couldn't tuck it into her pants. And the laced V, which probably only came halfway down his chest, reached clear to her navel. But the worst was the lacing, made of stiff rawhide that defied tight binding. No matter how hard she pulled, there was still a scandalous half-inch gap.

She kept her back to Chandos, and when she came to the fire for her coffee, she held her hat over her breasts, daring him with a single furious look to say anything. He didn't. In fact, he did his best not to look at her at all.

Courtney cast about for a subject that would get her mind off her discomfort, and her gaze fell on the extra horse that was tethered with their three.

"Wasn't that a bit harsh, making that Trask fellow walk all the way back to Kansas?"

The mild rebuke got her more than she bargained for. Chandos fixed her with icy blue eyes, and she had the feeling he was actually on the verge of violence.

"Since you don't know what he's guilty of, lady, how can you know what he does or doesn't deserve?"

"You know for a fact that he's guilty?"

"Yes."

"Of what?"

"Rape. Murder. The slaughter of men, women, and children."

"My God!" Courtney blanched. "If you

knew all that, why didn't you kill him outright?"

Saying nothing, he stood up and moved away toward the horses.

"I'm sorry!" she called after him. Had he heard?

God sakes, she was always saying she was sorry for something. Why didn't she just keep her mouth shut in the first place?

She would put Dare Trask out of her mind. He ought to've been drawn and quartered, as civilized countries had practiced for terrible crimes. But she wouldn't think of it again.

She doused the small fire with the remaining coffee and then went to her horse, which Chandos had been nice enough to saddle for her. She quickly pulled her hairbrush through her hair, which was a mass of tangles, though clean.

Chandos came up behind her as she was working on a particularly difficult knot. "Since you think I have a talent for such things, I could cut that off for you." There was a strong trace of humor in his voice, and he added, "How many scalps was I supposed to have taken? I can't remember."

Courtney swung around. He was grinning at her. How quickly he got over a bad mood!

She remembered everything else she'd said about him last night, and she felt her cheeks heating up. "How long were you out there listening?"

"Long enough."

"I hope you don't think I believe any of what I said," she assured him quickly. "It's just that when they asked me if you were part Indian, I thought I'd better say yes. I wanted to unsettle them. After all, they claimed they'd never seen you, so how would they know you don't look anything like an Indian?"

"I don't?" Chandos ventured softly, disturbingly. "You've seen so many Indians that you're qualified to make the distinction?"

Courtney paled. He was teasing her, but she didn't find it at all amusing.

Slowly, she felt the total seriousness of his manner. "You aren't part Indian, are you?" she whispered, then immediately regretted the question. Anything that farfetched didn't deserve an answer. He didn't give one, anyway, only stared at her in that unsettling way he had.

She lowered her eyes. "Forget I asked. If you're ready to go . . . ?"

Taking her hand, he slapped into it the

leftover meat from last night. "That ought to hold you till lunch."

"Thank you." But as he turned away, she asked, "Chandos, do you know what '*bella*' means?"

The look he fixed on her was intense. "The Mexican call you that?"

"Yes."

"It means beautiful."

"Ah."

Once more Courtney found herself in a state of acute, blushing discomfort.

Chapter 22

"If you've got any more wash, you'd better get it done tonight," Chandos informed Courtney as soon as they stopped to make camp that evening. "We leave off following the Arkansas tomorrow, and won't be near water again for at least three days."

Courtney didn't have much more to wash, but she did have to air out and dry her whole wardrobe. Chandos quickly finished taking care of his horse and Trask's, and headed for the river with his wash. He finished that quickly too, before Courtney was even ready to start. When she was done, their campsite looked like the backyard of a boarding house. Clothing was spread out over every available bush and tree and rock.

Courtney found it humorous that their campsite, smack in the middle of Indian Territory, could look so homey. But it did. It gave her a warm feeling that turned into deep contentment, surprising her. Part of that feeling came from just being close to Chandos, and feeling totally safe because he was there. He hadn't gone away to hunt tonight, and she was certain it was because he didn't want to leave her alone. He sensed she wasn't up to that yet, and she was grateful for his kindness.

So that he would know she appreciated him, she worked hard to make a savory stew out of their dried beef and vegetables, using the few spices she had bought, and loading the stew with fat dumplings. There wasn't a single bean in it, either.

While Courtney prepared the meal, Chandos leaned back against his saddle and closed his eyes. When she began humming, the tune played over his body and he closed his eyes tighter against it. She was doing it again, working on his senses just when he least expected it. Where Courtney Harte was concerned, he seemed to have no defenses.

How much more could he take of this constant wanting her without fulfillment? Having to fight his own natural inclinations was new to Chandos, as was wanting a woman so badly he could hardly think of anything else. She had him wound up so tight he was ready to burst, and there was no way to escape her.

But he wouldn't touch her. Even if she offered herself, he wouldn't . . . Well, wait a minute, he wasn't that noble. There was only so much he would demand of himself, after all.

Oh, who did he think he was kidding? She *had* offered, and he was still suffering over it. This ridiculous notion of his that he had to protect her—even from himself—was sheer torture. She had put out one signal after another with her sultry looks, her soft, yielding kisses. She wanted him, and knowing she wanted him fired his blood like nothing ever had.

But did she know she was tempting him beyond endurance? She couldn't know. He had taken pains not to let her know—until last night. And if she did know, then she obviously didn't care, for she'd made no effort to curb those looks that seared his flesh.

"Chandos, how do they manage to drive such large herds of cattle over these hills? Do they go around them?"

"They don't." He was surprised by the sharpness in his voice and quickly softened it. "The cattle trail is about fifty miles west of here."

"But I thought the quickest way to reach Waco was to follow the cattle trail?"

"It is."

"And we're not?"

"I've got business in Paris, a town in northeast Texas. It'll take us five days or so out of our way, but it can't be helped. It's where I was headed in the first place, and I don't feel obliged to lose a week taking you to Waco first, then doubling back. Any objections?"

He said it so defensively that she didn't dare object. "No. I wouldn't ask you to change your plans on my account. A few more days shouldn't matter." She stirred her stew one last time. "Food's ready, Chandos."

While she ate, Courtney found herself both delighted to learn that she'd be with Chandos longer than she'd supposed, and angry that he hadn't bothered telling her his plans. She peeked at him a few times until he caught her at it, unnerving her with his gaze so that she hastily finished her meal and rushed off to check her clothing.

Enough of her things were dry that she could finally wear something else, so she went down to the river to change. Stripping out of her pants and shirt, she hesitated only a moment before taking a plunge into the water. It was past sunset, and Chandos was still eating. This would be the last water they would camp near for several days, so it was her last bath for a while.

Moonlight shimmered over the water. Courtney dug her feet into the river bottom beneath the shadow of an overhanging tree and let the current wash over her. She felt utterly wicked being stark naked. It was delightful.

At last, reluctantly, she left the river. Drying off posed a problem because she had no towel, so she wiped herself off with her hands—Lord, hadn't she wanted to do that to Chandos's back? *Don't think about that, Courtney.* Then she dressed quickly and headed back to camp.

To her surprise, she found that he had cleaned up their meal and laid out his bedroll and was already banking the fire. She sighed. She wasn't the least bit sleepy after her invigorating bath, but he was ready to sleep.

He stood up as she reached him. His eyes swept over her pale green silk gown, and she was suddenly aware that she hadn't completely dried off before dressing. The silk clung to her in places. Too, some of her hair had gotten wet, though she'd pinned it up. It was obvious that she had bathed, and the memory of bathing stark naked suddenly embarrassed her.

"If I'd known I wouldn't have to clean the dishes," she blurted out, "I wouldn't have bothered to get dressed." Oh, why did that sound so awful? She hadn't meant . . . "What I meant—oh, never mind. Here." Courtney handed him the shirt she had aired. "And thanks again."

She turned away, but Chandos alarmed her by grabbing her wrist. "Next time let me know what you're doing, woman. You could have been bitten by a water snake, or hit by a floating log and swept downriver, or carried off by Indians, or worse."

"What could be worse than Indians?" she said flippantly, defensive because she hadn't considered any of that.

"There's worse."

"But you weren't that far away," she said. "You would have heard me call for help."

"If you could have called. A man wouldn't give you that chance."

"If you're suggesting I not wash—"

"No."

Her eyes rounded as the obvious alternative hit home. "If you mean to—to—"

"Hell, no," he growled, as appalled by her conclusion as she was. "I don't have to watch you. I just need to be close by, close enough to protect you." He realized there was no way out of this embarrassing conversation. "Forget it," he finished curtly.

"Forget what? Letting you know before I—?"

"Forget washing, just forget it."

"Chandos!"

"A lady's got no business bathing on the trail, anyway."

"That's unreasonable and you know it!" she challenged him. "It's not as if I removed all my clothes. I did tonight, but I—"

She got no further. The image her words conjured up in Chandos's mind undid him. With a low growl, he brought her against him, and the full force of his passion was unleashed.

At the first touch of his mouth, Courtney

felt a shock of excitement deep inside that stole the strength from her limbs. Thinking her legs wouldn't support her, she held tightly to Chandos, wrapping her arms around his neck.

One of his arms held her like steel, pressing her so hard her breasts melted against his chest. His other hand gripped the back of her head, so she couldn't escape his ravishing mouth. There was something very savage in the fierce, brutal way his lips moved on hers, bruising, forcing her lips apart. And then the stabbing of his hot tongue slashed across hers.

Misunderstanding the violence of his assault, Courtney could only think he was trying to hurt her again, and she became frightened. She tried to move away from him, but he didn't release her. She pushed against his shoulders trying to break free, but his hold only strengthened. She twisted and squirmed, but she couldn't budge him.

Chandos was dimly aware that Courtney was fighting him. He had lost his personal battle, and he knew it. But it hadn't occurred to him yet that he might be frightening her with the power of his desire. Her continued struggling brought him up short, enough to bring him to his senses.

His assault on her mouth ended, and she gasped for breath. He loosened his hold on her, just enough that she could put a little space between them.

"Was that another one of your lessons?" she said, panting.

"No."

"But you hurt me again!"

Chandos stroked her cheek. "That was the last thing I meant to do, little cat."

He was now so gentle—his voice, his gaze, his hand on her face. But Courtney wouldn't let her guard down. She was still afraid of him.

"Why did you attack me, Chandos?"

The accusation wrenched him. "Attack?"

"What would you call it?"

"Storming your defenses?" he suggested wryly.

"Don't you dare laugh!" she cried. "You're hateful, and—and—"

"Shh, cateyes, and listen to me. If I frightened you, I'm sorry. But when a man wants a woman as much as I want you, it's not easy to go slowly. Do you see?"

After a shocked silence she asked in wonder, "You—you want me?"

"How can you doubt it?" he said gently.

Courtney lowered her eyes so he couldn't see her joy, her confusion.

"You didn't want me before," she said in a small voice. "Don't do this to me, Chandos, just because you—you need a woman, and I'm all that's available out here."

He tilted her chin up, forcing her eyes to meet his. "What have I done to you with my foolish battle to resist you?" He sighed with self-reproach. "Doubt the wisdom of my desire if you will, but don't doubt that I have wanted you from the moment you walked into that store in Rockley. Do you think I would have bothered with that no-account Jim Ward except for you?"

"No—don't say that."

"Do you know how close I came to killing your friend Reed because you *let* him kiss you?"

"Chandos, please!"

He gathered her close to him, very gently this time, ignoring what was now only a halfhearted resistance. "I can't help what I feel any more than you can, cateyes. I tried to leave you behind and put you from my mind, but I couldn't. I tried not to touch you. I can't fight it anymore, especially now that I know you want me, too."

"No, I—"

He wouldn't let her deny it. He took away her will and reason with another kiss, as tender now as the first one had been brutal. But it was his confession that worked magic on her, more than any kiss could have done. He wanted her—had always wanted her! Oh, Lord, how that thrilled her.

Courtney melted into him, returning his kiss with utter abandon. This was her fantasy come true, and she wanted it to go on and on. It did, as he rained kiss after kiss on her.

She wasn't thinking what all this kissing would lead to, not even when Chandos carried her to his bedroll and laid her gently on it.

His kisses became more amorous, and he started to undress her. She moved her hands to stop him, but he brushed them away, moving his lips down along her neck. Oh, Lord, it felt so good, so tingly.

A decision had to be made, she told herself. Would he be angry if she let him go so far and then stopped him? Could she stop him?

A tiny tremor of fear began to rise in her and she gasped, "Chandos, I—I'm not . . ."

"Don't talk, little cat," he whispered

209

huskily by her ear. "It's past wanting now—I *have* to touch you. Like this—and this."

His hand slid down her open dress, finding first one breast and then the other. Her thin chemise was no protection against such intense heat. And then, as the pleasure became unbearable, he began nibbling at her ear.

He was bombarding her with passion, and she couldn't think. There was no protest from her as he quickly removed her gown. A dizzying kiss followed, and then her chemise was whisked over her head and she was pressed back down, naked from the waist up.

His mouth covered her breast and her body jerked at this new blaze of heat. Her hands flew to grasp his head and hold him there. Her fingers entwined in his hair, she moaned as his tongue enflamed the hard kernel of her nipple, flicking it, stabbing at it. And then he began sucking, and she heard the sound of deep feline pleasure in her throat. The purring made Chandos groan.

Courtney had never dreamed of anything so wonderful, so deeply satisfying, but there was more, and Chandos was impatient to show her all of it.

She hadn't even felt him untying her petticoat, but as his hand slipped inside, the muscles of her belly quivered. Those gentle fingers glided on their downward path, and suddenly she realized how far they'd gone. Could she stop him? Her tug on his arm was only a token resistance.

And then his finger plunged inside her, and she cried out, "No!"

His lips came quickly to silence her, but he didn't remove his finger. It was the idea of it being there inside her that had made her cry out, not the feeling he was causing, certainly not that. A churning, violent eruption reverberated through her, obliterating her resistance.

When she was finally still, when her hand no longer pulled at his arm, but moved slowly up to clasp his neck, Chandos paused to look down at her. The fire in his eyes mesmerized her, giving her an inkling of what it had cost him to hold his passion in check thus far. It was an almost unbearable revelation.

He kept his gaze on her face as his hand caressed the hard knot at the apex of her mound. She gasped, blushing furiously when she saw he was watching her.

"Don't—"

"Shh, kitten," he whispered. "Imagine me inside you. You're wet for me. Do you know what it does to me to know you're so ready for me?"

He kissed her, once, twice, and his eyes smoldered as they locked with hers. "Let me love you, kitten. Let me hear you purring when I'm deep inside you."

He didn't let her answer but kissed her again. And then he moved away and in a moment her remaining clothing slid down her legs and was tossed aside.

"Don't cover yourself," he said when she tried to, adding in a reverent whisper, "You're more beautiful than any woman I've ever known. Don't hide your beauty from me."

Courtney suffered the embarrassment because he had asked her to. And then he was kneeling beside her, pulling off his shirt, and she forgot her shyness as she watched him.

He shocked her again.

"Touch me, little cat. Your eyes have told me countless times that you want to."

"That's not true!" she gasped.

"Liar," he said kindly.

There was no time to muster indignation. She watched as he unfastened his pants. Her first sight of all of him brought a sharp intake of breath. Surely, she couldn't accommodate all of him, could she?

Fear returned, but an exciting kind of fear.

Chandos knew she was frightened. Once his clothes were shed, he immediately moved her legs apart and stretched his long body over hers until she could feel the tip of his manhood at her portal. And then he groaned, and his lips crushed hers. He plunged inside her, absorbing her cry of pain with his mouth, and the spasms of her body with his.

He impaled her deeply, fully, but the pain didn't last, the hurt didn't last. All through it, he was kissing her thrillingly, his tongue teasing a response from her. He held her so tenderly, his hands cupping her face, caressing her, his chest grazing her breasts.

For a long time only Chandos's mouth and hands moved, and then when at last his hips began to move as well, Courtney moaned her disappointment. She loved the feel of him inside her, and she thought it was over. She soon learned otherwise. He glided in and out, forcefully, yet with exquisite care.

"Ah, yes, kitten, tell me," he groaned

against her mouth as she purred with the exquisite pleasure of it.

She did. She couldn't help it. Her arms closed tightly around him and her hips rose to meet him. She discovered that if she raised her legs she could take more of him into her, and the higher she raised them, the deeper he could plunge. She raised them higher and higher, exploding with the sudden burst of unbelievable, pulsating ecstasy that tore his name from her.

She was unaware that he had watched her the whole while, that only now did he give himself over to the passion that had ruled him for so long.

Chapter 23

All the next day, Courtney was in love. Nothing bothered her, not the heat and insects, not the monotonous riding. Nothing penetrated her bliss.

Two days later, she wasn't sure. And three days later she had changed her mind. She couldn't possibly love an exasperating man like Chandos. She could still want him—and despise herself for it—but she couldn't love him.

What had Courtney fuming was that he returned to his enigmatic self. He had made her his, transported her to the heights of ecstasy, and then treated her with the same old indifference! She was stupefied.

There was no escaping the truth. She had been used. Everything Chandos had said to her that night was a lie, everything. He had satisfied his lust, and now he had no more need of her.

The evening of the seventh day on the trail, they crossed another river, as Chandos had predicted they would. Since Courtney was already wet, she decided to bathe after supper, *without* telling Chandos. She took particular pleasure in this bath because she was spiting Chandos by disobeying his orders.

But when she started to leave the water, her underclothes plastered wetly to her body, her hair dripping, she sensed rather than saw that she wasn't alone. After a heart-stopping minute, she saw him. It was Chandos. She wasn't exactly relieved, however. He was hunkered down in the shadow of a tree and had been watching her, for how long she couldn't guess.

He rose, stepping out of the shadows toward her.

"Come here, cateyes."

He hadn't called her that in three days, nor spoken in that husky voice, either. He had gone back to calling her "lady"—when he spoke to her at all.

Courtney's nostrils flared and her eyes sparked.

"Damn you!" she shouted. "You're not using me again!"

He took another step toward her, and she moved back into the water. She might have gone farther, but he stopped. She glared at him, every line of her body defying him. Then he swore in that other language he often used, and turned and went back toward camp.

She had done it. She'd stood her ground with daring and courage, and she was proud of herself.

Courtney decided not to leave the water just yet, even though she began to shiver. It wasn't that she was afraid to face Chandos, exactly. She just wanted to give him time to cool his anger. And when she heard a gunshot coming from the direction of their campsite, she didn't budge. She wasn't stupid. If he was using such a ploy to make her come running to see what had happened, then he hadn't cooled off.

Another ten minutes passed before Courtney began to worry. Maybe she'd been wrong. He might have killed a wild animal. Or someone might have shot Chandos. He might be dead!

Courtney rushed out of the water, but she didn't go running up the slope as she was. She changed her wet underclothes for dry ones, and put on her skirt of beige and white stripes, along with the white silk blouse she had recently repaired. She carried everything else, including her boots, which were still wet from the river crossing. Offering up a quick prayer that she wouldn't step on anything crawly or poisonous, she hurried to the camp.

She ran until the light from their fire became visible, and then she slowed, cautious. Even so, she nearly tripped over the snake lying in her path. It was long and yellowish red, a copperhead, deadly. It was quite dead, but she cried out anyway.

"What?" Chandos called sharply, and her relief knew no bounds.

She ran until she saw him. He was alive, and he was alone. He was sitting by the fire and . . . Courtney stopped short, her color draining. Chandos had one boot removed, his pantleg cut open to the knee. Blood was running down the back of his calf, where he was squeezing at an incision. He had been bitten by the snake!

"Why didn't you call me?" she gasped, horrified that he was trying to treat himself.

"It took you this long to get here after the gunshot. Would you have come if I'd called?"

"If you told me what happened, I would have!"

"Would you have believed me?"

He knew. He knew what she had been thinking! How could he sit there so calmly—no, he had to remain calm, otherwise the poison would spread quicker.

Courtney dropped her things and rushed forward, grabbing Chandos's bedroll and spreading it out next to him. Her heart was racing.

"Lie down on your belly."

"Don't tell me what to do, woman."

She gasped at the surly tone, then realized he must be in pain. A wide area on his calf had turned violent red. He had his belt strapped tightly a few inches above the bite, which was in the middle of his calf. An inch or so lower and the snake would have bitten Chandos's boot. What awful luck!

"Have you sucked out most of the poison?"

Chandos's eyes, brighter than usual, stabbed at her. "Take a close look, woman. If you think I can reach that, you're crazy."

Courtney blanched again. "You mean you haven't even . . . you should have called me! What you're doing is only a last resort!"

"You know all about it?" he snapped.

"Yes," she retorted hotly. "I've seen my father treat snakebite. He's a doctor and—Have you loosened that belt yet? You should, every ten minutes or so. Oh, please, Chandos, lie down, for heaven's sake. Let me get the poison out before it's too late!"

He stared at her for so long, she almost thought he would refuse. But he shrugged and lay down on the bedroll.

"The cut is good," he told her, his voice getting weaker. "I could see to do that. I just couldn't reach it with my mouth."

"Do you feel anything besides the pain? Any weakness yet? Or nausea? Do you see clearly?"

"Who did you say was the doctor?"

She was relieved that he still had his wry humor. "It would help if you would answer the questions, Chandos. I need to know if

219

the poison went directly into your blood-
stream or not."

"None of the aforementioned complaints,
lady," he said with a sigh.

"Well, that's something, anyway, considering how much time has passed."

But somehow Courtney wasn't sure he
was telling the truth. If he were feeling
weak, it would be just like him not to admit
it.

She positioned herself by his calf and
went to work, feeling no squeamishness
about what she had to do—it had to be done.
But she was terrified because of the amount
of time that had passed.

Chandos remained perfectly still while she
worked on him, except to tell her at one
point to get her hand off his goddamn leg.
Courtney didn't pause from her steady sucking and spitting, but she blushed furiously
and was careful not to place her hand so high
on his leg again. She would fume about that
later, she told herself. Why, the man's lust
couldn't be controlled even when he was
suffering!

She worked on him for an hour, until she
simply couldn't do it anymore. Her lips
were numb, and her cheeks ached painfully.
The wound was no longer bleeding on its

own, but it was an angry red, and terribly swollen. She wished she had some kind of drawing salve to put on it. For that matter, she wished she knew anything about medicinal plants, for there might be something along the river or in the forest that would help draw out the poison or relieve the swelling. But she didn't know what to look for.

She fetched water from the river and applied a cold, wet cloth to the wound. And every ten minutes she continued to loosen the belt that was restricting Chandos's blood flow, leaving it off for a minute, then tightening it again.

She didn't relax for a moment. When she finally got around to asking how he was feeling, it was too late for an answer. He had lost consciousness, and panic began to overwhelm Courtney.

Chapter 24

"Cut my hair, old man, and I'll kill you!" Courtney had heard him say that before, that and so many other things that, altogether, painted a sad picture of Chandos's life. He was talking in his sleep and running a fever.

At some time during the night she had fallen asleep, though not for long. She had leaned her head on the back of Chandos's legs, and the next thing she knew, Chandos was shouting at something in his mind, saying he couldn't die until *they* were all dead. She tried to wake him, but he pushed her away.

"Goddammit, Calida, leave me alone," Chandos growled. "Go crawl into Mario's bed. I'm tired."

After that, she didn't try to wake him again. She changed his cold compress once more, and listened to his rambling as he relived gunfights, a beating, and encounters with the one he called "old man." And there were women he spoke to—Meara, respectfully, and White Wing, gently admonishingly. There was such a change in his voice when he talked to them that she knew he cared for them a great deal.

White Wing wasn't the only Indian name he mentioned, either. There were several others, and one he repeatedly called "friend." He even defended the Comanche man to the "old man," defending with such passion that suddenly Courtney remembered that Chandos had never answered the question when she'd asked if he was part Indian or not.

She hadn't given it much thought before, but it *was* possible. She realized that the strange-sounding language he sometimes used might be an Indian dialect.

Surprisingly, it didn't disturb her. Indian or not, he was still Chandos.

When rose streaks of dawn heralded the morning, Courtney began to have serious doubts about Chandos's recovery. She was exhausted. She didn't know what more she could do for him. His wound was just as ugly as it had been last night, and the swelling had barely lessened. He was still running a fever, and his pain seemed worse, but he groaned and thrashed about so weakly that it seemed he had no strength left.

"Ah, God, he broke her arms so she couldn't fight him . . . Goddamn bastard . . . only a child. Dead, they're all dead." His ramblings were whispered now, as if he barely had the strength to speak. "Break the link . . . cateyes."

She sat up, staring. It was the first time he had mentioned her.

"Chandos?"

"Can't forget . . . not my woman."

His difficulty breathing terrified Courtney more than anything else. And when he wouldn't wake up when she shook him, she began to cry.

"Chandos, please!"

"Goddamn virgin . . . no good."

Courtney didn't want to hear what he thought of her. She couldn't bear it. But what he had already said hurt, and she took refuge in her anger.

"Wake up, damn you, so you can hear me! I hate you, and I'll tell you so just as soon as you wake up! You're cruel and heartless, and I don't know why I've wasted a whole night trying to save you. *Wake up!*"

Courtney pounded on his back, then sat back, shocked and appalled. She had hit an unconscious man!

"Oh, God, Chandos, I'm sorry!" she cried, rubbing his back where she had struck him. "Please don't die. I won't be angry with you anymore, no matter how despicable you are. And—and if you get well, I promise I'll never desire you again."

"Liar."

Courtney nearly choked. His eyes were still closed.

"You're detestable!" she hissed, getting to her feet.

Chandos rolled slowly onto his side and looked up at her.

"Why?" he asked quietly.

"Why? You know why!" And then she said irrelevantly, "And I'm not a goddamn virgin, not now, am I?"

"Did I say you were?"

"About five minutes ago."

"Shit, was I talking in my sleep?"

"Abundantly," she said, sneering, then twirled around and stalked away.

"You can't take seriously what a man says in his sleep, cateyes," he called. "And to set things straight, I haven't thought of you as a goddamn virgin for a while now."

"Go to hell!" she tossed over her shoulder and kept walking.

But Courtney went no farther than the dead snake. Beside it lay a leather drawstring pouch that she knew very well hadn't been there last night.

A cold chill moved down her spine, and she took a quick, furtive look around the area, but there were so many plants and bushes and trees that anyone could stay hidden.

She stared at the pouch, afraid to touch it.

It was finely made, of buckskin, about double the size of her fist. There was something in it, for it bulged.

If someone had come by their camp at some point in the night while she was tending Chandos, why wouldn't she have seen him, or sensed his presence? And why hadn't the person declared his presence? Could someone have just accidentally dropped it? Even so, they'd have seen the campfire and come forward . . . unless they didn't want to be seen.

It gave Courtney a creepy feeling to know that someone *had* been there sometime in the night, and had probably watched her while she was unaware of it. But who? And why leave the pouch?

She picked it up carefully by the drawstring, holding it away from her body as she returned to camp. Chandos was where she had left him, lying on his side, and she reminded herself that he wasn't really better, only awake. Dear God, the things she had said to him when he was weak and suffering! What was becoming of her?

"That doesn't look like it bites, cateyes."

"What?" she asked, slowly approaching him.

"The pouch. You're holding it so far away

from you," he said, "but I don't think that's necessary."

"Here." Courtney dropped it in front of him. "I'd rather not open it myself. I found it beside your dead snake."

"Don't mention that goddamn viper to me," he said furiously. "I wish to hell I could kill it again."

"I imagine you do," she sympathized. Then she lowered her gaze. "I—I'm sorry I blew up like that, Chandos. There's no excuse for some of the things I said to you."

"Forget it," he replied, his attention on the pouch. He opened it. "Bless him!" he cried as he pulled out a drooping plant. The roots were still attached.

"What is it?"

"Snakeweed. Could I ever have used this last night! But better now than none at all."

"Snakeweed?" she said doubtfully.

"You crush it, mix some salt with the extracted juice, and put it on the bite. It's one of the better cures for snakebite." He held it out to her. "Would you?"

Courtney took the plant from him. "You know who left it, don't you?"

"Yeah."

"Well?"

He returned her stare for so long, she

thought he wasn't going to answer. Finally he said, "A friend of mine."

Her eyes widened. "But why couldn't this 'friend' come forward and give me the plant? He could've told me what to do with it."

Chandos sighed. "He couldn't tell you what to do with it. He doesn't speak English. And if he had come forward, you probably would have run away."

"He's an Indian?" It wasn't really a question, because she somehow knew their visitor had been an Indian. "Leaping Wolf, by any chance?"

Chandos frowned. "I really did do some talking, didn't I?"

"You held conversations with many different people. Do you always talk in your sleep?"

"How the hell should I know?"

The sharp retort turned her away. She prepared the snakeweed, then came back to him. "You want to turn back on your stomach, please?"

"No. Give me that stuff."

"I'll do it!" Avoiding his reach, she moved around behind him, saying, "You did enough damage by trying to treat yourself last night—unnecessarily, I might add."

"I didn't ask for your goddamn help."

"You would rather have died than have my help, I suppose?" she retorted.

He didn't answer. He didn't say anything else.

Courtney was stung. After all she'd done, he might have been a little appreciative. But he obviously didn't give a damn. And he didn't like having to accept her help.

"Is your friend still out there, Chandos?"

"You want to meet him?"

"No."

He sighed tiredly. "He wouldn't be nearby now, if that's what you're worried about. But he'll probably show up again to see if I've recovered. You won't see him, though, cateyes. He knows you frighten easily."

"I do not," she replied stonily. "How does he know?"

"I told him."

"When?"

"What the hell difference does it make?"

"None." She finished with his leg and came back around to face him. "I would just like to know why he's following us. That was him I saw that time, wasn't it? How many other nights has he sneaked—" Her eyes widened as she realized the possibilities.

"He wasn't around *that* night, cateyes," Chandos said softly, knowing her thoughts. "And he's not following us. We . . . happen to be going in the same direction."

"But you would be riding with him if I weren't here, wouldn't you? Yes, of course you would. No wonder you didn't want to bring me along."

His brows drew together. "I told you the reason I wanted to leave you behind."

"Yes, you did, didn't you?" she replied frostily. "But you'll have to forgive me if I no longer believe half the things you told me the other night."

Instead of reassuring her—as she'd hoped he would—Chandos said nothing. She was torn between screaming at him and crying. She did neither, however. She squared her shoulders and walked away.

"I'm going to the river to wash up. If I'm not back in a few minutes, you'll know I've run into your friend and fainted dead away."

Chapter 25

Chandos watched Courtney as she reheated the broth she'd been forcing on him all day. The late afternoon sun played with her hair, streaking the thick brown tresses with golden lights. He didn't think he could ever get enough of watching her. And he was finding he was a glutton for punishment where she was concerned.

He had played her a bad turn, his cateyes, and she was going to make him suffer for it. But he couldn't have done anything differently. She was not for him. If she'd known all there was to know about him, she'd have realized that. If she found out everything, he told himself, she would look at him with fear in her eyes.

What he saw in her now was fire, fire and the anger of a scorned woman. Now, if only her anger would stop feeding his male pride. But there was no getting around it—he was pleased by her reaction. He would have been terribly hurt if she'd accepted his pretended indifference. But he discovered that ignoring her made her furious, and that delighted him.

He hadn't wanted to steal her innocence.

He had tried his damnedest not to. But having lost that battle with himself, having made her his for that one incredible night, he'd believed his burning craving was satisfied. Well, he'd learned better. He'd only had to see her taking a bath in the river and his resolves were forgotten.

He was almost grateful to the snake for putting an end to his madness, for he'd surely have made love to Courtney again last night if he'd been able to. And that would be no good. It was going to be difficult enough to part with her as it was. Any further involvement would only make it worse.

She didn't realize that yet, of course. She was in the grip of her first passion, and she was thoroughly vexed with him. She thought he had used her. He sighed. It was better she thought so. It would be even better if she hated him.

The truth was, if he thought for one minute that he could make her happy, he would never let her go. But what kind of life could he offer her? He'd made his decision four years ago to forsake the white world and return to the Comanche way of life. Fifteen evil men had changed that life forever, and when it was all over, what would be left for him? He had roamed so long he didn't think he could settle anywhere, not even with the Comanche people. Could a white woman accept a life like that? Could his cateyes? He knew he couldn't ask her to.

He was startled out of his reverie as Courtney knelt down next to him, handing him the tin cup of hot broth. "How are you feeling?"

"Just as shitty as the last time you asked."

She frowned. "God sakes, Chandos, must you be so vulgar?"

"Vulgar? You want vulgar, I'll give you vulgar—"

"Thank you, no," she interrupted. "Last night I heard enough of the extremes of language you're capable of."

"Did I miss all your blushes, cateyes?" he teased. "That's too bad. I do enjoy them, you know. If all it takes is a little vulgarity—"

"Chandos!"

"There, that's better. It doesn't take much to bring color to your cheeks, does it?"

"If you can be so obnoxious, then you're not at Death's door," she said primly. And then she caught him unawares. "So tell me—are you part Indian?"

After the briefest pause, he said, "You

know, your doctoring was all right until you got it into your head that this weak soup was going to give me any strength."

Courtney sighed loudly. "A simple yes or no is all I want. However, if you don't want to answer, don't. It doesn't matter to me even if you *are* part Indian."

"How tolerant of you."

"How snide you are, Chandos."

That closed-off look came over his features, and he murmured, "You think I don't know Indians scare you half to death?"

Her chin went up. "I can't help it if the only experience I've had with Indians was a bad one. But you're not like them, for heaven's sake."

Chandos almost laughed but forced himself not to.

"I warned you not to try to second guess me, woman. If you're going to make me an Indian, I can damn well act the part."

"Then you aren't really—"

"No, but I don't have to be an Indian to be a savage, do I? Shall I prove it?"

Courtney jumped to her feet and hurried to the other side of the fire. With that barrier between them, she glared at Chandos, her hands on her hips. "Do you get some kind of perverse pleasure in frightening me?"

"Did I frighten you?" he asked innocently.

"Certainly not," she retorted. "But you tried—didn't you?"

"Certainly not," Chandos mimicked.

He was enjoying her fit of temper. He couldn't help it. She was so goddamn beautiful when her honey brown eyes sparked with fire and she rose to her full dignity, tossing her hair and throwing her shoulders back.

He had named her appropriately, for his cateyes could be a tiger. This journey was good for her—if not for him. She had come into her own. There was no telling how much more she would discover about herself before they reached Texas. A week ago she'd been so timid she couldn't stop stammering in his presence. Now, well, he knew damn well she *wouldn't* have fainted if she'd seen Leaping Wolf.

"I'd like to know what you think you could do to me, Chandos, when you can barely raise your head to drink your soup?"

That hit a nerve. "Be careful, lady. You'd be surprised what a man can do when he's riled."

Courtney shrugged.

"I was only curious," she assured him.

"Then come over here, and I'll appease your curiosity," he said smoothly, and her eyes flared.

"You might not be concerned with your condition, but I am! You should be conserving energy, not fighting. Now, please, drink your soup, Chandos. Then rest while I make something substantial for your dinner."

He nodded. Why upset her any more?

Chapter 26

It was going to rain. There might even be a storm, if the gathering dark clouds were an indication.

That was the first thing Courtney noticed when she woke. The second thing she saw was that Chandos was still asleep, so she took the opportunity to fill their canteens at the river, wanting to get the coffee started before he awoke.

The track to the river was darker than usual because there was no morning sun. The gloom began to affect her, and she certainly didn't feel like riding all day in the rain, even if Chandos was up to it. But then, sitting the rain out with only a rain slicker for shelter wasn't a very cheerful prospect, either. She didn't dare complain, though. This was just another aspect of riding the open trail.

The threatening sky received a withering look from Courtney as she bent to fill the canteens. Rain. It wasn't the end of the world, she told herself. Chandos was recovering. She ought to be grateful for that. There was so much to be grateful for, she had no business being depressed by a little rain.

"You Courtney Harte?"

She froze, bent toward the river, her canteen still in the water. Her whole body went rigid, and she forgot to breathe.

"You deaf, honey?"

Her eyes widened with the sudden realization. "He said you didn't speak English!" she wailed.

"Who? What the hell you talkin' 'bout?"

She swung around, her eyes fixing on the man's face. Relief nearly did her in. "God sakes, I thought you were a *Comanche!* There's one around here," she babbled.

"How do you know? You seen him?"

"Well . . . no."

"Well, neither have I. I guess he ain't

around anymore, then. Now, are you the Harte woman?"

What was going on? He didn't look frightening. He had the kind of face that was used to laughing, heavily creased around the mouth and eyes, a pleasant face, with well-fleshed cheeks and eyes the color of pale smoke. He was of average height, and a little stocky, about thirty-five years old.

"Who are you?" she demanded.

"Jim Evans. Bounty hunter."

"But you don't look like—I mean—"

"Yeah, I know." He grinned broadly. "Gives me the edge, see. I don't fit the general image. Now, are you going to own up to who you are?"

If he hadn't said he was a bounty hunter, she might have. But she could only think that a bounty hunter would be looking for Chandos.

"I'm not Courtney Harte."

He grinned again. "You wouldn't lie to me, now would you? The odds on there bein' two women out here who fit the description I have are pretty poor. I'd stake my life I found me the one and only Courtney Harte."

"Then why did you bother to ask?" Courtney retorted.

238

"Had to. Can't afford to make mistakes. I don't get paid for mistakes. And what you're worth ain't chicken feed, believe you me."

"Me? Then you're not after— What do you mean, what *I'm worth?* I'll have you know I am *not* wanted by the law, Mr. Evans."

"Didn't say you were."

"But you're a bounty hunter."

"I collect rewards," he told her. "Not just on folks wanted by the law. I'll hunt down anyone for any reason if the price is right. For you, it was. Your man is real anxious to get you back, honey."

"My *man?*" Disbelief was fast turning to anger as understanding dawned. "How dare he! Reed Taylor hired you, didn't he?"

"He's paying the price."

"But he's not my man. He's nothing to me!"

Jim Evans shrugged. "Whatever he is don't matter to me. He wants you back in Kansas, and that's what he'll get, 'cause I don't get paid until you're delivered."

"I'm sorry to disappoint you, mister, but I'm not going back to Kansas, not for any reason—and certainly not because Reed Taylor wants me to. I'm afraid you've wasted your time. Of all the—"

"And I'm afraid *you* don't *understand*, honey." He used the same agreeable voice, but his expression had hardened. "I never waste my time. You're going back to Kansas. Whatever objections you have, you can take up with Mr. Taylor, not with me."

"But I refuse—"

He drew his gun and pointed it at her. Courtney's heart did triple leaps. And before she even remembered that she had her own gun tucked in her skirt, he'd found it and taken it from her.

"Don't look so surprised, honey." He grinned. "I'm good at what I do."

"So I see. But would you really shoot me? I doubt Reed would pay if you brought me back dead."

"True," he drawled, "but he didn't say anything about what kind of condition you had to be in."

Courtney didn't mistake his meaning. Could she take the chance and run for it? But he was one step ahead of her.

"Don't even think about running or screaming. If the man you're with comes rushing down here, I'll just have to shoot him."

He motioned upriver. "Let's go."

"But, my things! Surely you don't expect me to leave without—"

"Nice try, but forget it. After what the Mexican told us 'bout that breed you're riding with, I'd just as soon not meet him at all. And if we just leave, he won't know what happened to you."

She began to panic. What he said was true. By the time Chandos got around to looking for her, it would be raining and her tracks would be washed away.

She stalled for time, hoping Chandos was up by now and wondering what was taking her so long. "The Mexican you mentioned wouldn't happen to be Romero, would he?"

"Yes. We came across him and two others a while back. Quite a story they told 'bout your friend. Made him sound like a one-man army. 'Course, you can't believe everything a fella says when he's making excuses for his own shortcomings. Or covering for whatever they did. Thought they mighta done you in and just weren't owning up to it. Pretty Boy was all for killing them and turning back to Kansas, but the Mexican offered to show us where they'd last seen you, and we picked up your tracks easy enough from there."

"Who is Pretty Boy?"

"You don't think I'd be fool enough to enter this territory alone, do you? The others are waiting up the river, with the horses. We figured your friend would be less suspicious if only I came in, and I'd have a better chance of getting the drop on him."

"I suppose you saw me heading down here alone, though?"

"Yeah, lucky wasn't I?" he said, grinning. "'Cause I tell you, honey, I sure wasn't looking forward to meetin' the breed."

He pulled her along with him, and she realized this was her last opportunity to scream. She couldn't do it, however. If Chandos had been himself, she wouldn't have hesitated. But he was weak from the snakebite, and might have gotten killed. And it wasn't as if she were in any danger. She was only being forced to return to Kansas, that was all.

It wasn't long, however, before she regretted her decision to go along quietly and not scream for Chandos.

Chapter 27

Pretty Boy Reavis was aptly named, with thick, silver blond wavy hair and eyes of deepest violet. He was in fact amazingly handsome, even beautiful. Twenty-two, lean, just under six feet tall, he presented a fantasy feast for the female imagination.

Courtney was so struck by the sight of him that she didn't even notice the two men with him. And Pretty Boy found her just as interesting.

"Taylor said you were beautiful, darlin', but he didn't do you justice."

He'd probably been away from women for a long time, Courtney thought, for she was standing there in her mussed riding skirt and the white silk blouse that was now a mass of wrinkles after being washed but not pressed. Her hair fell in wild disarray to her waist. And she hadn't washed since the night Chandos was snakebit.

"You'll ride with me," Pretty Boy said, coming forward to take her from the bounty hunter.

"Pretty Boy—"

"She rides with me, Evans," he said, grit in his voice.

There was a good deal more to Pretty Boy than his face.

Jim Evans heeded the unmistakable warning, letting go of her arm.

Courtney started to wonder who was in charge, but just then Evans told them all to mount up, and they did. Evans was in charge. Yet Pretty Boy had gotten what he wanted without an argument.

Pretty Boy was feared. From the way Evans had backed off so quickly, Courtney had the feeling that nobody challenged Pretty Boy. Maybe he wasn't just another gunman, but the kind that enjoyed killing for its own sake.

She was tossed up onto Pretty Boy's horse, after which he mounted, sitting behind her. Only then did she notice the Mexican. He met her startled gaze with the darkly serious look she remembered. That look had the ability to infuriate her in an instant.

"You don't learn from your mistakes, do you, Romero?" she asked caustically.

He had the audacity to smile. "You are still full of fire, *bella*. But, *sí*, I learn." He glanced over at Jim, who was just mounting up. "We heard no shots, *señor*. What have you done with Chandos?"

244

"Not a thing," Jim replied. "Didn't have to get near him. She was down by the river."

"You mean he don't even know we got her?" This from a long-faced fellow with an even longer red handlebar mustache. "I like that! He'll be hanging around waiting for her to return, and she won't!" He laughed. "Breeds ain't smart. Wonder how long it'll take him to figure she's gone."

"You are wrong," Romero said quietly. "My *amigos* and I made the mistake of underestimating that one. I for one will not be able to sleep until he is dead. If you will not see to it, then I will."

Courtney almost cried out, but she realized that wasn't the way to stop the Mexican. Chandos had gotten the better of Romero, and he had a score to settle. No amount of pleading would sway him. It might even goad him on.

Thinking quickly, she said, "Oh, thank you, Romero. I was afraid Chandos would think I had fallen in the river and wouldn't even bother looking for me."

"Is she serious?" Long-Face asked. And then he said to Courtney, "You want to see the breed dead?"

"Don't be ridiculous," she replied with a touch of haughtiness. "Chandos isn't going to die. He's too clever to be taken unawares. But how else is he to know what's happened to me unless he sees one of you?"

"You don't like Romero much, do you, darlin'?" Pretty Boy chuckled. Then he said to the others, "Forget him. If the breed follows us, I'll take care of him."

Apparently, no one doubted his ability, including Romero, for they moved out. Courtney breathed a sigh of relief. Chandos was safe.

But she wasn't. Not long after they crossed the river, Pretty Boy's hands began to roam. One hand drew alarmingly close to her breasts, and Courtney gasped in outrage as that hand did in fact clamp over a breast. She yanked the offending hand away, only to have both of her hands caught and twisted up behind her back, the pain bringing tears to her eyes.

"Don't play with me, darlin'." Pretty Boy's voice was an angry whisper. "We both know you've been givin' it to the Comanche breed. That makes you fair game."

The hand holding the reins moved up her belly and over her breasts. The horse side-stepped, shaking his head. Courtney squeezed her eyes shut against the pain in her shoulders and arms, still twisted behind her.

"Consider yourself lucky that I've taken a likin' to you, darlin'," he continued. "I'll keep the others away from you—but only as long as you show your appreciation. Taylor wants you back, but before we get there, I mean to take a bonus for my trouble. *How you want it is up to you.*"

He released her arm. Courtney stayed silent. What could she say? And she had no defense.

Yet she was in no way resigned. Incredibly handsome though he was, his cruel touch repulsed her. And as soon as the pain in her shoulder eased, she let him know what she thought of his mauling, consequences be damned.

Her elbow slammed into his stomach, and a tussle followed as she tried her best to jump off the horse. He gave her a blow to the side of her head, but she kept on fighting until, at last, his arms circled her like steel bands and she couldn't move at all.

"All right," he growled furiously. "You made your point. I'll keep my hands off you for now. But you better start praying I've cooled off by the time we make camp tonight."

As if to emphasize the warning, a flash of lightning streaked across the sky, and a rumble of thunder followed. A burst of hard rain drove down on them, ending further threats as Pretty Boy fished out his slicker and tossed it over them both, then kneed his horse to catch up with the others.

Chapter 28

"What happened to Dare Trask?"

Courtney considered not answering Romero. She didn't have an answer anyway.

She was sitting close to the fire, managing to take only a few bites from her plate of beans. Her stomach wouldn't stop churning with fear.

It had stopped raining in the late afternoon, and they made camp in the thicker part of a forest, high in the Sandstone Hills. She had almost expected to be beaten by Pretty Boy, and indeed he had nearly thrown her off the horse. But he tended the horse first, and now was rolling dice with Long-Face, who, she'd learned, was called Frank. Both men occasionally glanced at her, just often enough to keep her tensed up.

"What is wrong, *bella?*"

"That angelic-looking killer is going to rape me and you ask me what's wrong?" she answered Romero.

Her eyes were bright with anger, and the fire flecked her hair with golden lights. She had no idea how lovely she looked, or how much Romero wanted her in that moment.

"I am afraid I cannot sympathize. I would like you for myself. My *amigos,* they would have shared you, but Pretty Boy will not."

"Can you stop him?"

"You joke, *bella.*" He drew back, looking amazed. "No one challenges that one or gets in his way. He is loco. He does not care who he kills or why."

"Chandos wouldn't hesitate to challenge him."

"But he is not here."

"He will be, Romero," she warned. "Don't doubt it."

His eyes narrowed. "The last time we met, you swore he did not care for you."

"A lot has changed since then." She looked at the fire before adding, "I'm his woman now."

"*¡Dios!*" Romero swore. "I think my chances would be better if I did not ride

with you and these *hombres*. This is dangerous."

"You're probably right." Courtney tried
for a casual tone. "But unless you leave now,
it's not going to matter much."

Courtney wondered briefly whether she
might be able to get them all to abandon her.
She doubted it. Pretty Boy wouldn't be easy
to intimidate. He was too confident of his
own abilities. Still, the fewer of them, the
better her chances of escape.

"Chandos would have found our tracks
before the rain started," she said to Romero.
"He'll know how to find me."

"You were not so confident of that this
morning when you would have sent me in to
die."

"I only said that so you wouldn't get
yourself killed." She shrugged. "You don't
think I want anyone to die, do you? But I
don't see what I can do about it now . . ."

After a long, tense silence, Romero repeated his first question. "What happened
to Dare?"

"Chandos never told me."

"You were there."

"No I wasn't. He sent me on ahead of
him. He said he had some things to say to
Trask, things I shouldn't hear."

"He sent you ahead, alone, when he knew there were Indians out there?" Romero was incredulous.

"I wasn't in any danger. He assured me of that." She decided to stretch the truth a bit, since he couldn't know there had been only one Indian around. "I found out only yesterday that they are friends of his, and he usually travels with them. They've been out there ever since we left Kansas, but they've kept their distance because, well, Chandos knows I'd be scared out of my wits if I saw them."

"*Si*. If we did not see three of them, I would have returned to rescue Trask that night."

"You saw *three?*" Courtney gasped. It seemed she'd been telling the truth after all. "I just never . . . I mean I assumed . . . now that I think about it, I don't see how Trask could have gotten out of there alive. Chandos took Trask's horse. He said he didn't kill him, but—but he also said Trask was guilty of some atrocious things, and that he deserved anything he got. I thought he was forcing him to walk back to Kansas, but it's possible he just left him there for . . . ."

She swallowed hard. Yes, it *was* possible,

and that showed how cold-blooded Chandos could be.

What could Trask have done to deserve being left to Comanches? Could he have killed the people Chandos had talked to in his sleep?

"These Comanches are still around?" Romero asked uneasily, looking out into the trees surrounding them.

"Yes. In fact, when Jim Evans snuck up on me this morning, I thought he was one of them."

"It is possible, then, that they might ride with Chandos to get you back?"

Hope flared. She hadn't thought of that.

"No, no, they wouldn't ride with Chandos," she told him. "Why should they? He doesn't need help facing four men. Hasn't he already proved that?"

Romero nodded curtly.

"I think I shall bid you *adiós, bella*. It is not healthy to be around you."

"You're not leaving, are you?" she called as he walked away.

The others heard. Pretty Boy stood up, confronting Romero. "What's goin' on?"

"I helped you find the woman. It was a mistake. You should have left her with her man."

"Taylor?" Jim asked, puzzled.

"No, *señor*, she is Chandos's woman, and therefore he will come for her. I do not care to be here when he does."

"You'd rather ride out now, at night—alone?" Jim was incredulous. "You're loco."

Pretty Boy broke in. "What'd she tell you to spook you?" he demanded.

"She admits she is Chandos's woman."

"You expect us to believe a half-breed would give a damn what happens to a white woman?" Frank called over to them.

Courtney was taken aback by the contempt in Romero's dark eyes as he looked them over and said slowly, "I saw what this half-breed did to my *amigos*, and that was before she was his woman, when he was only her guide. But he has claimed her now. Do you know what a Comanche does to someone who steals his woman?"

"He's only half Comanche," Jim pointed out.

"No, *señor*, that makes him twice as deadly, for he can kill as a white man *or* as a Comanche. We are deep in Comanche territory, and I fear when he comes for the woman, he will not come alone."

Jim looked at Courtney, his expression hard.

"Then you'll stay, Romero," Jim said firmly. "We'll need every gun—"

"Let him go," Pretty Boy interrupted, sneering. "I don't need a coward backin' me up. I don't need any backup at all. I'm the best there is, Evans. That's why you wanted me along. Remember?"

Romero heard himself being called a coward, and every line in his body tensed. Courtney knew he was grappling with his pride, and she cried out, "No!" then covered her ears against the sound of the gunshot.

Romero went for his gun, but Pretty Boy proved his claim. Courtney watched in horror as blood spread across Romero's chest. He toppled over slowly, and lay still.

Pretty Boy was smiling. It was the kind of smile that made her feel ill.

"Quite a commotion you stirred up, darlin'."

Courtney doubled over with spasms that emptied her stomach. When it was over, Pretty Boy came to stand beside her.

He laughed cruelly. "Didn't think you had such a delicate constitution, darlin', or I would've warned you not to watch."

"You—you deliberately baited him," she said.

"Maybe."

"There's no maybe about it," she cried. "You wanted to kill him! Why?"

"I wouldn't be so high-and-mighty about it," he said coldly. "You're the one who stirred him up to show his colors. I just don't like cowards, that's all."

Courtney groaned. It *was* her fault. No! It wasn't! She might have told a few lies, but she hadn't forced Romero into a showdown. Pretty Boy had done that all on his own.

"I thought the Comanches were savages, but *you're* the savage," Courtney hissed.

She was sure he was going to hit her, but he only yanked her to her feet. "I think the problem is, I've ignored you too long, darlin'." His grip on her arm hurt and she squirmed, but he held her tightly while he turned his attention to the others. "Frank, get rid of the Mexican—and take your time about it. And Jim, if you're so worried about Indians, why don't you go scout around a bit?"

Courtney blanched.

"No!" she cried. "Evans, don't you dare leave me here with this monster! Evans!"

Jim Evans didn't even look at her as he

caught up his rifle and left the camp. Frank likewise ignored her as he dragged Romero's body away and out of sight. Courtney had Pretty Boy's full attention then. His grip tightened and the fury in those violet eyes terrified her.

"I—I didn't really mean—what I called you," she offered fearfully.

"'Course you didn't, darlin'."

He didn't believe her, of course, and she intuitively understood that there was no mercy in this man. Once before, long ago, Courtney had prayed for the courage not to beg. That had been during the attack by Indians, when her life was at stake. This time, with Pretty Boy, seemed no less horrible, and she ordered herself not to grovel or plead.

She took courage in anger.

"All right, I *did* mean it! You're a vicious—"

Fire exploded in her cheek. No sooner had he slapped her than he dragged her down to the ground, the weight of his body holding her so she couldn't move at all. Stunned, she found his mouth grinding against hers, cutting off her breath.

She was being shown the difference between passion and brutal lust. Pretty Boy was hurting her deliberately, and she knew the pain was only just beginning. There would be more, much more.

His teeth slashed across her cheek, then sank into the side of her neck. Courtney cried out, grabbing a handful of his hair and yanking his head back. It didn't bother him. He grinned down at her.

"You go any farther," she gasped, "and Chandos will kill you!"

"Haven't you got it straight yet, darlin'? Your half-breed don't scare me."

"If you're not scared of him, you're a fool!"

His hand closed on her throat, cruelly squeezing while she fought for air. He let her struggle for nearly a minute before finally letting go. In the next instant, her blouse and chemise were ripped open in one movement, and a long red line ran down her chest where his nail had cut the skin.

"You'd do better to keep your mouth shut," he told her coldly. "I've taken more crap from you than I've ever taken before."

"Then no one's ever told you the truth before, is that it?"

Courtney couldn't believe she had said that. It got her another slap, this one bringing tears to her eyes, but there was a devil riding her and she couldn't stop herself.

"There's one thing you've overlooked, Pretty Boy," she said, panting. "You've killed the last man you'll ever face in a showdown. Comanches don't fight that way. If they want you, five or six will come at you at once. What will your fast gun avail you then?"

"Is that what you told the Mexican to make him run scared?" he said, sneering.

"No." She shook her head. "I told him Chandos would probably come alone 'cause he wouldn't need help to dispose of vermin like—"

She screamed as his fingers dug into her breast. His other hand quickly covered her mouth, but she bit him and he snatched the hand away.

"Chandos!" Courtney screamed, knowing it wouldn't do any good, but needing the small bit of hope.

"Bitch!" Pretty Boy growled. "I ought to—"

He broke off as they heard a horrifying scream. It silenced Pretty Boy and froze them both. It was a death cry, a cry of pain, a man's scream. And then there was another scream, even more horrible than the first.

On the heels of it they heard someone charging through the brush, and then Frank burst into the camp.

"Goddamn!" Frank gasped, nearly out of breath. "They got Evans!"

Pretty Boy had leaped up, gun in hand. "Could've been a bear. Or a wildcat."

"Sure, but you don't believe that any more than I do," Frank said. "It's an old trick. They'll torture him all night long so we can hear him scream. It's supposed to drive us crazy so that, come morning, we'll be easy pickings."

Pretty Boy turned his gun on Courtney.

"Get up. We're gettin' out of here."

She rose slowly. "I thought you wanted to face them," she said innocently.

That got her another slap, and she went reeling over backward and landed hard on the ground. She stayed there, holding her face with one hand and her blouse closed with the other. Her eyes met Pretty Boy's, and her hatred was unmistakable. He was a bit taken aback, despite himself.

"Go easy, will you?" Frank said. "She's all we got to bargain with."

"We're leavin'," was Pretty Boy's confident answer. "Won't need to bargain if we ain't here."

"We don't dare. You don't think there ain't one of them out there watching us right now? We'd be cut down if we tried to leave. This is one we'll have to fight our way out of—and they're calling the shots."

Pretty Boy knew Frank was right. He whirled around, trying to spot a target. Courtney took a perverse pleasure in Pretty Boy's fear despite her own fear. They all had good reason to be afraid, but for different reasons.

Frank was wrong about Evans. Ten minutes passed with no further screams, and they assumed Evans was dead. The two men also assumed that the Indians out there were after Courtney, but Courtney knew it was just as likely these were Indians who'd just happened across them, not friends of Chandos's. And if they weren't friends of Chandos's, then she would soon be as dead as Pretty Boy and Frank.

"I'll need a gun," Courtney suggested as she got to her feet.

"Like hell!" Pretty Boy snarled.

"God sakes, are you going to be a fool to the bitter end?" she snapped. "I might not have much experience with guns, but at least I can hit what's right in front of me."

"Yeah, like me."

Frank snickered, and Courtney gritted her teeth in exasperation.

"Look, hasn't it dawned on either of you that *anyone* might be out there?" she asked sharply. "It might even be a wild animal—there haven't been any more screams. Or maybe Evans had an accident."

"Man don't scream like that over accidents," Frank said.

"All right," Courtney conceded, hesitating a moment before she said, "But I have to tell you something. It's not likely to be Chandos out there, not this soon anyway. He was snakebit, and still recovering when Evans got me. That's really why I didn't want Romero to confront Chandos. Chandos wasn't up to it yet. And although there were some Indians in the area, it's pretty far-fetched to think they would come to rescue me. Can you imagine a full-blooded Comanche riding to rescue a white woman?"

"I can imagine a white woman would say anything to get her hands on a gun. You know you would, darlin'," Pretty Boy replied. "You can talk till you're blue and the answer's still no."

"You—"

His temper flared. "Shut your god-

261

damn mouth so I can hear what's going on out there!"

Courtney clamped her mouth shut. And just then, Frank gasped, "I don't believe it! The bastard's crazy. He's coming in *alone*."

Pretty Boy and Courtney turned to look. It was Chandos, and he was alone, astride Surefoot, winding slowly through the trees as he came into view about ten feet away. Courtney's heart lurched. He had come for her! Sick as he was, he'd come to rescue her!

He looked terrible. Two days' growth of whisker stubble and rumpled clothes exaggerated his haggard appearance. He hadn't even changed clothes.

Pretty Boy was grinning. Frank held his gun firmly.

Chandos held his reins, his gun holstered. When his gaze moved over Courtney, taking in her torn clothes, he tensed, his jaw hardening.

"You alone, mister?"

Chandos didn't answer Frank's question. He dismounted and stepped slowly in front of his horse. Courtney held her breath, for he hadn't drawn his gun yet, and it would be so easy for Frank to raise his gun a little and shoot. But then she saw that Frank seemed intimidated by Chandos's boldness and was hesitant. Pretty Boy made no move, either. Courtney realized then that both men probably thought there were arrows trained on them. They didn't believe Chandos would walk into their camp alone unless he was being covered by his Comanche friends. Was he?

"You Chandos?" Frank ventured.

Chandos nodded. "Your tracks read there's four of you. Where's the fourth?"

Pretty Boy smiled. "Wouldn't you like to know."

"The Mexican's dead, Chandos," Courtney said.

"I told you to keep your mouth shut!" Pretty Boy yelled, moving to hit her.

"I wouldn't."

Chandos's voice stopped him, and Pretty Boy lowered his hand slowly, turning so he faced Chandos squarely. Courtney suspected he was about to draw his gun. Frank stalled him, however, for Chandos had revealed something.

"You don't ask about Evans, so that means it was you who killed him."

"He's not dead," Chandos told him.

"Then what the hell did you do to him to make him scream like that?"

"I didn't like some of the things he had to say, so—"

"I don't want to hear this, Chandos!" Courtney screamed.

"Yeah, never mind," Frank agreed. "But he's not dead?"

"I left his rifle near him."

Courtney didn't understand the significance of that, but the men did. It was the goad needed to end the parley, for there was no longer any doubt about Chandos's intentions. The air became electric as the three men faced off, waiting for the first move. It came from Frank, who jerked his gun up and fired.

Courtney screamed. Frank's nervousness ruined his aim, and the bullet flew wide of its mark. Chandos's gun cleared leather in that instant. Pretty Boy's did too, but Chandos hit the ground as he fired off two shots, the first taking Frank center chest. He was dead in a moment. The second shot made Pretty Boy jerk forward, eyes wide with disbelief. He hadn't fired a single shot. He pulled the trigger, and his gun flew out of his hand as Chandos fired a third shot. The impact spun Pretty Boy around, so that when he dropped to his knees, he was facing Courtney.

"Guess I . . . should've . . . believed you, darlin'. The bastard's . . . killed me."

He wasn't dead yet. He wouldn't be dead for some time to come. But he would die. There wasn't anything to be done for gut-shot and he knew it. His lovely violet eyes filled with horror.

Chandos rose and walked forward, his expression hard as granite. He retrieved Pretty Boy's gun, then came to stand in front of him. With his eyes on Pretty Boy, Chandos slowly holstered his own gun and then stuck Pretty Boy's gun in his belt. Through the haze of pain, Pretty Boy understood.

"You left Evans his rifle," Pretty Boy said with a groan. "Leave me my gun."

"No."

"Chandos, you can't leave him like that!" Courtney cried.

He didn't even look at her. His eyes were locked with Pretty Boy's. "He hurt you. He pays."

"It should be up to me!"

"It isn't." He gave her a quick look, then gazed back at Pretty Boy. "Get on my horse, lady. We're leaving."

She ran toward his horse, but he sensed her intention. She wasn't going to wait for him. She wanted to get away from him and his ruthless justice. He charged after her and caught her.

"He hurt you, didn't he?" His voice was like steel.

"Yes, but he didn't do what you think. Evan's screaming stopped him."

"But he still hurt you, so don't question the penalty. I could have made his death a lot worse. I could have made it last much longer."

He let go of her, and she cried, "Why are you so vengeful? *You're* not the one he hurt."

"Are you sorry I came for you, cateyes?"

Courtney lowered her eyes. "No."

"Then get on my horse and don't even think about leaving without me. I'm angry enough with you. You didn't signal me this morning that you were in trouble. Don't make me have to chase after you again, because there's no way in hell you can get away from me, lady."

Courtney nodded briefly, then turned toward Surefoot. She was so angry with Chandos that she almost forgot how grateful she ought to be. He had saved her from Pretty Boy . . . but all she saw in her mind's eye was his granite face and cold expression.

266

Chapter 29

This was the second time Courtney had left a scene of bloodshed during the night. She rode in front of Chandos, enveloped in the warmth of his protection. Again, he had killed for her. He only wounded men who were after him. He killed men who were after her.

But he was angry with her. And only moments after they finally stopped riding, his passion erupted. He lifted her down from his horse, and her blouse spilled open. Perhaps that triggered it. Or maybe it was the killing. He hadn't only killed but had himself come close to dying. It was as if he needed a reaffirmation of life, and found it in her soft, yielding body.

Courtney was overpowered. There was to be no denying Chandos. But she wasn't frightened. What she felt was a trembling excitement, his intensity overwhelming her. If Chandos needed to exert his male dominance this way, she was happy to let him. She had her own anxieties to release, after all, and she could think of no better way to release them.

And in the back of her mind was the

comforting thought that if he wanted to love her, he couldn't be *that* angry with her.

He lowered her to the ground, and she clung to him, pulling him down with her. Grass and stones spiked through her clothes, but she barely felt it as his lips fastened on a nipple and he began to suckle hungrily.

Sounds of pleasure gurgled in her throat. Chandos groaned and settled his weight between her legs, his arms wrapping beneath her to hold her even closer. His belly pressed against her groin, moving against it, a stimulation that sent exploding sparks of pleasure into her deepest core.

She was wild for him, there was no other way to put it. She bit, scratched, pulled him toward her. He yanked off her skirt and petticoat, piling them beneath her hips. It didn't really make their bed any softer, but she didn't care. Her eyes, slanted more than usual by her passion, were caught and held by his fiery gaze as he knelt between her legs and unbuckled his belt and holster. Even in the dark his look had the power to take her breath away. She couldn't bear it when he moved away, and she pulled him back to her the moment he finished shedding his clothes.

Penetration was immediate. A hungry

growl accompanied his fierce thrust, matched by her own sigh. She gasped as he withdrew, then impaled her again. He pounded her depths and she met him with equal fervor, glorying in their mating until she reached a shattering, explosive climax. Her ultimate ecstasy was prolonged as he buried himself deep, pressing, straining, until she felt the gushing warmth of his release filling her.

Courtney lay sprawled beneath him, his weight beginning to hurt. But she wouldn't have stirred him for the world. Her heart was pounding, and her breathing hadn't returned to normal yet. Thoughts drifted through her mind, and suddenly she had a clear picture of how she had just behaved— almost as savagely as Chandos!

He stirred. His lips brushed her neck and he sat up, taking most of his weight off her chest. He looked down at her.

"You screamed."

"Did I?" She was amazed by how nonchalant she managed to sound.

He smiled and kissed her and his lips were soft as they slid back and forth, teasing.

Courtney sighed. "*Now* you're gentle."

"You didn't want gentleness, kitten," he

declared, and the truth of it made her blush. "But you do now, don't you?"

She was too embarrassed to answer. He rolled over onto his side and pulled her against him. Her breasts pressed comfortably into his side. A breeze caressed her, and she shivered.

"Cold?"

"Only a little—no, don't get up."

She threw her arm across him. A puny effort to restrain a man like him, but it worked. His arms locked around her in a protective circle.

"Chandos?"

"Yes, cateyes?"

There was silence as she struggled to put her thoughts in order.

"Couldn't you call me Courtney?" she finally said.

"That isn't what you were going to say."

No, it wasn't. "Do you think he's dead yet?" This in a hesitant, childish voice.

"Yes," he lied.

Her fingers glided through the hairs on his chest. There was another long silence while Courtney debated whether to ask why it was necessary for Pretty Boy to die so cruelly. But there was that primitive elation in the realization that her man had avenged her.

"Chandos?"

"Yes?"

"You really did come for me alone, didn't you?"

"You expected me to gather a posse out here?" he asked dryly.

"No—no, of course not. But there was your friend, Leaping Wolf. I know he was nearby. I didn't think you were up to finding me yourself."

The muscles across his chest grew tight, and she realized that she had questioned his masculinity—and after he had proved himself so heroically!

"So you thought I couldn't protect you? Is that why you didn't bother to call for my help this morning, when they took you?"

Courtney groaned.

"I'm sorry, but you weren't exactly in blooming health, you know," she defended herself. "I was afraid they would kill you."

"You'd be surprised what a man can do when he's got a reason. Didn't I tell you that last night?"

"What was your reason, Chandos?" she challenged. It was a brazen question, she knew that.

"You're paying me to protect you, or did you forget that, too?"

Disappointment was a thick knot in her throat. She was paying him. Was that the only reason? She started to get up. He held her fast.

"Don't ever sell me short again, cateyes."

His hand came around to her cheek, moved to the silken hair by her temple. He pressed her face back down against his chest. His voice had been warm, and the lump in her throat eased a little.

It was something, anyway, that he didn't want her to get up. But she wanted more—much more. She wanted him to care.

"Don't be angry with me, Chandos. You found me. I never really doubted that you would."

After a while she asked, "Then you really are recovered from the snakebite?"

"You can ask me that—now?"

She pressed her face harder against his chest, wondering if he could feel the heat of it. "I mean . . . does it hurt anymore?"

"It still hurts like hell."

But he'd come riding after her in spite of it. She smiled, unaware that he could feel the movement against his skin. Her finger absently twirled circles around his nipple.

"Chandos?"

"What now?"

"What happens if I get pregnant?"

He let his breath out in a long sigh.

"Are you?"

"I don't know. It's much too soon to tell." She hesitated. "But what happens if I am?"

"If you aren't, you won't be." There was a long pause before he ended. "If you are, you are."

A thoroughly unsatisfactory answer. "Would you marry me if I am?"

"Could you live the way I do? Always on the go, never staying in one place for more than a few days?"

"That's no way to raise a family," she pointed out irritably.

"No, it's not," he said with finality. Then he moved her aside and got up.

Anger and disillusionment tore through her as she watched him dress and then lead Surefoot away to unsaddle him. As he moved away, he tossed his bedroll down and she sat staring at it for a long while. How cold and unfeeling Chandos could be!

Chapter 30

Even with an average ride of twenty-five to thirty miles a day, Courtney had managed to avoid the deplorable blisters Mattie had predicted. But today, she was sure she'd have some at last. Chandos rode hard and fast to make up for the time they'd lost, and Courtney began to wonder if he was making the ride hard for her on purpose.

It seemed he did everything he could to make her uncomfortable, and had done so since they woke up that morning. He hurried her out of bed and straight into the saddle, to ride behind him this time, which was most uncomfortable.

They reached their camp late in the afternoon and found the other horses well tended and a fire burning—a fire that couldn't possibly have lasted since yesterday morning. Chandos let out a shrill whistle that, ten minutes later, produced an Indian.

Leaping Wolf was not overly tall, but then the Comanches were known for their horsemanship, not their height. He was dressed in an old army shirt with a carbine belt strapped low on his waist. His moccasins were calf-high, his legs otherwise bare except for a wide breechcloth that fell to his knees. His hair was glossy black, long, and loose. His eyes were jet black, set in a broad face. His skin was the color of old leather. He was young and lanky, but powerful across the shoulders. He carried a rifle cradled in his arms like a baby.

Courtney, who had stopped breathing when he walked into camp, watched as the two men greeted each other and then hunkered down by the fire to talk. They spoke in Comanche, of course.

They pointedly ignored her, but she couldn't start dinner with them by the fire anyway, so she went through her things instead to see if anything was missing. Nothing was.

Soon, Leaping Wolf left, giving her the same appraising look he'd given her when he entered, long and intense. But where there'd been wariness in his expression before, his guard was relaxed now and she could have sworn he was almost smiling.

He said something to her, but he didn't wait for Chandos to translate. Once he was gone, Chandos hunkered back down by the fire, chewing on a blade of grass, watching the place in the trees where his friend had disappeared.

Courtney decided he wasn't going to volunteer what Leaping Wolf had said, so she went to see what their supplies held for dinner.

When she brought the usual beans and dried beef and biscuit fixings to the fire, Chandos fixed his attention on her.

"I want you to burn that blouse," he said, startling her.

Courtney didn't take that seriously. "Do you want biscuits or dumplings?"

"Burn it, cateyes."

He was looking at the deep V that plunged down to a knot where she'd tied the blouse together. Her torn chemise was under it, turned around so that the rip was in the back and the back was in the front, covering her breasts, but just barely.

"Did your friend say something about my blouse?"

"Don't change the subject."

"I wasn't. But I'll change the blouse if it will make you happy."

"Go ahead. Then bring it—"

"I will not!" What was wrong with him? "There's nothing wrong with this blouse that I can't repair. I fixed the other . . ." She paused, her eyes narrowing. "Oh, I see. It's all right if *you* rip my blouse, but now

276

that someone else has, you want it burned. That's it, isn't it?"

He glowered at her, and her anger mellowed into a warm glow. Jealousy, possessiveness, whatever it was, this meant he felt *something* for her. She decided she was willing to do as he asked.

She fetched a blouse of coral pink and went behind a tree to change. Returning a few minutes later, she quietly dropped the torn white blouse into the fire. Of fine, delicate silk, it was consumed in seconds. Pieces of ash floated up and were caught in the breeze.

Chandos continued to stare, brooding, into the fire.

"What did your friend say to me?" Courtney finally asked.

"He wasn't talking to you."

"But he was looking at me."

"He spoke *of* you."

"Well?"

The silence went on, broken only by the crackle of the fire.

"He commended your courage," he finally answered.

Courtney's eyes widened. The reaction was lost on Chandos, however, as he got up then and left the camp, walking toward the river. She sighed, wondering if he had told her the truth.

He hadn't exactly. He didn't want to tell her that Leaping Wolf's actual words had been, "Your woman has more courage now. That is good if you decide to keep her."

Oh, hell, Chandos knew she had more courage, but that made no real difference. She still wanted and deserved things Chandos could never give her, so he couldn't keep her. Yet when Leaping Wolf had called her "his woman," it had sounded so right. Damn her and her cat eyes!

He wished this journey were over, wished he'd never started it. Enduring another two weeks with this woman would be hell. The only good thing was that she had given him a reason to not touch her again when she'd mentioned pregnancy. Of course, that didn't mean he would stop wanting her . . .

He was afraid. When she was taken, he'd felt fearful in a way he hadn't felt for years. It was an emotion he'd been immune to these last four years. You had to *care* about something to feel such a fear of losing it.

Thinking about that only increased his frustration, so Chandos directed his thoughts to what he would do to Wade Smith when he found him. That was at least a frustration he was used to, for the man had slipped through Chandos's fingers so many times. Would Paris, Texas, be the end of the trail at last?

Chandos spent a very restless night, between one frustration and another.

Chapter 31

Two days away from Paris, Texas, Courtney sprained her ankle. It was a stupid accident. She stepped on a large rock, using only her instep for support, and the rest of her foot buckled right under. If she hadn't been wearing boots, it might have been a lot worse.

Her foot swelled so fast she had difficulty getting her boot off. And once it was off, it wouldn't go back on. The pain wasn't too bad as long as she didn't move her foot. But staying off her feet and delaying the journey was out of the question. Even if Chandos had suggested it, she wouldn't have agreed.

Chandos's disposition changed when she was injured. Now he was indifferent only half of the time. He became quite solicitous. She got the impression that he welcomed the opportunity to discharge the debt he'd incurred when she took care of his snakebite injury.

The man was so exasperatingly independent, he'd probably resented her help. Well, that debt was quickly cancelled as he saw to all her needs, cooked their food, and took care of all four horses. He made her a crutch out of a sturdy limb. He helped her mount and dismount. And he kept their pace slow, cutting their daily distance by a third, after all.

They had been traveling along a creek in a southeasterly direction when she sprained her foot, and after the injury, Chandos veered sharply southwest. Courtney didn't know it, but he changed direction because of her injury. They crossed the Red River, then skirted around a town—much to her disappointment. She hadn't seen civilization for weeks!

They reached another town a few hours later, and Chandos went straight in, stopping in front of a restaurant called Mama's Place. Courtney was dying for a meal that didn't include beans, and she was delighted when Chandos led her inside, dusty and unpresentable though she was. The large, bright dining room held a dozen tables covered with check tablecloths. Only one was occupied, since it was the middle of the afternoon. The couple at that table gave Courtney and Chandos the once-over, the woman becoming alarmed as she looked Chandos over. Dusty and travel-worn, he was every inch the gunfighter in black pants and dark gray shirt open halfway down his chest, a black neckerchief tied loosely around his throat.

Chandos gave the middle-aged couple a brief glance, then dismissed them. He seated Courtney, told her he'd be back in a minute, then disappeared into the kitchen. Courtney was left to endure the couple's scrutiny, feeling utterly self-conscious, knowing how disheveled and dirty she looked.

A moment or so later, the front door of the restaurant opened and in strode two men who had seen the strangers ride down the street and wanted a better look. Courtney's nervousness increased. She always hated being the center of attention, and it was impossible to be invisible in Chandos's company. He couldn't help but arouse curiosity.

Just then, imagining what these people were thinking about her, she suddenly realized what her father would think. Hadn't he married his housekeeper just for the sake of propriety? Courtney was traveling alone with Chandos! God sakes, her father would think the worst—and the worst was true!

When Chandos returned, he immediately noticed her high color and rigid posture. Her eyes were glued to the table. What was wrong? Had the two fellows who'd come in after he left been bothering her? He gave them such a hard look that they immediately left the restaurant. A few moments later, the couple at the table also left.

"Food will be here in a minute, cateyes," Chandos said.

The kitchen door opened, and a round woman strode toward them. "This is Mama. She'll be taking care of you for a few days," Chandos announced casually.

Courtney's eyes riveted on the rotund Mexican woman, who began speaking rapid Spanish to Chandos. She was short and comfortable looking, with salt-and-pepper hair woven into a tight bun. She was wearing a brightly colored cotton skirt and white blouse with an apron over them, and woven leather sandals.

"What do you mean, she'll be taking care of me?" demanded Courtney of Chandos. "Where will you be?"

"I told you. I have business in Paris."

"This *is* Paris!" she said, exasperated.

He sat down across from her, giving Mama a nod of dismissal. Courtney watched the woman waddle away, then gazed at Chandos, waiting for him to explain.

"What are you up to?" she said, glaring. "If you think you can—"

"Settle down, woman." He leaned across the table and caught her hand. "This is not Paris. It's Alameda. Because of your ankle, I figured you could use a few days' rest while I take care of my business. I didn't want to leave you alone, so I brought you here."

"Why would you have to leave me alone? What is it you have to do in Paris?"

"That, lady, is none of your business."

Oh, how she hated it when he took that tone with her! "You're not coming back, are you? You're just going to leave me here. Is that it?"

"You know me better than that," he said. "I brought you this far, didn't I? I'm not going to abandon you a few miles short of your destination."

That didn't alleviate her frustration. She didn't want to stay with strangers, and she didn't want Chandos to leave her.

"I thought you were going to take me

283

with you to Paris, then we would go on from there."

"I changed my mind."

"Because of my ankle?"

He felt he'd already answered that. "Look, I'll only be gone about four days. It'll do you good to stay off your foot that long."

"But why here? Why not in Paris?"

He sighed. "I don't know anyone in Paris. I pass through Alameda often, coming and going through Indian Territory. I know Mama. I know I can trust her to look after you while I'm gone. You'll be in good hands, cateyes. I wouldn't leave you unless—"

"But, Chandos—"

"Goddamnit!" he exploded. "Don't make me feel—"

He stopped as Mama entered, carrying a large tray of food.

Chandos stood up as Mama reached the table.

"I'm leaving now, Mama. See that she gets a bath after she eats, then put her to bed."

He marched halfway to the door, then stopped, turned, and came back. Towering over Courtney, he lifted her out of her chair and wrapped his arms around her. His kiss was heady stuff, leaving her breathless.

"I'll be back, kitten," he murmured huskily against her lips. "Don't scratch anyone while I'm away."

And then he was gone. Mama was staring at Courtney, but Courtney was watching the door that had just closed and trying to hold back her tears.

If she could feel such desolation now, when he would be gone only four days, how was she going to feel when he left her, for good, in Waco?

Chapter 32

For two days Courtney just sat in front of her bedroom window above the restaurant, looking at the street out front. When Mama Alvarez scolded that she should be in bed, Courtney smiled vaguely, refusing to argue. Mama meant well. And Courtney knew it was stupid to keep watch by the window when Chandos probably hadn't even reached Paris yet, but she wouldn't budge.

Her foot propped on a cushioned stool, she sat and watched the activities of the small town, which was only a little bigger than Rockley. She did a lot of thinking in that bedroom, and no matter how she argued with herself, one truth could not be denied. She loved Chandos. She loved him more than she thought it was possible to love anyone.

It wasn't just one thing. It wasn't only that he made her feel safe. That was important, but there was also the wanting. Lord, how she wanted him. It was also the way he could be gentle when she needed gentleness, loving when she needed loving. And it was his lonely independence too, his don't-get-close attitude. How vulnerable that made him seem.

But as much as she would have liked to, Courtney didn't deceive herself. She knew she couldn't have Chandos, no matter how much she wanted him. He wanted no permanent relationship, and had made that clear. She had to be realistic. There would be no marrying Chandos.

As far back as she could remember, she had doubted she would ever find true love and have that love returned. That she was right gave her no satisfaction now.

The second day of her stay at Mama's, Courtney met Mama's daughter. The girl barged into Courtney's room without knocking and introduced herself. It was hate at first meeting—for both of them—for Courtney recognized the girl's name from Chandos's tortured dreams, and Calida Alvarez knew Chandos had brought Courtney there.

Calida was beautiful, vibrant, with glossy black hair and brown eyes that sparkled with malice. She was older than Courtney by only four years, but those few years made a great difference. The older girl, passionate by nature, exuded the confidence and self-assurance Courtney had always lacked.

That is what Courtney saw. Calida, on the other hand, saw her first real rival, a young lady who was coldly formal, calmly in control, and whose sun-kissed features were so unusual she was stunning. Golden skin, brown hair that flashed with golden streaks, eyes that slanted upward at the corners like a cat's and were the color of warm whiskey. Courtney was tawny gold all over, and Calida wanted to scratch her eyes out. In fact, she attacked with words.

"I hope you have a good reason to travel with my Chandos."

"*Your* Chandos?"

"*Sí*, mine," Calida said flatly.

"He lives here, then?"

The older girl hadn't expected a counter-attack, and she faltered, then recovered.

"He lives here more than he lives anywhere else."

"That hardly makes him yours," Courtney murmured. "Now, if you'd said he was your husband . . ." She gave Calida a vague smile and let the insinuation hang in the air.

"*I* am the one who has refused marriage! If I want to marry him, I have only to snap my fingers." She did, loudly.

Courtney found her temper rising. Did Chandos know how certain of him Calida Alvarez was? Did she have good reason to be so certain?

"That's all very well, Miss Alvarez, but until you do have that ring on your finger, my reasons for traveling with Chandos are none of your concern."

"It is my concern!" Calida shouted loudly enough to be heard in the street.

Courtney had had enough. "No it is not," she said slowly, with a furious undertone. "And if you have any more questions, I suggest you save them for Chandos. For now, get out."

"*Puta!*" Calida spat. "I will have words

with him, all right. I will see he leaves you here, but not in my mama's house!"

Courtney slammed the door shut behind the girl, then realized that her hands were trembling. Was there anything real in Calida's threat. Could she talk Chandos into abandoning Courtney here? There was enough doubt to make Courtney worry. Calida had known Chandos a long time. She knew him intimately. Courtney did too, but Chandos came back to Calida often, while he resisted Courtney with all his might.

Calida flounced into Mario's Saloon, where she worked in the evenings. She lived with her mama, but her life was her own and she did as she pleased, worked where she wanted to, and turned a deaf ear to her mama's pleas.

She worked in the saloon because that was where excitement was. There were occasional gunfights and brawls—many of them fought over her. Calida thrived on excitement, and was happiest when she instigated action, whether by pitting two men against each other, or stealing a man from another woman so she could watch the drama unfold. Calida had never been thwarted, never failed to get what she wanted, one way or another.

At that moment, she was fuming. The *gringa* had not given her the answers she wanted. Nor had she seemed upset to learn that Chandos had another woman.

Maybe there was nothing between Chandos and the *gringa*. Could that be? Maybe the kiss Mama had witnessed meant nothing. But Calida told herself there had to be something between Chandos and Courtney. He'd never traveled with a woman before, Calida knew. Chandos was a loner. That was one of the things Calida liked about him, that and the dangerous aura about him.

She knew Chandos was a gunfighter, but she believed he was also an outlaw. She'd never asked, but she was sure he was. Outlaws excited Calida more than anything else. Their lawlessness, their unpredictability, their dangerous lives. Many of them passed through Alameda on the run, usually to hide out in Indian Territory. She knew many outlaws, had bedded many, but Chandos was something special.

He never said he loved her. He never tried to bamboozle her with words. She couldn't deceive him in any way. If he said he wanted her, he wanted her. If she tried to play hard to get or inflame his jealousy, he walked away.

It was his indifference that intrigued her and made her always available when he came to town, no matter who else she was bedding or pursuing at the time. And Chandos always came to her. He stayed at her mama's house, too, which was convenient.

Chandos didn't like hotels, and the first time he came to Alameda, he'd talked Mama into renting him a room. Mama liked him. She didn't like Calida's other men, but she liked Chandos. And there were empty bedrooms in the house since Calida's brothers had grown and left home. Mama knew what Chandos and her daughter did late at night. Calida brought other men to her room, even Mario, but the older woman had long since given up trying to reform Calida. Her daughter did as she liked and always would.

And now, the man she considered exclusively hers had brought another woman to town with him and asked *her* mama to look after the woman! What nerve!

"What has put that spark in your eye, *chica?*"

"That—that—" She stopped, staring at Mario thoughtfully. She smiled. "Nothing important. Give me a whiskey before I start serving—without the water."

She watched carefully as he poured her drink. Mario, a distant cousin, had come to Alameda with her family nine years ago. The family had been forced to leave one town after another, towns that didn't tolerate Mexicans running businesses. Alameda, farther north, was tolerant because there had never been any Mexicans there before. Everyone loved Mama's cooking, so no one objected when Mario opened a saloon across from Mama's restaurant. The saloon was a success because Mario's liquor was good and cheaper than his competitors'.

Mario was Calida's lover when Calida felt generous. He'd have married her in a minute, as would several other men, but Calida didn't want a husband. Certainly she didn't want Mario. He was handsome enough, with velvety brown eyes and a pencil-thin mustache that made him look like a Spanish grandee. And his brawny strength was impressive. But at heart Mario was a coward. Mario would never fight for her.

Calida favored Mario with another smile as he handed her the glass of whiskey. An idea was taking shape in her mind, one that had numerous possibilities.

"Mama has a guest, a beautiful *gringa*," Calida said casually. "But Mama doesn't know she's a *puta*."

"How do you know?"

"She confided that she plans to stay at our house only until her injured foot is better. Then she will move to Bertha's house."

Mario's curiosity was aroused. He visited Bertha's whorehouse often, though only a few girls there would accept him. A new whore would be much in demand at Bertha's, especially a beautiful new whore. But, Mario thought, he would probably be the last to bed her.

"Are you going to tell your mama?" he wanted to know.

Calida's mouth formed a little moue and she shrugged. "I don't see why. She was very friendly, that one, very talkative, and—and actually, I feel sorry for her. I can't imagine what it must be like to want a man and not have one available. But that is her predicament."

"She told you *that?*"

Calida nodded, leaning across the bar to whisper. "She even asked me if I knew anyone . . . who might be interested. Are you?" He frowned at her and she laughed. "Come now, Mario. I know you will have her eventually. I do not mind, *querido*, because I know it will mean nothing to you. But do you wish to wait until she is worn out, or would you rather have her when she is desperate for a man?"

She had him. She knew that look. Mario was aroused by just the thought of being the first man in town to have the new woman.

"What about your mama?" he asked her.

"Wait until tomorrow night. Mama is invited to Anne Harwell's birthday party, and she plans to go as soon as her last customer leaves the restaurant. Of course, she won't stay out very late, not with church the next day. But if you're quiet, I'm sure the *gringa* will want you to stay with her all night, and you can leave in the morning while Mama is at church."

"Will you tell her to expect me?"

"Oh, no, Mario." Calida grinned. "You must surprise her. I do not want the woman to feel indebted to me. Just make sure she doesn't scream before you have a chance to tell her why you're there."

And, Calida thought, if things went well, Chandos would return in time to be part of the surprise. It would be quite a scene, and she wished she could be there to watch. She felt better just thinking about it.

Chapter 33

A pool of yellow light fell on the hard-packed dirt street behind the little house. The back street was quiet that evening because it was removed from the Saturday night hell-raising going on along the main thoroughfare.

Chandos had been told that it was mainly dance-hall girls who lived on this lane. One of those girls was Wade Smith's woman. Her name was Loretta.

Chandos had wasted a damn lot of time locating her, because Smith was using an alias here in Paris. Also, Smith had lived very quietly in town because he was wanted by the law. No one at all knew him as Wade Smith, and only a few people knew him by his alias, Will Green.

This Will Green might be the wrong one, Chandos knew that. But he might also be the right one. Chandos was taking no chances. He stood in the shadows across the lane, watching the little house for a long time before he approached it. His gun was palmed, held close to his side. His heart beat fast. He was exhilarated. This was it, the showdown he'd desired for so long. He was about to come face-to-face with his sister's killer.

Moving stealthily to the door, Chandos carefully tried the knob. It wasn't locked. He waited, his ear to the door, hearing nothing inside. He heard only his own blood pounding in his head, nothing else.

He turned the knob slowly again, then quickly kicked the door open. The whole front wall shook as the door flew inward. Several dishes on a shelf toppled over and a cup rolled out into the middle of the dirt floor. On the bed, a blond head turned and looked down the barrel of Chandos's gun.

The breasts outlined against the sheet were tiny, barely formed. Why, the girl couldn't be more than thirteen or fourteen, Chandos realized. Was this the wrong house?

"Loretta?"

"Yeah?"

The girl cringed.

Chandos exhaled heavily. It was the right house. He should have remembered that Smith liked them young.

She had been badly beaten. One side of her face was dark and swollen. There was a black eye on the other side. An ugly dark bruise spread from her collarbone to her left shoulder, and smaller bruises ringed her upper arms, as if she had been brutally gripped. He hated to think what the rest of her would look like under that sheet.

"Where is he?"

"Wh-ho?"

She sounded pathetically young, and frightened. It made him realize how he must look to her. He hadn't bothered to shave since leaving Courtney, and he was still pointing his gun at the girl. He holstered it.

"I'm not going to hurt you. I want Smith."

She stiffened. Heat flashed in the one open eye as anger replaced fear.

"You're too late, mister. I turned that bastard in. The last time he beat me up was the last time."

"He's in jail?"

She nodded. "Sure as hell is. I knew there was a ranger in town, or I wouldn't've turned him in. I didn't trust the jail here to hold him, so I told my friend Pepper to ask the ranger to come see me. I told the ranger who Wade really was. See, Wade told me 'bout this girl he killed in San Antonio. He threatened once that he'd kill me just like he did her. I believed him."

"Did the ranger take him?" Chandos asked, trying not to sound impatient.

"Yeah. He come back here later on, him an' the marshal, an' caught Wade with his pants down. The bastard still wanted me, lookin' like this. I think he likes it better when I look like this."

"How long ago was that?"

"Three days, mister."

Chandos groaned. Three goddamn days. If it hadn't been for the snakebite and the bounty hunters coming after Courtney, he'd have gotten to Smith in time.

"If you wanna see him, mister," Loretta continued, "you'll have to hightail it. That ranger knew about Wade. He said they got enough evidence against Wade down in San Antonio to hang him right after a fast trial."

Chandos didn't doubt that. He'd been to San Antonio soon after the killing and heard all about it. That was where he'd first lost Smith's trail.

Chandos nodded. "I'm obliged, kid."

"I ain't no kid," she told him. "Leastwise I don't look young when I get my face made up. I've been working the dance halls a year now."

"There ought to be a law against it."

"Do tell," she retorted. "A preachin' gunslinger. If that don't beat all." When he didn't take up her challenge, but merely turned to leave, she called out, "Hey, mister, you didn't say why you wanted Wade."

Chandos glanced back at her. She could so easily have been a worse victim of Smith's. The girl didn't know how lucky she really was.

"I wanted him for murder, kid. That girl down in San Antonio wasn't the only young girl he's killed."

Even across the room he could see gooseflesh appear on her arms.

"You—you don't think he could get away from the ranger—do you?"

"No."

"I think maybe I'll move on, soon as my ribs heal." She said it more to herself than to him.

Chandos closed the door. He closed his eyes and stood outside the little house, thinking about trying to catch up with the ranger. He could probably manage it, but the lawman wouldn't turn Smith over to him. There would be a fight, and he couldn't see killing a ranger who was only doing his duty. He'd never done that and he wasn't ready to start now.

And then there was his cateyes. If he didn't get back to Alameda before the four days were up, she would think he'd lied. She might even try going on to Waco by herself.

That settled it—but he didn't like it one bit. When the hell had she become his first priority?

Chandos headed for the stables, frustration beginning to churn. He wasn't writing Smith off just because he'd come up empty-handed again. It certainly wasn't the first time. He would get Courtney to Waco first, and then he'd go on to San Antonio. He wasn't willing to give Smith up to the hangman. The bastard belonged to *him*.

Chapter 34

Courtney spent Saturday afternoon writing a letter to Mattie. She had left Rockley three weeks ago—God sakes, was that all? It seemed more like months had gone by.

She wanted to let her friend know that she didn't regret her decision to go to Waco. Mama Alvarez had assured Courtney that

300

many people came through Alameda on their way to Kansas, and one could surely be found to carry Courtney's letter.

So she wrote Mattie a long letter describing her adventures vividly, but refrained from saying she'd fallen in love with her escort. She finished the letter by expressing again her hopes of finding her father.

Waco was less than a week away, according to Mama Alvarez. Soon Courtney would know if her intuition had led her true, or she'd been just chasing rainbows. She didn't dare consider the latter for very long, for if she didn't find her father, she would be stranded in Waco, alone, and without any money, because she owed Chandos all she had left. If it turned out that way, she had no idea what she would do.

The day passed quietly. Courtney refused to watch for Chandos anymore. She had wanted to go downstairs to the restaurant for dinner, but Mama flatly refused, reminding her that Chandos's instructions were that she remain in bed to rest the ankle. It was better. She could even put some weight on it now and get around without the crutch, but she gave in. Mama Alvarez meant well. She was kindness itself—the exact opposite of her daughter.

Courtney had asked her questions and learned that Calida worked in a saloon at night serving drinks—just that, nothing else, Mama assured her. Courtney sensed that Calida's mother didn't approve at all. Mama said emphatically that Calida didn't have to work at all, that she worked only because she wanted to.

"Stubborn. My *niña* is stubborn. But she is a grown woman. What can I do?"

Courtney understood working in order to feel useful, for extra money—but in a saloon? When she didn't have to?

Courtney counted herself fortunate that another day had passed without her being bothered again by the unpleasant Calida, and she dismissed her with that thought.

She went to bed early that night. Mama had gone to a party, and Calida was working, so the place was quiet. It was very noisy out in the street, however, because it was Saturday night, and Alameda was no different from other frontier towns. Men caroused all night, knowing they could sleep it off Sunday morning. Most of them didn't have wives to drag them to church.

She smiled to herself, remembering how, in Rockley, she had often seen men nodding off in church, seen the bleary, reddened eyes, even seen some men holding their heads in pain when the sermon got too loud. It was probably the same here in Alameda.

She finally dozed off, and it wasn't long before she was dreaming. The dream became unpleasant. She was hurt. There was a weight crushing her chest. She was crying and she couldn't breathe. And then Chandos was there, telling her not to cry, soothing her fears the way only Chandos could do.

Soon he was kissing her, and she woke slowly, finding that he really *was* kissing her. It was his weight pressing on her that she'd been dreaming of. She didn't stop to wonder why he hadn't wakened her, only to rejoice that he wanted her. He gave in to his desire so seldom.

She wrapped her arms around his neck and pulled him close to her. His mustache tickled her face. Courtney went cold.

"You're not Chandos!" she cried, struggling against him.

Horror had made her voice shrill, and a hand covered her mouth. His hipbone knocked against hers and she felt his manhood hard against her belly. He was naked. The realization tore a scream from her, but his hand muffled it.

"Shh . . . *Dios!*" She bit his hand. He

jerked the hand loose, then quickly put it back. "What is wrong with you, woman?" he hissed, exasperated.

Courtney tried to speak, but his hand was pressed against her mouth.

"No, I am not Chandos," he said irritably. "What do you want with that one anyway? He is *muy violento*. Besides, he is not here. I will do, *sí*?"

She shook her head with such force that she nearly dislodged his hand.

"You do not like Mexicans?" he said sharply, and the anger in his voice caused her to remain perfectly still.

"Calida told me you want a man," he went on. "She says you are not particular. So I come here to do you a service—not force myself on you. Do you wish to see me first? Is that what is wrong?"

Stunned, Courtney nodded slowly.

"You will not scream when I take away my hand?" he asked, and she shook her head. He removed his hand. She didn't scream.

He moved off her, watching her carefully as he got off the bed. She still didn't scream, and he began to relax again.

Courtney knew how little good it would do her to scream. There was no one in the house and so much noise outside in the street that nobody would pay any attention. Instead, she reached under her pillow very carefully, feeling for her gun. That was one habit developed on the trail that she was thankful for. Not that she meant to use the gun. She didn't think she would have to shoot the stranger.

Just as he struck a match, looking around for a lamp, Courtney managed to tug the sheet up over her without a sound and aim the gun. He saw the gun and stopped moving. He didn't even breathe.

"Don't drop that match, mister," Courtney warned. "If that light goes out, I shoot."

Courtney felt her blood begin to warm. It was a heady thing, the power a gun gave. She'd never fired it, but he didn't know that. Her hand was steady. She wasn't afraid now, and he was.

"Light the lamp, but don't make any sudden moves . . . slowly, slowly, that's right," she directed. "Now you can blow out the match. Good," she said after he had followed her instructions. "Now, just who the hell are you?"

"Mario."

"Mario?" Her brow knitted thoughtfully. "Where have I heard . . . ?"

She remembered. Chandos had mentioned the name in his nightmare that night. What had he said? Something about Calida going to Mario's bed.

"So you're a friend of Calida's?" she said scornfully.

"We are cousins."

"Cousins, too? How nice for you."

Her tone made him even more nervous. "My clothes, *señorita?* May I put them on? I think I have made a mistake."

"No, you didn't make the mistake, Mario, your cousin did. Yes, yes, put your clothes on." She was beginning to get flustered. "Be quick about it."

He was, and once she felt it was safe to look at him other than directly at his face, she appraised him. He was a big man, not so much tall as brawny, and most of his weight was in his chest. No wonder she'd felt crushed. God sakes, he probably could have snapped her in two with his hands. Certainly he could have finished what he'd come for, if he'd been inclined to use force. Thank God he wasn't a really bad man.

"I will go," he said hopefully. "With your permission, of course."

It was meant as a cue for her to lower her gun. She didn't.

"In a moment, Mario. What exactly did Calida tell you?"

"Lies, I think."

"I don't doubt that, but what lies, exactly?"

He decided to be blunt and get it over with. "She said you were a whore, *señorita*, that you had come to Alameda to work in Bertha's house."

Courtney's cheeks flamed. "Bertha's is a whorehouse?"

"*Sí.* A very fine one."

"What am I doing here, then, if I intend to live there?"

"Calida said you had an injured foot."

"That's true."

"She said you were staying here with her mama only until you recovered."

"That's not all she told you, Mario. Finish."

"There is more, but you will not like it, I fear."

"Let me hear it anyway," Courtney replied coldly.

"She said you wanted a man, *señorita*, that you . . . could not wait for . . . until you moved to Bertha's. She said you asked her to find you a man, that you were—desperate."

"Why that lying . . . " Courtney exploded. "Did she really *say* 'desperate'?"

He nodded vigorously, watching her closely. Fury was evident in every line of her face, and her gun was still pointing at his heart.

She surprised him.

"You can go. No, don't stop to put your boots on. Carry them. And Mario." Her voice stopped him at the door. "If I find you in my room again, I'll blow your head off."

He didn't doubt that.

Chapter 35

Calida waited all night for Mario to return to the saloon. When the saloon closed, she waited in his room. Around four o'clock in the morning, she finally fell asleep.

Courtney waited too, waiting for Calida to come home. She paced her room, anger feeding on itself. She heard Mama return from her party at ten o'clock, but after that the house stayed quiet. Finally, she gave up. Short of going to the saloon to confront

Calida, which she wouldn't do, she might have to wait until morning. She fell asleep.

Despite their lack of sleep, both Calida and Courtney woke early Sunday morning. For Calida, this was a near miracle, for she always slept late. But she was anxious to learn the results of the drama she had set in motion.

Mario had never returned, so she assumed he had seduced the *gringa* after all and had spent the whole night with her. That being the case, she set her mind to figuring out the best way to break this news to Chandos. Smiling, she left the saloon.

Mario watched her sashay down the street. He loved that *puta*, but he hated her, too. She had played her last trick on him. He knew what she was thinking. He'd refrained from going home so she *would* think it. Knowing she would be there, waiting to learn what had happened, he'd gone to Bertha's instead and gotten drunk. He hadn't slept at all.

He could barely keep his eyes open. Since dawn he'd stood at the window at Bertha's, waiting for Calida to appear. Bertha's house was at the end of town, so he had a clear view of the whole street.

Fifteen minutes ago, he'd seen the window open at the *gringa*'s bedroom in his cousin's house, so he knew she was up. And five minutes ago Mama had left for church.

Mario wished he could be there to see what would happen now, but he would have to be satisfied just knowing Calida's scheming had not turned out the way she wanted it to, for once. Let her see what it was like to face the gun of an angry woman! At last, he allowed himself to end his vigil at the window and fall asleep beside the whore snoring in the bed behind him.

Courtney stood at the kitchen stove, pouring a cup of the coffee Mama had made before leaving for church. Her temper was as hot as the coffee. Every time she thought of what might have happened last night, her anger boiled over.

When Calida entered the kitchen, there was Courtney. Calida was surprised to find her up, and surprise showed in her eyes. Courtney was alone.

Calida sauntered forward slowly, hips swaying. She grinned, taking in Courtney's haggard appearance.

"How was your night, *puta?*" she asked, giggling. "Is Mario still here?"

"Mario didn't stay," Courtney said slowly

and quietly. "He was afraid I would shoot him."

Calida's grin faded. "Liar. Where is he if not here? He did not come home, I know that."

"He's probably in some other woman's bed, since he didn't get what he came to this house for."

"That is what you say, but I wonder if Chandos will believe it," Calida said viciously.

Courtney understood now. So this had been for Chandos's benefit. She ought to've guessed.

She took Calida by surprise, slapping her as hard as she could, dropping the coffee cup as she did so. Calida growled as the two women reached for each other, nails bared. In moments they were rolling on the floor. Calida was an old hand at brawling. She fought dirty. Courtney, on the other hand, had never even imagined what fighting would be like. But this was an outlet for her fury, and she had never in her life been so angry. Used, abused, entirely for spite, she fought wildly.

Courtney got in two more solid slaps, and the second one gave Calida a bloody nose. But Courtney lost her hold when Calida jammed a knee into her stomach, putting all her weight behind the blow. The older girl then shot to her feet and ran to the kitchen cabinet. As Courtney rose, Calida swung back around, a savagely exultant expression on her face and a knife in her hand.

Courtney was stopped cold. Prickles raced across her scalp.

"Why do you hesitate?" Calida taunted. "You wanted my blood, so come and get it."

Courtney watched the knife waving hypnotically back and forth. She considered backing off, but Calida would win if she did. She would get away with her viciousness and have only a bloody nose in payment. That wasn't enough. Courtney's honor demanded that she win this battle.

Calida took Courtney's hesitation for capitulation. She thought she had her. The last thing she was expecting was for Courtney to lunge at the knife, latching onto Calida's wrist.

Calida's mind whirled. She didn't dare kill a *gringa*, no matter that Courtney had attacked her first. They would hang her because she was a Mexican. The *gringa* could, however, kill Calida. The look in Courtney's eye gave every indication that she would use the knife if she got her hands on it.

Calida became truly frightened. The girl was crazy.

Courtney's grip on her wrist tightened and she moved a step closer to Calida.

"Drop it!"

They sprang apart, shocked. Chandos stood in the doorway, his expression thunderous.

"I said drop the goddamn knife!"

It clattered to the floor, and the girls moved farther apart. Calida began straightening her clothes and wiping the blood from her face. Having no idea what else to do, Courtney moved to pick up the coffee cup she had dropped. She couldn't look at Chandos. She was mortified to have been found brawling.

"I'm waiting," Chandos said.

Courtney glared at Calida, but Calida tossed her head, glaring right back. She had always been able to lie her way out of anything.

"This *gringa* you bring here, she attacked me," Calida said hotly.

"That, true, Courtney?"

Courtney whirled on him, her eyes wide with astonishment. "Courtney?" she echoed with disbelief. "*Now* you call me Courtney? Why? Why now?"

He sighed and dropped his saddlebags to the floor, then walked toward her slowly. "What the hell's got you so fired up?"

"She is jealous, *querido*," Calida purred.

Courtney gasped. "That's a lie! If you're going to start lying, you bitch, then I guess I'll have to tell him the truth!"

"Then tell him about how you kicked me out of your room when we had only just met," Calida began hurriedly, then went on to embellish further. "She was horrible to me, Chandos. When I only asked why she was here, she shouted at me that it was none of my business."

"As I recall, you did all the shouting that day." Courtney bristled.

"Me?" Calida was wide-eyed with wonder. "I came to make you welcome and—"

"Shut up, Calida," Chandos growled, his small supply of patience wearing thin. He grabbed Courtney's arms, bringing her close to him. "Lady, you'd better do some fast talking. I rode all night to get back here. I'm dead tired, and I don't care to sift through lies to get the truth. Tell me now what happened."

Feeling like a cornered animal, Courtney

attacked. "You want to know what happened? All right. I woke up last night to find a man in my bed—as naked as I was—and your—your *mistress* sent him to me!"

His hands tightened. But his voice was oh–so–soft.

"Were you hurt?"

It cut through the haze of fury. She knew he was dangerously angry, and that he could ask that question before anything else warmed her.

"No."

"How far did he—?"

"Chandos!"

She couldn't bear to speak of it in front of Calida, but Chandos was losing his control.

"You must have been dead to the world if he could get your clothes off without waking you," he said. "How far did—?"

"God sakes," she snapped, "I took off my clothes before I went to bed. I had closed the window because of the noise, so it was hot in the room. I was asleep when he snuck into my room. I assume he had his clothes on, then took them off before he crawled on top of me."

"How far did he—"

"He only kissed me, Chandos," she interrupted again. "As soon as I felt his mustache, I knew he wasn't—" She stopped, and her voice became a whisper before she finished, "You."

"And then?" he asked after a silence.

"Naturally I . . . made my objections clear. He wasn't expecting that. He got up to light the lamp, and as soon as he was away from me I reached for my gun. He was frightened enough to tell me the truth."

They both turned and looked at Calida.

"A very pretty story, *gringa*," Calida said, "but Mario did not come home last night. If he did not spend the night with you, then where did he go?"

Chandos set Courtney away from him and turned to Calida, impaling her with his eyes. Calida had never seen Chandos like this. It was her first realization that he might not believe her so easily, and she began to clench her hands.

"Mario?" he demanded furiously. "You sent Mario to her?"

Calida backed away. "*Send* him? No," she hastily denied. "I told him she was here. I only suggested he come and meet her, maybe cheer her up, because she was alone. If the *gringa* invited him into her bed, this is not my doing."

"You lying bitch!" Courtney gasped, outraged.

Chandos wasn't buying it, either. His hand shot out, and the fingers closed around Calida's throat.

"I ought to break your neck, you conniving bitch!" he snarled into her terrified face. "The woman you turned your spite on is under my protection. I thought this was the one place I could leave her where she would be safe. But you had to play a vicious game, and now I have to kill a man I've got nothing against, because he fell in with your evil scheming."

Calida blanched. "Kill him?" she cried. "For what? He did nothing! She says he did nothing!"

Chandos shoved her away from him. "He broke into her room and frightened her. He put his hands on her. That's reason enough."

He headed for the door and Courtney ran after him, grabbing his arm and stopping him. She was frightened and angry and thrilled all at once.

"You take your job too seriously sometimes, Chandos—not that I don't appreciate it. But, God sakes, if I'd wanted him dead, I could have shot him myself."

"You don't have it in you, cateyes," he murmured, not without a trace of humor.

"I wouldn't be so sure," she retorted. "But you can't kill Mario, Chandos. It wasn't his fault. She told him lies about my coming here to work at Bertha's." Courtney assumed he knew who Bertha was. "She told him I was a—a whore and that I needed a man, that I was—was—" Courtney's temper exploded again. *"Desperate!"* Chandos nearly choked. "Don't you dare laugh!" she cried.

"I wouldn't dream of it."

She eyed him suspiciously. Oh, well, at least he no longer had murder in his eyes.

"Well, that's the story she told him. So he actually came here to do me a service, sort of."

"Oh, God. Trust you to see it that way."

"Don't be sarcastic, Chandos. It could have been a lot worse. He could have forced himself on me even after he knew I didn't want him. But he didn't do that."

"All right." Chandos sighed. "I won't kill him. But I still have some business to attend to. Wait for me in your room," he told her. She hesitated, tensing, and he touched her cheek softly. "Nothing you will object to, cateyes. Now go on. Fix yourself up, or get some sleep. You look like you could use it. I won't be long."

His voice soothed her, and his touch told her she had nothing else to worry about. She did as he said, leaving him in the kitchen with Calida.

Chapter 36

The moment Courtney stepped into her room, every ache and pain from her fight with Calida began to throb. Her ankle injury hurt worse than ever. She hobbled to the small oval mirror over the bureau, groaning when she got a good look at herself. Lord, Chandos had seen her looking like this. Like this! Oh, God.

Her hair was matted in thick tangles. Dark coffee stains spotted her skirt. There were several tears in her dress. One rip at the shoulder revealed three crescent-shaped punctures surrounded by dried blood. A few drops of blood had dried on her neck, and there was a scratch at the corner of her eye and another behind her ear, as well as half a dozen on the back of her hands.

She knew she would have bruises later on, too. Damn Calida. But at least Chandos believed her and had seen Calida for what she was. Courtney doubted he would be bedding that one again, about which Courtney felt grateful, and a little smug.

A bath was first, and she went back downstairs to find Chandos and Calida both gone. She mopped up the spilled coffee while she boiled water for her bath. Mama returned from church in time to help her carry it upstairs. Courtney said nothing about what had happened, mentioning only that Chandos was back.

She was fixed up, the bathwater waiting to be removed, when Chandos came in, not troubling to knock. She didn't mind, accustomed by now to a lack of privacy where he was concerned.

His condition startled her. Nearly as messed up as she had been, he was cradling his side.

"Just what I need," he said, eyeing her bathwater in the tub.

"Don't think you're not going to tell me," she said firmly.

"Nothing to tell," he evaded, then sighed. "I didn't kill him. But I couldn't just let it go, either. Calida took off the moment you left the kitchen, or I would have throttled her."

320

"But, Chandos, Mario didn't *do* anything!"

"He touched you."

She was amazed. It was a thoroughly possessive answer. She started to say so, then thought better of it.

"Who won?"

"You could say it was a draw," he said, sitting on the bed with a groan. "But I think the sonofabitch broke one of my ribs."

She hurried over and reached for his shirt buttons. "Let me see."

He caught her hands before she could touch him, and her eyes met his, questioning. There was a wealth of meaning in his bright blue eyes, but she couldn't quite fathom it yet. She didn't know what it did to him when she touched him.

She stepped back.

"You wanted a bath," she said, embarrassed. "I'll leave for a while."

"You can stay. I trust you to turn your back."

"It would hardly be proper—"

"Stay, goddammit!"

"All *right*."

Courtney whirled around and stalked to the window, where she pulled up a chair and sat, back stiff and teeth clenched, silently waiting.

"How's your ankle?" he asked.

"Better."

He frowned. "Don't pout, cateyes. I just don't want you running into Calida without me."

She listened to the sounds of his clothes dropping to the floor, piece by piece, and tried desperately to concentrate on the scene outside the window. Churchgoers were gathered in little groups, and two young boys in their Sunday best were tossing a ball back and forth. A little girl ran after a dog that was running away with her bonnet. Courtney saw it all—and saw none of it. Chandos's boots hit the floor, and she jerked in her chair.

It was all well and good his wanting to keep her within sight in order to protect her, but just then Courtney didn't appreciate it. Didn't he know she imagined his every move? How often she had seen him without a shirt? She knew what his body looked like, and right now she was picturing him in her mind vividly, as if she could see him. Her pulse raced.

Water splashed, and she heard him gasp. The water would be cold, and she imagined goosebumps spreading over his arms and chest, then saw herself rubbing them away.

Courtney shot to her feet. How dared he subject her to this? She felt like her insides were dissolving, and he blithely took his bath without a single thought for what he was doing to her! The insensitive beast!

"Sit down, cateyes. Or better yet, go lie down and get some rest."

His voice was deeply husky, rolling over her like a caress. Courtney sat down.

Think of something else, Courtney . . . anything else! "Did you settle your business in Paris?" Her voice was faint.

"Uh-uh. I've got to go to San Antonio."

"Before or after you leave me in Waco?"

"After," he replied. "And I have to hurry, so we'll be riding hard. Think you can manage it?"

"Do I have a choice?"

She cringed as she heard the resentment in her voice. But she couldn't help it. She was sure he was using fictitious business in San Antonio as an excuse to get her off his hands as soon as he could.

"What's wrong, cateyes?"

"Nothing," she said stonily. "Do we leave today?"

"No. I need some rest. And I don't think you got much sleep last night."

"No."

There was silence until he said, "Think you can rustle me up something to bind this rib with?"

"Like what?"

"A petticoat will do."

"Not one of mine," she retorted. "I've only got two. I'll go ask—"

"Never mind," he cut in. "It's probably not broken anyway, just bruised."

God sakes, couldn't she leave the room for just a moment? "Have I been threatened, Chandos? Is there some specific reason why I should stay here with you?"

"I would think you'd be used to being alone with me, cateyes. Why are you so skittish all of a sudden?"

"Because it's not decent, my being in here while you're taking a bath!" she exploded.

"If that's all that's bothering you, I'm done."

Courtney glanced around. The tub was empty and Chandos was sitting on the edge of the bed, naked except for a towel wrapped around his hips. Her eyes flew back to the window.

"God sakes, will you put some clothes on!"

"I left my gear down in the kitchen, I'm afraid."

"I brought your bags up," she informed him tightly. "They're over there, by the bureau."

"Then have a heart, will you? I don't think I can move anymore."

She had the impression suddenly that he was toying with her, but she dismissed it. Frowning, she fetched his saddlebags and put them on the bed, keeping her eyes averted.

"If you're so tired," she said, "then make use of my bed. I can get another room for tonight."

"Uh-uh." His tone left no room for argument. "This bed's big enough for two."

She drew in her breath sharply. "That's not funny!"

"I know."

She looked fully at him now. "Why are you doing this? If you think I can sleep with you lying next to me, you're crazy."

"You haven't been made love to on a bed yet, have you, cateyes?"

He gave her a lazy smile that stopped her

breathing. Her knees liquefied and she reached for the bedpost.

He stood up. His towel fell away, leaving her no doubt of his seriousness. His body was sleek and smooth and damp, and oh, Lord, she wanted to fly into his arms.

But she didn't. She wanted nothing more than to make love, but she couldn't bear his indifference afterward, not again.

"Come here, kitten." He lifted her face to his. "You've been hissing all morning. Now purr for me."

"Don't," she whispered just before his lips touched hers.

He leaned back, but didn't let go of her. His thumbs moved against her lips, and her body swayed toward his of its own volition.

His smile was knowing. "I'm sorry, little cat. I didn't want it to happen. You know that."

"Then don't do this," she pleaded.

"I can't help it. If you'd learn to be less obvious about what you're feeling, I wouldn't be in this predicament. But when I know you want me, it drives me crazy."

"That's unfair!"

"You think I like losing control like this?"

"Chandos, please—"

"I need you—but that's not all." He gathered her close, and his lips seared her cheek. "He touched you. I need to wipe that from your memory—I have to."

How could she continue to resist, after that? He might never admit it, but those words said how much he cared.

Chapter 37

The night sky was black velvet scattered with glittering diamonds. Far off there was the lowing of cattle, and even more distant, the howl of a bobcat. The night was briskly cool, though not cold, and gentle breezes stirred a tree on top of the hill ahead.

The horses plodded up the rise and stopped under the tree. Dozens of flickering lights stretched out over the flat plain below. Courtney sighed.

"What town is that?"

"It's not a town. That's the Bar M Ranch."

"But it looks so big!"

"It is," Chandos said. "Everything Fletcher Straton does, he does in a big way."

Courtney knew the name. She'd read it in

the newspaper article that had accompanied the photograph her father was in. Fletcher Straton was the rancher whose men had apprehended the cattle rustler who was turned over to the law in Waco.

"Why are we stopping?" Courtney asked as Chandos dismounted and came around her horse. "You don't intend to make camp here when Waco is nearby, do you?"

"It's a good four miles to town."

His hands closed on her waist to help her down. He hadn't done that since they'd left Alameda. He hadn't gotten this close to her since Alameda.

She moved her hands away from his shoulders as soon as her feet touched the ground, but his hands remained at her waist. "Couldn't we go to Waco?" she ventured.

"I'm not making camp, cateyes," he said gentle. "I'm saying good-bye."

Stunned, Courtney froze where she stood. "You—you're not taking me into Waco?"

"I never intended to. There are people in town I don't want to see. And I couldn't just leave you in Waco on your own anyway. I need to know you're with someone I can trust. There's a lady on the Bar M who's a friend of mine. It's the best solution."

"You're leaving me with another one of your mistresses?" she cried, incredulous.

"No, goddammit, Margaret Rowley is Straton's housekeeper. She's an English lady, a motherly kind of person."

"A little old lady, I suppose?" she snapped.

He ignored her sharpness, saying lightly, "Whatever you do, don't call her that. She boxed my ears once when *I* did."

There was a knot in her belly working its way up into her throat. He really meant to leave her. Walk out of her life, just like that. Somehow, she had believed she meant more to him than that.

"Don't look at me that way, cateyes."

He turned away. She watched, dazed, as he started a fire, angrily breaking sticks and throwing them together. Soon he had the fire going, and the firelight revealed the sharp angles of his features.

"I've got to reach San Antonio before it's too late!" he said forcefully. "I can't take time to see you settled in town."

"You don't have to see me settled. My father is a doctor. If he's there, he won't be hard to find."

"*If* he's there." Sparks shot into the air. "If he's not, at least here you'll have someone to help you figure out what to do next. Margaret Rowley is a good woman, and she knows everyone in Waco. She'll know if your father is there. So you'll know to-night," he offered soothingly.

"*I'll* know? You're not even going to wait around to find out?"

"No."

Her eyes widened with suspicion. "You're not even going to take me down there, are you?"

"I can't. There are people on the Bar M I don't want to see. But I'll wait here until I see that you're safely inside."

Finally, Chandos looked at her. His gut wrenched. Hurt, disbelief, confusion were all there. Her eyes were glassy because she was trying desperately to hold back tears.

"Goddammit!" he exploded. "Do you think I want to leave you here? I swore I'd never come near this place again!"

Courtney turned around to wipe away the tears that slipped past her defenses. "Why, Chandos?" she choked. "If you don't like it here, why leave me here?"

He came up behind her and put his hands on her shoulders. His closeness was too much for Courtney and more tears slid down her cheek.

"It's the people I don't like, cateyes—all except the old lady." His voice was calmer. "For some godforsaken reason I can't begin to imagine, Margaret Rowley likes working on the Bar M. If I knew anyone else around here, I wouldn't bring you here. But she's the only one I can think of to leave you with so I won't have to worry about you."

"Worry about me?" That was too galling. "Your job is done. You'll never see me again. What have you got to worry about?"

He pulled her around to face him. "Don't do this to me, woman."

"*You?*" she cried. "What about *me?* What about what *I* feel?"

He shook her. "What do you want from me?"

"I—I—"

No. She wouldn't say it. She wouldn't beg him. She wouldn't ask him not to leave her, no matter how much this good-bye was killing her. Nor would she tell him she loved him. If he could just leave her, just like that, then it wouldn't make any difference to him anyway.

She shoved him away. "I don't want anything from you. Stop treating me like a child. I needed you to get me here, not to see me settled. I can do that myself. God sakes,

I'm not helpless. And I don't like being palmed off on strangers and—"

"Are you through?" he asked.

"No. There's the matter of what I owe you," she said stiffly. "I'll go get it."

She tried to pass him and he caught her arm. "I don't want your goddamn money!"

"Don't be ridiculous. That's why you agreed—"

"Money had nothing to do with it. I've told you before not to assume things about me, cateyes. You don't know me. You don't know anything about me—do you?"

He didn't frighten her with this tack anymore. "I know you're not as bad as you'd like me to think."

"No?" His fingers tightened on her arm. "Should I tell you why I'm going to San Antonio?"

"I'd rather you didn't," she said uneasily.

"I'm going there to kill a man," he said coldly, bitterly. "There won't be anything lawful about it, either. I've judged him, found him guilty, and I mean to execute him. There's only one hitch. The law has him, and they mean to hang him."

"What's wrong about that?"

"He has to die by *my* hands."

"But if the law has him . . . you don't

mean to pit yourself against the law?" she gasped.

He nodded. "I haven't figured out yet how to get him loose. The main thing I have to do is get there before they hang him."

"I'm sure you have your reasons, Chandos, but—"

"Don't, goddammit!" He didn't want her understanding. He wanted her to turn against him—now—so he wouldn't try to come back later. "What does it take to make you open your eyes? I'm not what you think I am," he told her.

"Why are you doing this, Chandos?" she cried. "Isn't it enough that you're leaving, that I'll never see you again? Do you want me to hate you, too? Is that it?"

"You do hate me," he said darkly. 'You just don't know it yet."

A chill of premonition crawled up her spine as he unsheathed the knife from his belt. "Are you going to kill me?" she asked disbelievingly.

"I couldn't do it four years ago, cateyes. What makes you think I can do it now?"

"Then what . . . what do you mean? Four years ago?" Her gaze was fixed on the knife as he drew the blade across the forefinger of his right hand. "What are you doing?" she whispered.

"If I think you still want me, then the link will never be broken. It must be broken."

"What link?" Anxiety made her voice crack.

"The link we formed four years ago."

"I don't understand—" The blade sliced into his left forefinger now. "Chandos!"

He dropped the knife. Courtney stared as he raised his hands to his face. The two forefingers met in the center of his forehead and moved outward, toward his temples, leaving bright red smears of blood just above his eyebrows. His fingers then came together at the bridge of his nose and slashed downward across his cheeks and met at his chin, leaving more lines of blood.

For a moment Courtney saw only the blood-red lines dissecting Chandos's face into four parts. But after a moment the pale blue of his eyes began to come through, vivid against the bronze skin.

"You! It was you! Oh, my God!"

She could barely think for the old fear that welled up, and she ran, blindly. Halfway down the hill he caught her. The impact made them both fall, and he took the brunt of it. His arms around her, protecting her, they rolled all the way to the bottom of the hill.

When they stopped, Courtney tried to get up, but he pinned her to the ground.

Fear transported her back to Elroy Brower's barn.

"Why did you show me? Why?" she cried, terrified. "Oh, God, wipe the blood off! That's not you!"

"It's me," he said ruthlessly. "This is what I am, what I've always been."

"No." She shook her head wildly in denial, back and forth, back and forth. "No, no."

"Look at me!"

"No! You took my father. *You* took my father!"

"Now, that's one thing I didn't do. Hold still, goddammit!" He caught the hands beating at him and pressed them down onto her hair, spread out on the ground. "We took only the farmer with us. The rest we left for dead."

"The farmer." She groaned, remembering. "I know what the Indians did to him. Mattie overheard people talking about it one time and she told me. How could you be a part of that? How could you let them mutilate him like that?"

"Let *them?*" He shook his head. "Oh, no, you can't deceive yourself that way. The farmer was mine. He died by *my* hand."

"No!" she screamed.

He might have told her the reason, but he didn't. He let her struggle against him until she had freed herself, and then he let her run from him, disappearing in the direction of the Bar M. He watched her go, then slowly got to his feet.

He had done what he'd meant to do. Whatever she had felt for him, he had killed. Now he would never know if the life he had to offer her would have been enough. He'd set her free. If only it would be so easy to free himself of her . . .

Chandos wiped the blood from his face and headed back up the hill. The horses stirred as he approached. They had probably stirred earlier, when the cowhand approached, but Chandos had been too involved with Courtney to hear the man coming. Even now his distraction was so great that he was three feet from the fire before he noticed the fellow hunkered down there. He had never thought to see that man again.

"Easy now, Kane," the man said as Chandos's stance took on dangerous meaning. "You wouldn't shoot a man just 'cause he's late comin' in off the range, would you? I couldn't very well ignore your fire, could I?"

"You should have, Sawtooth," Chandos said, a warning in his tone. "For once you should have."

"But I didn't. And you're forgettin' who taught you how to use that gun."

"No, but I've had a lot of practice since then."

The older man grinned, flashing the even line of teeth that had gotten him his nickname. The story he told was that his teeth were once so lopsided they were more nuisance than help for eating, so he'd taken a saw to them just to see if he could come out with a better chomp.

He was a lean man, but solidly built, in his late forties, with gray hair intruding on the brown. Sawtooth knew cattle, horses, and guns, in that order. The Bar M foreman, he was about the closest friend Fletcher Straton had.

"Shit, you ain't changed a bit, have you?" Sawtooth grunted, seeing that Chandos didn't relax his tense stance. "I couldn't believe it when I saw that pinto of yours. I don't forget horses."

"I suggest you forget you saw him, and me," Chandos said, bending to pick up the knife he'd dropped earlier.

"I recognized your voice, too," Sawtooth grinned. "Couldn't help but hear it, the way you and the woman was shoutin' at each other. Mighty strange the way you put the scare into her. Care to satisfy an old man's curiosity?"

"No."

"Didn't think so."

"I could kill you, Sawtooth, and be miles from here before they found your body. Is that the only way I can assure myself you won't tell the old man you saw me?"

"If you're just passin' through, what's the difference if he knows?"

"I don't want him thinking he can use the woman to get to me."

"Can he?"

"No."

"You said that too fast, Kane. You sure it's the truth?"

"Goddamn you, Sawtooth!" Chandos snarled. "I don't *want* to kill you."

"All right, all right." Sawtooth stood up slowly, his hands outstretched and clearly empty. "If you feel that strongly about it, I reckon I can forget I saw you."

"And you stay the hell away from the woman."

"Now, that's gonna be kind of hard, ain't it, seein' as how you've left her here?"

"With Rowley. And she won't be staying long."

"Fletcher's gonna want to know who she is," Sawtooth drawled, watching him carefully.

"He won't make the connection. Just you keep your mouth shut, that's all."

"That why you scared her—so she wouldn't say nothin'?"

"You're pressing it, Sawtooth," Chandos rasped. "But you always did stick your nose into what didn't concern you. The woman means nothing to me. And there's nothing she can tell Fletcher, because she doesn't know who I am. If you change that situation, you'll only be starting a fire without water to put it out, because I'm not coming back this way."

"Where you headin'?"

"Goddamn bloodhound," Chandos hissed.

"That was just a friendly question." Sawtooth grinned.

"Like hell." Chandos stalked past him and jumped onto Surefoot. He grabbed the reins of Trask's horse, saying, "These other two horses are hers. You can take them in or leave them for someone else to hunt down. She'll probably claim she was thrown, so one of the hands will come looking for them—unless you can catch up with her before she reaches the ranch. But if you do, keep your goddamn *friendly* questions to yourself, hear? She's not up to an interrogation tonight."

As Chandos rode away, Sawtooth stomped out the fire. "Means nothin' to him, huh?" He grinned. "Who the hell does he think would believe that?"

Chapter 38

Lights flickered in the distance against the night sky. Cattle could still be heard gently lowing. Nothing had changed outside Courtney, though everything had changed inside her. The pain, oh, the pain of knowing she loved a savage . . . savage *Indian!*

At that moment, "Indian" meant everything vile and terrifying. A savage butcher! Oh, not him, not her Chandos! But it was true, it was.

Halfway to the ranch, her tears so blinded

her that Courtney dropped to her knees and sobbed her heart out in great sobs that tore all the way through her. There was no sound of him following her. There would be no strong arms to comfort her this time, no soothing voice to tell her it was a lie, or at least make her understand. Dear God, *why?*

She tried to remember the day of the attack at Brower's farm. That wasn't easy. She had worked so hard to put it from her mind. But she brought it back, her fear, her terror when the feed box was opened. Believing she was going to die and hoping she wouldn't beg. And then seeing the Indian—no, not an Indian, but Chandos. She had seen Chandos. But that day he'd truly been an Indian, his hair long and braided, the war paint, the knife. And he'd meant to kill her. His hand twisting in her hair, the terror, and then seeing his eyes, which weren't the eyes of an Indian. She had only known the eyes didn't fit that frightening face, didn't seem at all terrifying, as they should have.

Now she knew why, when she'd first seen the gunfighter, she could entrust her life to him.

Chandos said a link had been formed between them. What did that mean? A link?

And why had he been with those Indians that day, attacking, killing?

Courtney stopped crying so hard as more of that day came back. What was it Berny Bixler had said to Sarah about revenge? The Indians had wanted revenge for an attack on their camp. He said Lars Handley's son John, who had left Rockley so quickly, claimed he and a group of other men had wiped out every man, woman, and child of a band of Kiowas. But the dead Indians must have been Comanches, not Kiowas. They must have been Chandos's friends. She remembered Bixler saying the Indians wouldn't stop until they got every one of the men involved. She supposed they were all dead now, unless . . . Trask! Was he one of them? Chandos had said he was guilty of rape and murder. And the man in San Antonio? Was he one?

Who could Chandos have lost in that massacre to make him kill Elroy Brower the way he had? To make him still lust for revenge after all this time?

"These yours, miss?"

Gasping with shock, Courtney scrambled to her feet.

The man drew closer and she saw old Nelly and the pinto she had never named because she'd realized she wouldn't get to keep her. Chandos hadn't taken the mare with him after all, as she'd assumed he would.

"Where did you—find them?" she asked uncertainly.

"He's gone, if that's what you're wonderin'."

"You saw him leave?"

"Yes, ma'am, I did."

Why did that make her feel dread? Was it only because Chandos had said he didn't want to see anyone here? She had no business worrying on his account, not anymore.

"I don't suppose you know him?" she found herself asking.

"Matter of fact I do."

She reached for the pinto and mounted, feeling even gloomier. This was just great, just what Chandos didn't want to happen. If anything came of it, she supposed he would blame her.

"Do you work at the Bar M?"

"Yes, ma'am. Name's Sawtooth, or that's what they call me, anyhow."

"I'm cat—" she began, then corrected herself. "Courtney Harte. I'm not here by choice. I would much prefer going on into

Waco and getting a room . . . They do have hotels, don't they?"

"Yes, ma'am, but it's a good four miles."

"I know, I know," she said impatiently. "But would you oblige? I'd be most grateful."

Sawtooth was silent. He wasn't one to turn down ladies in distress. Fact was, he usually went out of his way to be helpful to the gentler sex. But this one, well, there were just too many unanswered questions. It was more than likely, damned likely, that Fletcher would skin him alive if he found out who'd brought her here, and that Sawtooth had let her slip away.

"Look, ma'am," Sawtooth said reasonably. "I'm just in off the range. I ain't had a chance to chow down yet, and you probably ain't, either. All things considered, tonight's not the time to be headin' for town. And you must have some reason for comin' out to the Bar M?"

"Yes," Courtney replied, disappointed. "I'm supposed to turn myself over to Margaret Rowley, a woman I don't even know, simply because *he* said so. God sakes, I'm not a child. I don't need a keeper."

A match flared, and they each got a fairly good look at the other for a second.

Sawtooth nearly burned his fingers. He grinned.

"Come on, and I'll take you in to Maggie."

"Maggie?"

"Margaret. She's got her own place out back, though she's probably still at the big house now. And don't worry, you don't have to know Maggie to like her. And I'm sure she'll take to you."

"It's kind of you to say so, but . . . oh, very well." Courtney kneed the pinto forward, knowing she had no choice. After a moment she ventured. "Would it be too much to ask if you wouldn't tell anyone who brought me here, or even that you saw him?"

"Would you mind tellin' me why?"

"Why?" Courtney's defenses went up. "How should I know why? Chandos doesn't explain himself. He said he didn't want to see anyone around here, and that's all I know."

"Is that what he's callin' himself now? Chandos?"

She glanced at him. "I thought you said you knew him."

"When he was here last, he would only answer to some godawful long Indian name nobody could pronounce or remember."

"Sounds just like him."

"You've known him long?" he asked.

"No . . . well, if you take into account . . . no, that doesn't . . . oh, dear, I'm not making much sense, am I? Actually, I've known him about a month. He brought me here from Kansas."

"Kansas!" Sawtooth whistled. "That's one hellofa long way, beggin' your pardon, ma'am."

"Yes, it was."

"Long enough for you two to get to know each other pretty well?" he said casually.

"You'd think so, wouldn't you?" Courtney said in a small voice. "But I found out tonight I didn't know him at all."

"Do you know where he's headin', Miss Harte?"

"Yes, to—" She stopped, looking at the dark shape of the man riding next to her. For all she knew, Chandos might be a wanted man here. "I'm sorry, but I can't seem to remember the name of the town he mentioned."

Sawtooth's deep chuckle surprised her. "He means that much to you, does he?"

"He means nothing to me," she assured him haughtily, and he laughed again.

Chapter 39

Even before they reached the front yard, Courtney heard the lovely strains of a guitar floating on the night air. And then the big house came into view, brightly lit inside and on the front porch as well, where a group of men were lounging on chairs, railings, and even the wide steps leading up to a large front door. There was laughter and soft bantering accompanying the guitar music. It was a warm scene of comradery, and spoke well for the Bar M. This was obviously a nice place to live.

But Courtney was uneasy when she saw that there were only men on the porch, many men. And the moment they saw her, the music stopped on a discordant note.

As Sawtooth led their horses to the porch, silence reigned. Not a whisper could be heard.

In the stillness, Sawtooth's laugh grated on Courtney. "Ain't you saddlebums ever seen a lady before? Goddamn—beg pardon, ma'am—she ain't no apparition. Dru, get off your tail and go tell Maggie she's got a visitor—out back, mind you." A curly-haired young man shot to his feet and backed himself in through the front door, his eyes never once leaving Courtney.

"The rest of you cowpushers, this here's Miss Harte," Sawtooth continued. "Don't know how long she'll be visitin'. Don't know if you'll even see her again, so tip your hats while you got the chance." A few men did, while the others continued to stare, making Sawtooth laugh again. "I ain't never seen such a bunch of pea brains. Come on, ma'am."

Courtney managed a quick smile, then gratefully walked her mare to follow Sawtooth around the side of the house. She heard a mad scrambling of boots on the porch and knew if she looked back she would see all those cowboys hanging over the porch railing, staring after her.

"You enjoyed that, didn't you?" she hissed at Sawtooth, riding just ahead of her.

"I love shakin' the boys up." He chuckled, delighted. "But I didn't think they'd lose their tongues as well as their brains. You're a mighty pretty woman, ma'am. They'll be pokin' fun at each other for a month now, 'cause not one of 'em had the sense to say howdy when they had the chance." They rounded the back of the house. "Here we are. I expect Maggie'll be along any moment."

Sawtooth dismounted in front of a cottage that looked like it belonged in the New England countryside instead of the Texas plains. Courtney was instantly charmed by the little whitewashed house. It had a picket fence, flower-lined walkway, shutters at the windows, even flowerpots on the sills. Quaint and lovely, it was out of place behind the huge Texas ranch house. There was short stubby grass in the front yard, with a big old tree on the left side. There was even an arborlike trellis curving over the front door, a scrubby vine trying valiantly to cover it.

"Miss Harte?"

"What? Oh."

Courtney reluctantly drew her eyes away from the cottage and let Sawtooth help her down from the pinto. He wasn't an overly tall man, she saw now, and he had a rangy body, but the gray eyes that met hers were kind.

A door closed at the back of the ranch house. "That'll be Maggie."

And it was. A small woman came hurrying across the backyard that separated the two houses, pulling a shawl over her shoulders as she moved. There was ample light from the bigger house for Courtney to see the salt-and-pepper hair, the soft, rounded body, and, when Maggie reached them, the bright, lively green eyes.

"So who is my visitor, Sawtooth?"

"I'll let her tell you," he replied. Then he added, "A friend of yours brought her."

"Oh? Who?"

Courtney glanced at Sawtooth, relaxing when she saw he wasn't going to say. "Chandos," Courtney answered. "At least that's what he calls himself—now."

Maggie repeated the name to herself thoughtfully, shaking her head. "No, no, I don't recognize the name. But then so many young men come and go from here, and I do like to think I've made an impression on at least some of them. It's so nice to be thought of as a friend."

"Listen to you," Sawtooth scoffed. "As if everyone on the ranch didn't love you, Maggie."

Courtney had the pleasure of seeing someone else blush for a change. She warmed to Maggie right then. But pride, she told herself, was pride.

"If you don't remember Chandos, then I really can't impose—"

"Nonsense, and I do mean nonsense, child. I'll remember him once you tell me a little bit about him to refresh my memory. I never forget anyone, do I, Sawtooth?"

"You surely don't." He chuckled. "I'll just get your bag, ma'am," he told Courtney.

Courtney followed him to the horses, whispering, "Can I tell her about him? He didn't say . . . oh, God sakes, I don't know *what* it is he wanted to avoid here. But you know, don't you?"

"Yes, I do. And yes, you can tell Maggie. She was always on his side."

That made her so curious she wanted to say more, but he said, "I'll see to your horses, ma'am. And I hope, well, I guess I hope you'll be here a while."

She didn't mistake his meaning. "Chandos won't come back because of me."

"Are you sure, ma'am?"

He led the horses away. Courtney stood there holding her bag, until Maggie came to steer her down the flower-lined path to the cottage.

"You don't look at all happy, lass," Maggie remarked gently. "This man who brought you to me, is he important to you?"

Courtney couldn't bear to answer that.

"He—he was my escort. I paid him to bring me to Waco, but he wouldn't take my money. He wouldn't take me to Waco, either. He brought me here instead, because he said you were a friend, that you were the only one he could trust around here, and he didn't want to worry about my being alone. God sakes, that's a laugh! Him worrying about me, now that he's rid of me." That awful lump was starting to rise in her throat again. "He—he just *left* me here! I was so—"

The tears came in a torrent, and when Maggie offered her shoulder, Courtney took advantage of it. It was so embarrassing. But the hurt was too strong to be pent up.

Courtney knew she had no claim on Chandos, and knew he wasn't what she'd thought. There was this terrible vengeful side of him that she couldn't begin to understand. Yet despite that, and despite knowing she should be glad never to see him again, she felt an agony of abandonment, of betrayal, even, and it hurt. God, how it hurt.

Maggie sat Courtney down on a sofa, an expensive Chippendale Courtney would later admire, and handed her a lace-edged hanky. She left her young guest only long enough to light a few lamps in the parlor, then returned to wrap Courtney in her arms until the girl began to quiet.

"There now." Maggie replaced the wet hanky with another. "I've always said a good cry does wonders for the system. But you can't tell men that, and goodness, men are all we have around here. It's so nice to be able to mother a female for a change."

"I'm sorry I did that," Courtney said, sniffling.

"No, lass, don't be sorry. When a body needs to cry, they ought to. Do you feel better?"

"Not really."

Maggie patted her hand, smiling gently. "Do you love him so much?"

"No," Courtney said quickly, adamantly, then groaned, "Oh, I don't know. I *did*, but how can I anymore after what I learned tonight? The savagery he's capable of . . ."

"Goodness, what did he do to you, dear?" she whispered.

"Not to me. He—he mutilated a man in revenge and killed him."

"He told you about it?" Maggie was taken aback.

"I already knew about it. Chandos just confirmed that he was the one who did it.

And he's on his way now to kill another man, probably in the same horrible way. Maybe these men deserved his vengeance, I don't know. But to kill so—so cruelly!"

"Men will do terrible things, child. God knows why, but they will. At least most men have a reason for what they do. Does your young man?"

"I'm not exactly sure," Courtney said quietly, explaining as much as she knew about that long-ago Indian raid. "I know he had friends among the Comanche," she finished. "Maybe he even lived with them. But is that enough reason for such hideous violence?"

"Maybe he had a wife among those people," Maggie suggested. "Many white men do take Indian wives, you know. And if she was raped before she was killed, that would account for the mutilation."

Courtney sighed. She hadn't wanted to consider a wife, but Maggie was probably right. It would explain why Chandos knew the Indians so well. Of course, Maggie was only guessing.

"It doesn't really matter whether I can condone what he did, or understand it," Courtney murmured. "I'm never going to see Chandos again."

"And that makes you very unhappy—no, don't bother saying no, lass. So now I have to admit to a terrible curiosity about who this young man is. Can you describe him to me? I'm dying to remember him."

Courtney looked down at her hands, which were clenched tightly in her lap. "Chandos is a gunfighter. He's very good at it. That's one reason I felt safe traveling with him. He's tall and dark, and really very handsome. His hair is black, but his eyes are blue." Maggie said nothing, and she went on, "He's quiet. He doesn't like to talk much at all. Trying to get any information out of him is like pulling teeth."

Maggie sighed. "You've just described a dozen men I've seen come and go from this ranch, my dear."

"I don't know what else I can tell you . . . Oh, Sawtooth said Chandos used an Indian name while he was here."

"Well, that does narrow it down. There have been two young men here with Indian names. One was a half-breed . . . and yes, he did have blue eyes."

"Chandos could pass for half Indian, though he claims he isn't."

"Well, if he isn't, then—" Maggie

paused, frowning. "Why didn't he come in with you?"

"He wouldn't. He said there were people here he didn't want to see. I'm afraid he's done something here. Maybe he's wanted by the law or something like that."

"Did he say anything else, lass?" Maggie asked, her soft voice urgent now.

Courtney smiled sheepishly. "He did warn me not to call you an old lady. He said when he did, you boxed his ears."

"Dear God!" Maggie gasped.

"You know who I mean?" Courtney asked, joyful now.

"Yes, yes. It was the day I boxed his ears that we became friends. He wasn't . . . easy to know."

"*Is* he wanted by the law?" Courtney asked very softly. She had to know.

"No, unless you consider Fletcher's 'law.' He didn't leave here under the best of conditions, and Fletcher, well, he said some pretty terrible things in the heat of anger. They both did. But that was four years ago, and Fletcher regrets—"

"Four years?" Courtney cut in. "But that was when he rode with the Comanche."

"Yes, he returned to the Comanche then . . . " Maggie stopped, her hand going to her chest. "Dear God, that attack, it was, it must have been . . . His mother lived with the Comanche, lass. And a young half-sister he adored. Then they must be dead, both of them . . . Oh, that poor boy."

Courtney went pale. His *mother?* A *sister?* Why didn't he tell her? He had mentioned a sister once, said she gave him the name Chandos. He said he would use that name until he finished what he had to do . . . so his sister could stop crying and sleep in peace.

Courtney gazed, unseeing, out the window. She hadn't understood. Those men had killed his mother and his sister. She couldn't begin to imagine what he'd suffered. Why, she had never believed her own father was dead, but look how she had suffered just from their separation. But Chandos had probably seen the bodies . . .

"Ma'am, I . . . can we talk about something else, please?" Courtney pleaded, feeling a new fountain of tears too close to the surface.

"Of course," Maggie said soothingly. "Perhaps if you told me why you have come?"

"Yes." Courtney latched onto that. "I'm here to find my father. Chandos said you would know if he's living in Waco. He said you know everyone. Oh, God sakes, I haven't even introduced myself. I'm Courtney Harte."

"Harte? We do have a Dr. Harte in Waco, but—"

"That's him!" Courtney cried, jumping up in her excitement! "I was right. He *is* alive! He's here! I knew it!"

Maggie shook her head, bewildered. "I don't understand, lass. Ella Harte told Sue Anne Gibbons at the last church picnic that Dr. Harte's only daughter had died in an Indian attack."

Courtney stared wide-eyed at the older woman. "He thought I died?"

"In a fire that burned the farmhouse down," she said. "He said you'd taken shelter in the house with your stepmother. That's what he told Sue Anne."

"But we were in the barn, in the feed box!"

Maggie shook her head, wholly confused. Before she could think what to say, Courtney asked, "Who is Ella?"

"Why, Dr. Harte's wife. They were married about two months ago."

Courtney sat down again, sobering fast. A wife. No, *another* wife! It wasn't fair, it just wasn't. Would she *never* have him to herself, even for a little while? And to be only a few months too late!

Thoughtless in misery, she uttered one of Chandos's expletives. "God*damn!*"

Chapter 40

The kitchen was brightly lit, empty except for Sawtooth, who sat at the table with a tall glass of milk and a piece of cherry pie. When the back door opened and Maggie slipped inside, he didn't move. He knew by the footsteps who it was. Her expression was anxious.

Sawtooth sat back in his chair and surveyed her.

"You gonna tell him?"

Maggie stood looking down at him. "You knew. Weren't you thinking about telling him?"

"Nope. I was waitin' to see what you'd do. Besides"—Sawtooth grinned—"the boy made me swear I'd forget I seen him. He was real persuasive about it. You know how he can be."

Maggie folded her arms, staring at the door that separated the kitchen from the rest of the house. "Is he still up?"

"Reckon so." Sawtooth nodded. "It's early. How's the little lady?"

"I put her to bed. Did you know she's Dr. Harte's daughter?"

"That right? Well, that relieves my mind on one score. Least now I know she'll be stickin' around a while, if not out here, then in town."

"I'm not so sure." Maggie sighed. "The lass was awfully shook up to hear that her father had married. That is a very unhappy young lady, Sawtooth."

"That'll change, soon as Kane comes back."

"You think he will?"

Sawtooth nodded. "I ain't never seen him give a damn about anything, Maggie, but I seen it tonight. That gal's mighty important to him. You must think so too, or you wouldn't be thinkin' about tellin' Fletcher."

"That isn't my reason," Maggie said softly, sadly. "If that was all there was to it, I wouldn't take the chance of stirring him up when he might wind up disappointed. But I learned from Miss Harte that four years ago in Kansas a band of Comanches were massacred by white men, and since then, the lad has been seeking the murderers in vengeance."

"Goddamn," Sawtooth whispered. "Then Meara's dead."

"It seems so," Maggie replied. "Murdered. And Fletcher has a right to know."

Loud voices woke Courtney, getting louder as they neared the cottage. Then the cottage door burst open and Courtney sat up in alarm, holding the covers up over her chemise. One hell of a big man was standing in the doorway. Behind him was Maggie, who shoved him aside and came into the room. She eyed Courtney carefully, then turned to the man.

"See what you have done?" Maggie said loudly, and with a good deal of exasperation. "You've frightened the poor lass! This could have waited until morning."

The man came farther into the room now and gently but firmly set Maggie out of his way. His eyes were on Courtney, his expression a mask of determination.

He was tall and brawny, with massive shoulders and chest, and thick arms. He had expressive brown eyes and dark brown hair with a streak of gray smack in the center above his brows. A thick mustache was dotted with gray. He would be a handsome

361

man, thought Courtney, if he didn't look so forbidding.

Courtney sat up straighter on the sofa. This was a one-bedroom cottage and she had refused to put Maggie out of her bed.

"Who are you, mister?" she demanded.

Her directness threw him. He even glanced at Maggie as if to ask, Is this your poor frightened lass? He seemed the kind of man who had long been used to people jumping to obey him. Was this the owner of the Bar M?

"I'm Fletcher Straton, Miss Harte," he confirmed, his voice gruff. "I understand you know my son, Kane, quite well."

"No I do not," Courtney retorted. "And if that's the reason you barged in here—"

"You know him as Chandos."

Her eyes narrowed. "I don't believe you. He mentioned you by name. If you were his father, he would have said so, and he didn't."

"Kane hasn't called me Father since Meara took him away," Fletcher replied. "That's his mother—Meara, a stubborn black-haired Irish lass who hasn't got a forgiving bone in her body. He's got her eyes. That's how I knew him when he

362

showed up here ten years after I had given them both up for dead."

Stunned, Courtney glanced at Maggie for confirmation.

"It's true, lass," Maggie said softly. "And I wouldn't have betrayed your confidence except that he has a right to know." Her gaze went to her hands. "Fletcher, you didn't give me a chance to finish what I had to tell you, before you rushed over here to see Miss Harte. There is no easy way to tell this. I'm afraid Meara is dead, along with the Comanches she lived with. From what Miss Harte has told me, it appears that when Kane left here, he returned to find them all massacred, and he's been hunting down the whites who did it ever since."

The man's composure crumpled. The bleakest pain crossed his features, making him suddenly look much older. But control returned in a moment, and his expression hardened.

"Did Kane tell you his mother was dead?" he asked Courtney.

She would have liked to give him some hope. She wasn't sure why, but she wished she could. She wondered why. Her first impression was that he was a hard man. God sakes, even his son apparently didn't like him. But still . . .

"Chandos never once mentioned his mother to me," she said truthfully. "I knew there was a massacre. I saw Chandos ride with the surviving Comanches after the massacre, when they attacked the farm I was staying at. Chandos spared my life that day, when nearly everyone else was killed. What he did to the farmer who had participated in the Indian slaughter was horrible. But if his mother was ra—killed, I can at least understand what drove him to do it." She paused, then said carefully, "But if you're asking me for proof that his mother is dead, I can't give you any. You'll have to ask Chandos."

"Where is he?"

"I can't tell you that."

"Can't—or won't?" he demanded.

Courtney's sympathy was vanishing under his belligerence. "Won't. I don't know you, Mr. Straton. But I do know that Chandos didn't want to see you. Considering that, why should I tell you where you can find him?"

"Loyal, aren't you?" he growled, not accustomed to being thwarted. "But let me remind you, young lady, whose roof you're sleeping under."

"In that case, I'll leave!" Courtney snapped. She rose, dragging the blanket with her, for cover.

"Sit down, goddammit!"

"I will not!"

In the bristling silence, Maggie laughed softly. "I think you had better change your tactics, Fletcher. The lass has been in the company of your son for the past month. His defiance has rubbed off on her—at least where you're concerned."

Fletcher scowled at Maggie. Courtney scowled at Maggie. With a dramatic sigh, Maggie stood up.

"I would think, Fletcher Straton, that an old codger like you would learn from your mistakes," Maggie said sternly. "Haven't you been this route before? Haven't I heard you say a hundred times that if you had the chance you would do things differently? Well, you might get that chance, but from what I can see, you will make the same mistakes again. You've already made a big one. Instead of asking the lass, explaining, telling her how much it would mean to you to hear about Kane, you bully her. Why should she talk to you at all? She is only spending the night here—under *my* roof, I might add. She's not dependent on you,

Fletcher, so why should she talk to you at all? If it were me, I wouldn't."

Having said her piece, Maggie walked out the cottage door. The ensuing silence in the little parlor was uncomfortable to say the least. Courtney sat down on the sofa again, beginning to feel embarrassed over losing her temper. After all, this *was* Chandos's father. And they each had knowledge of Chandos that the other wanted.

"I'm sorry," she began, then smiled as Fletcher said the same words at the same time. "Perhaps we can start over, Mr. Straton. Would you tell me why Chandos wouldn't come near this place?"

"Chandos." He grunted the name in distaste. "Goddamn, beg pardon, but that boy will use *any* name other than the one I gave him. While he was here, he wouldn't answer to Kane. You could call him anything, even 'hey you,' and he'd at least look at you. But call him Kane and he ignored it."

"Don't ask me to call him Kane," Courtney said firmly. "To me he's Chandos, simply Chandos."

"All right, all right," Fletcher grumbled softly. "But don't ask me to call him Chandos, either."

"I won't." Courtney grinned.

"About what you asked," he said, pulling up a chair and sitting in it. "It's not surprising that Kane didn't want me to know he was near here. When he took off, four years ago, I sent my men out after him to bring him back. They never caught up with him, of course. He led them a merry chase for nearly three weeks, playing with them, I think, before he got tired of it and lost them.

"He's got no reason to think I wouldn't try to keep him here again. That's probably why he didn't want anyone to know he was close by."

"Would you try to keep him here?"

"Goddamn, beg pardon, right I would," Fletcher said obdurately. "But"—he hesitated, looking down at his large hands—"not in the same way. This time, I'd ask him to stay. I'd do my best to show him it'd be different, not like before."

"How was it—before?"

"I made one mistake after another," Fletcher admitted ruefully. "I see them all now. I started by treating him like a boy when, to the Comanche, eighteen is a man already. He was eighteen when he returned here. The next dumb thing I did was, I tried to make him forget everything he'd learned from the Comanche, the very things that came natural to him after being with them for so long. I let him rile me, time and again. I couldn't accept that he didn't want what I had to give him."

"You said you thought he was dead for ten years. Was he living with the Comanche all that time?"

"Yes, with his mother. She ran off from me, you see. Oh, I can't blame her for leaving. I wasn't exactly the most faithful of husbands. But she didn't have to take the boy with her. She knew how much he meant to me."

"You can't expect a mother to abandon her child."

"No, but there are other ways of separating when two people don't get along. I would have given her anything she wanted. I would have set her up anywhere she wanted. All I would have asked was to have Kane half the time. Instead, she disappeared. I never did understand how she managed it, until Kane showed up. Then I knew where they'd hidden all those years.

"Oh, at first it wasn't hiding. What happened was, they were captured by Kiowas and sold to the Comanches. Some young Comanche buck bought them both. He married Meara, and adopted Kane." He shook his head.

"The way Kane rode in here on that pinto of his, bold as you please, looking every inch an Indian in buckskin and with those long goddamn, beg pardon, braids that he refused to cut, it's a wonder one of my men didn't shoot him."

Courtney could just imagine young Chandos riding into the Bar M looking like that, and facing a bunch of white strangers. Unlike her, he would have been unafraid, defiant even. And what must his father have felt? A son returned to him as a savage? She could see where there would be trouble.

Suddenly she recalled Chandos's dream.

"Did he call you . . . ah, 'old man,' Mr. Straton?"

He grunted. "That's the only thing he'd call me. Did he tell you that?"

"No. He was bitten by a snake while we were on the trail," she explained. Remembering more, irritation came back. "The stubborn fool wouldn't even call me to ask for help. We'd had a disagreement, you see . . . Well, anyway, he had bad dreams that night when he was fighting the poison, and he did a lot of talking in his sleep. One of the things he said—" She stopped, not wanting to repeat Chandos's exact words. "Well, he was against your cutting his hair. Did you actually try to?"

Fletcher began fidgeting. "That was my biggest mistake, the one that drove him off. We'd had another argument, one of hundreds, and I was furious enough to order my men to corral him and hack off those cursed braids of his. It was a hellofa fight. Kane wounded three of the boys with his knife before Sawtooth shot the knife out of his hand. That's who taught him to shoot, Sawtooth. Kane wouldn't wear a gun while he was here, though, just that knife. It drove me crazy the way he refused to act, goddammit, beg pardon, refused to act white! He wouldn't wear anything 'cept them buckskins, and sometimes a vest. When it got cold, maybe he'd wear a jacket. But that's all. Wouldn't put on a shirt, though I bought him dozens. I think he did it just to rile me."

"But why? Didn't he want to be here?"

"That's just it." There was a long, drawn-out sigh, full of regret. "When Kane came here, I thought he was here to stay. I thought he'd wanted to come. That's why I could never understand the hostility he showed, right from the start. He kept to himself, even ate his meals alone, 'cept when he was working out on the range. And there wasn't a day that he didn't bring in meat for the table, even if he had to get up before dawn to do his hunting. He wouldn't even accept my goddamn, beg pardon, food without replacing it."

"Please, Mr. Straton," Courtney broke in. "You don't have to keep begging my pardon for a word I've picked up myself—thanks to your son."

"Did you?" For the first time, he smiled. "When he first showed up, he never swore at all, 'cept in Comanche. I'm glad to know he learned *something* around here."

Courtney rolled her eyes. God sakes, what a thing to be proud of!

"You were saying?"

"Yes, well, like I said, he kept to himself, wouldn't get to know the men, let alone me. You couldn't have a conversation with him unless you carried the whole thing yourself. I can't remember him ever once speaking to anyone first. And yet I know damn well he was full of questions, 'cause I could see it in his eyes. But he had the damnedest patience. He would wait until his questions got answered without his having to ask. You see, he wanted to learn anything and everything we could teach him. And he did. After a year, there wasn't anything he couldn't do on this ranch. That was another reason I thought he was here by choice."

"But he wasn't?"

"No. He didn't tell me, though. I had to hear it from Maggie, hell, two years after he'd come here. He'd opened up to her by then. She was the only one, in fact, who learned anything at all about him."

"Why did he come here?"

"His mother," Fletcher said simply. "You could say she forced him, but the fact is, he would've done anything for her. See, he had reached the age where he would have been a full-fledged member of that band of Comanches, with all the privileges that went with being a man, including taking a wife. I guess she figured that before he settled down in that world, he ought to have a taste of this one so he wouldn't have any regrets later on. I give Meara credit for that," he said, more to himself than to Courtney. "She was thinking of the boy, not of herself.

"She'd asked him to give it five years here. He took off after three. She wanted him to enjoy all the advantages of wealth, and I don't mind telling you, I'm a rich

372

man. But he scorned my money. She was probably hoping he'd be open-minded and really give it a chance before making any decision. But the boy's mind was made up before he even got here.

"After ten years with those Indians, Kane *was* a Comanche, in every sense but blood. He never tried to fit in here. He was just biding his time, and learning what he could from us whites, as he surely thought of us. Well, at least his mind wasn't closed to knowledge. Who knows, he might even have stayed the full five years if I hadn't made an issue over them goddamn braids of his."

"Chandos doesn't have them anymore," Courtney offered quietly.

"No? Well, that's something, anyway. But he doesn't have that band of Comanches anymore, either."

"That isn't exactly true," Courtney said, explaining briefly. "He hasn't been alone in hunting down those men who attacked the Comanche camp. In fact, there were Indian friends of his close by on our whole trip through Indian Territory. He would have traveled with them if he hadn't agreed to escort me to Waco."

"Why did he agree to that, Miss Harte?"

Fletcher asked, very curious. "That doesn't sound at all like the Kane I know."

"He didn't want to. He tried his best to convince me not to make the journey at all. In fact, I had given up trying to persuade him, when he suddenly changed his mind. I thought it was because he was coming to Texas, anyway. I had offered him all the money I had if he would take me along. I thought we had a deal. But when I tried to pay him tonight, he got angry and said the money had nothing to do with it." She shrugged helplessly, then said softly, "He said I shouldn't assume anything about him or try to understand what motivates him. He's right, too. I don't begin to understand what makes him do the things he does. He's the gentlest man I've ever known—and the most savage. He can be loving and protective, then turn on me and try to make me hate him."

"Loving? Protective? I never thought to hear those words used to describe Kane."

"Four years is a long time, Mr. Straton. Are *you* the same man *you* were four years ago?"

"Yes, unfortunately. Old dogs never change."

"Then you still want to make Chandos into something he isn't?"

"No. I think I learned better than to try that again. He may be my son, but he's his own man. But goddamn—did you say 'gentle'?"

Heat rose in Courtney's cheeks, and her defenses rose, too. She had practically confessed to their intimacy, for why else would a man like Chandos be gentle?

"I said Chandos is the most gentle man I know, Mr. Straton, but the occasions when he was were rare. Most times he's cold, curt, thoroughly exasperating, stubborn, and don't let me forget dangerous, deadly, and merciless. Oh, and heartless. Also, unpredictable—"

"I get the picture." Fletcher cut in with a chuckle. "So he hasn't changed all that much. But if he's all those things, little lady, how did you fall in love with him?" he said quietly.

She considered denying it, but what was the use? Maggie had probably told him that she'd admitted loving Chandos.

"Not by choice, I assure you," Courtney said stiffly. "But you, Maggie, even Sawtooth—I'm afraid you've all gotten the wrong impression somehow. You seem to think I will draw Chandos back here. That won't happen. I said he was loving, not that he loves me. If he ever does come back here, it won't be because of me."

"I'd like you to stick around anyway, Miss Harte, at my expense."

"Well, I mean to stay in Waco, Mr. Straton."

"I meant here at the ranch."

She shook her head.

"Didn't Maggie tell you my father lives in Waco? He's the reason I came to Texas. I came to find him."

"Yes, I know. Edward Harte. But that doesn't mean you'll want to live with him. He's got a new bride. Are you sure you'll be happy staying with them?"

She wished he hadn't asked that. "I won't know anything until I've seen my father. But in any case, I couldn't stay here."

"I don't see why not. We're not exactly strangers now. And we've got one thing very much in common, Miss Harte. We both love my son."

Chapter 41

"It's a nice, fair-sized town now," Sawtooth was saying as he drove the buckboard down Waco's main street. "It wasn't this big before the war, but afterward, a goodly number of Southerners moved here to start new lives. The cattle drives stop here on the way north, and that's helped, too."

"It's not another cowtown, is it?" Courtney asked with considerable dread.

"Like the ones in Kansas? No, ma'am." He chuckled. "The cowboys ain't built up wildness when they come through here, not like after they cross the Indian lands."

Courtney smiled. Of course Texas wouldn't be anything like Kansas. She remembered how glad she'd been to finally reach a town after crossing more than two hundred miles of unsettled territory, to finally have a hot bath, eat real food, sleep in a bed. She understood now why trail drivers needed to celebrate and raise a little hell. She just hoped they didn't raise any here.

There were dozens of men wearing guns, but as they rode down the main street, she saw only a few who truly looked like gunfighters.

At least Waco had a town marshal to uphold the law, which Rockley didn't. And though many men wore guns, there were just as many who didn't. There were finely dressed ladies strolling down the boardwalks too, with gentlemen escorting them. Courtney noticed Mexicans too, a couple of Indians, and even a Chinese man. It made Waco almost seem like a city.

"There's your pa's place." Sawtooth pointed up ahead. "He has his office there, too."

It was nothing like their home in Chicago, but it was a nice two-story house, well tended, with newly planted flower borders running around the house and along the fence that circled the small yard. The house was on the corner of a side street. There were chairs on the covered porch and a padded bench chained to the overhanging roof, which made a swing. She imagined it would be nice to sit there on warm evenings, since you could see all the way down the main street from there, yet you were secluded enough to be inconspicuous yourself.

"What's his wife like, Sawtooth?" Courtney asked nervously. As they stopped in front of the house, he answered.

"Miss Ella? Why, she's a real nice lady,

378

least everyone says so. She teaches school. She came here after the war with her brother. He's a lawyer. He lost an arm in the war. Miss Ella was helpin' him out in his law office until the teacher we had moved back East. She offered to take the teacher's place, and she's been at the school ever since."

Courtney's nerves were getting the best of her. Lord, another stepmother to contend with! All she could think of was how intolerable the last one had been. But her father must have *wanted* to get married this time, which made a big difference. He hadn't married for reasons of propriety, so maybe he loved Ella.

"Well, ma'am?"

Once again she had let Sawtooth stand there waiting to help her down. "I'm sorry," she said as she took his hand and stepped to the ground. "I guess I'm a little nervous. It's been so long since I've seen my father. And I've changed a good deal these last four years. Do I look all right," she asked, her voice shaky.

"You look pretty enough to marry, even for a confirmed bachelor like me."

"Does that mean yes?" She grinned up at him.

He just chuckled. Reaching for her carpetbag behind the buckboard, he then nodded toward her horses, tied to the back of the wagon.

"I'll take your horses over to the livery," he said. "I know your father keeps a buggy there."

"Thank you." Courtney leaned forward to kiss his cheek. "And thank you for bringing me to town. Do you think I'll see you again soon?"

"Most likely." He grinned. "Fletcher will probably have me or one of the men come to town every day to pay you a call."

"To see if Chandos has shown up?"

"Yup. Either that, or he'll set someone to watch your father's house. I wouldn't put that past him."

Courtney shook her head ruefully. "It will be for nothing. I wish he'd see that."

"What he sees is another chance to get his son back. And that's *all* he sees. He's hopin' Kane might even be willing to settle down now, because of you. He'd give anything to have him livin' close to home, not necessarily on the ranch, but close enough so he could see him sometimes. You wouldn't know it, seeing the way they used to go at each other, but Fletcher loves that boy."

"Chandos asked me once if I could live

the way he does, always moving, never staying in one place for more than a few days. I don't think he will ever settle down, Sawtooth."

"How'd a subject like that come up—*if* you don't mind my askin'?"

She turned pink. "I asked him if he would marry me. He won't."

Sawtooth wasn't as surprised that she had done the asking, as he was that Kane said no. "You mean he turned you down flat?"

"No. He just asked if I could live like he does."

"Then you turned him down?"

"No. I told him that's no way to raise a family. He agreed. That ended the discussion."

"Could you live like he does?" Sawtooth ventured.

Her brow creased. "I don't know. I used to think that the safety and security of a home were more important than anything. But I've learned these last few years that the home depends on the people living in it and not on anything else."

She knew she was telling an awful lot to a near stranger, but she decided to go right ahead. "I always felt safe with Chandos, even in the middle of Indian Territory. But

I do want children someday, and children can't keep moving around all the time. So I just don't know." She ended with a sigh.

"Men are known to change their minds about what's important, too," Sawtooth offered.

Some men maybe, Courtney thought, but not Chandos.

Knowing how nervous she was about seeing her father again, Sawtooth left her.

Determinedly, because that was the way Chandos would have done it, Courtney marched straight up to the house and banged on the door. It opened almost instantly, a tall, spindly woman standing there expectantly.

"Ella?"

"Goodness, no." The woman chuckled. "I'm Mrs. Manning, the housekeeper. If you want Mrs. Harte, you'll find her at the schoolhouse this time of day."

"No, uh, actually, I'm here to see Edward Harte."

"Come in, but you'll have to wait a while. He's across town visiting a patient."

Mrs. Manning led Courtney into the patients' waiting area, a room filled with straightbacked chairs. Courtney didn't mind. She didn't want to explain herself to this woman, and she needed time to compose herself before seeing her father. Fortunately the room was empty. So she sat there alone, waiting for the doctor's return.

It was the longest twenty minutes of her life. She fidgeted, she fussed with her green dress and her hair. She got up and paced, then sat down in a different chair.

Finally, she heard the front door open and her father's voice calling to Mrs. Manning that he was back. He passed by the open doorway on his way down the hall to his office.

To her surprise, Courtney couldn't seem to find her voice. She wanted to call to him, but could not make a sound.

A moment later he came back, filling the doorway. She stood up, staring at him, still unable to utter a sound. There she stood in the middle of the room like a dolt, her mouth open, the words stuck behind the tight swelling in her throat.

He didn't recognize her for a full minute. But something about her kept him from speaking. He simply returned her stare. Perhaps it was her eyes that did it. Her eyes hadn't changed, and they were enormous at the moment, pleading with him.

"My God—*Courtney?*"

"Daddy," she cried.

He ran toward her. She flew into his arms. And when those arms closed around her, she felt the most incredible joy she'd ever known. Her father was holding her as she had so often yearned to be held by him.

After a long, long time, Edward set her back from him and looked at her. His hands touched her face, smoothing away her tears. His own face was wet with tears, and in that moment Courtney knew he really did love her. He had always loved her. It had only been her own doubts that had made it seem otherwise. God sakes, what a foolish child she had been, so wrapped up in misery that she couldn't see what had always been there.

"Courtney?" he whispered. "How? I thought you were dead."

"I know, Daddy."

"You weren't taken. I saw the Indians leave, and they had only the farmer with them."

"I was in the barn."

"But I looked for you in the barn. I shouted for you until I lost my voice."

"You didn't look in the feed box." There was no accusation in her voice. She was simply stating a fact.

"Of course not. It wasn't big enough to conceal . . . my God, how?"

"Mr. Brower had dug out a hole beneath it. He made it for his wife. He was in the barn when the attack started and he told us to get in it. And Sarah and I had both fainted. I guess that's why we didn't hear you calling."

It took a moment for the obvious to register with him.

"Sarah is alive, too?"

Courtney nodded. "And married again."

She explained that everyone had thought him captured, that it was considered impossible for him to have survived. She told him she'd never stopped hoping, never, and then quickly recounted the last four years, and told him about seeing his picture in the old newspaper.

"Sarah thought I was crazy, but to tell you the truth, I think she didn't want to believe it was you. She likes being married to Harry."

"I've remarried again, too, Courtney."

"I know. I spent last night at the Bar M with Margaret Rowley. She told me about Ella."

Hands on his daughter's shoulders, he gazed out the window. "Good Lord, I've got two wives! I'll have to do something about that."

"And Sarah has two husbands," Courtney said with a grin. "But I'm sure she'll agree that one annulment is better than two divorces, don't you think?"

"I can only hope so."

"Daddy," Courtney asked. "Why did you leave that farm? You were wounded. Why didn't you wait there for help?"

"I couldn't bear it, honey, thinking you'd died in that burning house. I had to get away from there. I know it was the wrong thing to do, but I wasn't exactly thinking coherently at the time. I didn't even take a horse with me, which shows you the state of my mind. I wandered as far as the river, and then I collapsed. A preacher and his family found me. We were well into Indian Territory before I was lucid enough to realize they were taking me to Texas with them."

"So that's how you came to Waco."

"Yes. I tried to forget. I made a life for myself. There are good people here." He stopped suddenly, then asked, "How was it you stayed at the Bar M instead of coming into town last night?"

"That was as far as Chandos would take me."

"Chandos? What kind of name is that?"

The name I'll use until I finish what I have to do. "It's the name his sister gave him. He's actually Fletcher Straton's son, or rather estranged son. It's kind of hard to explain about Chandos, Daddy."

"Tell me how you got here from Kansas."

"Chandos brought me."

"Just him?" he exclaimed, and she nodded. "You traveled alone with him?"

The code of morals that had forced him to marry his housekeeper was evident in his shocked expression. Courtney surprised herself by getting angry with her father.

"Look at me, Daddy. I'm not a child anymore. I'm old enough to make my own decisions. And if I chose to travel alone with a man because it was *the only way* I could get here, then that's that. It's done, anyway," she said in a quieter tone. "I'm here."

"But were you—all right?"

"Chandos protected me. He didn't let anything happen to me."

"That's not . . . what I meant."

"Oh, Daddy." Courtney sighed.

" 'Daddy'?" came a shocked voice from the doorway behind her father. "Edward, I thought you had only the one daughter."

Courtney was delighted with the interruption, timed as it was. She was afraid her father would take a typically parental attitude toward Chandos. But she wasn't the timid creature she'd once been. She wasn't going to apologize for something she wasn't at all sorry for. And yet this wasn't the way to start a new relationship with her father.

So even though she was fully prepared to dislike the lady standing in the doorway, she stepped around her father and extended her hand graciously.

"You must be Ella." Courtney's smile was warm. "And yes, he does have only one daughter—me—alive and well, as you can see. But I'll let him tell you all about what happened. I left my bag on the porch, and if Mrs. Manning could show me to a room . . . ?"

She was trying to maneuver her way around the surprised Ella and get through the doorway when her father stopped her, a warning note in his voice. "We will continue this discussion later, Courtney."

"If we must." She tried to sound cheerful. "But I really would like to get settled. And I'm sure Ella doesn't have much time right now—or is school finished for the day?"

"No, no, I do have to get back."

Courtney smiled at the bewildered lady before leaving the room. Outside the closed door, she leaned against the wall, her eyes shut. She could hear them talking inside the next room, her father explaining, and Ella sounding so pleased for him.

Ella was quite a pretty woman, and young. Courtney hadn't expected her to be so young, only about twenty-five. With bright red hair and pale green eyes, a vivid combination, Ella certainly didn't look like any teachers Courtney had ever known.

Her father probably loved Ella. And they didn't need the upset Courtney would be bringing into their lives.

She sighed, pushing herself away from the wall, and went to fetch her bag.

Chapter 42

With a cunning she hadn't realized herself capable of, Courtney managed to put off any discussion of Chandos for several days. She kept her father distracted by asking him all about his life in Waco, how he'd met Ella, and so forth. Patients kept him busy—how familiar that was—so she got to see him only in the late afternoon and evenings, and even then he was often called away.

She got to know Ella too and found she actually liked her. It was a big change, after Sarah. But Ella was busy too, with school, and Courtney found herself alone too long every day.

It didn't take long for her to become bored. She considered asking for Mrs. Manning's responsibilities. After all, she was capable of running a house. But she heard Mrs. Manning's life story one morning, and saw how utterly happy she was to be working for the Hartes, so that was that. But Courtney had worked too many years to be able to just laze away her days. She had to do something.

For a few days she helped her father with his patients. He was pleased. She had always wanted to be involved in his work, but had never had a chance to learn how draining it could be. She was too sympathetic, her feelings too easily aroused. When she broke down at the sight of a crippled child, she stopped working in her father's office.

Ten days after Courtney arrived, she decided to leave. It wasn't only that she felt so useless here. Fletcher Straton had been right. She wasn't at all comfortable intruding on a new marriage. Edward and Ella had so little time together as it was, and now they were forced to spend much of it with her. They were still getting to know each other, and her presence there was often awkward.

The nights were the worst. Courtney heard her father and Ella talking companionably in the room next to hers, then heard them make love. She blushed when she saw them in the morning. It was more than she could bear. Even a pillow over her head didn't help. And there was no getting away from it because there were only three bedrooms, and Mrs. Manning had the third.

Those were her reasons for leaving, or so Courtney told herself. But the fact was, she missed Chandos so much that she was utterly miserable, and it was too hard to keep on pretending otherwise.

She told her father she was going to visit Maggie for a few days, but she had every intention of coaxing a job out of Fletcher Straton. A ranch that size, there had to be something she could do.

Fletcher was delighted when she arrived and told him what she wanted. She'd known he would be, what with his sending a man to watch her father's house day after day.

She had to come up with enough courage to tell her father she wouldn't be returning to his house after all. He would be disappointed. He would tell her she didn't have to work. He would remind her that they'd only just been reunited. But it wasn't as if they couldn't see each other and as often as they liked, she would tell him. She was only four miles away from him.

That was what she would tell her father, but the truth boiled down to one thing: she wanted to live on the ranch and draw on Fletcher Straton's certainty that Chandos would come back. She needed that hope more than anything.

Dinner that evening with Fletcher was enjoyable. He tried hard to make her feel at home. Maggie and Sawtooth dined with them, and everyone made suggestions as to what Courtney could do around the ranch. These suggestions included cataloging Fletcher's library, decorating the big house and even naming the newborn calves. Sawtooth nearly choked on his food as Fletcher swore he always named every calf.

After dinner there was lively, affectionate reminiscing. Maggie told how Fletcher had found her in Galveston. He'd been looking for a housekeeper for a long time and knew she was the one he wanted. But she had no intention of staying in Texas, and was on her way to New Hampshire to live with her sister.

Fletcher promised she could rule his household any way she pleased, and she knew she wouldn't have that privilege with her sister, so Maggie agreed. But Fletcher claimed she hadn't agreed until he'd promised her her own house, exactly like the one she had left behind in England. He kept his word, all right. She got the very cottage she left behind, shipped all the way from England, contents and all!

With much laughter, Sawtooth told the story of how he and Fletcher had met, fifteen years ago. It was nighttime on the plains, and each thought the other was an Indian. It was a dark night, too dark to go investigating, and they'd each heard a noise. Was it an animal? An Indian? Each spent a sleepless night lying, tense, in a bedroll twenty feet from the other! Come morning, they'd had a look at each other and a good laugh over it.

Courtney went to bed feeling better than she had in days. She needed to be near these people who were close to Chandos. Well, maybe not close. He didn't allow that. But they all cared for him. And none of them would ever tell Courtney he wasn't the man for her, as her father surely would if he knew she was in love with a gunfighter.

A soft breeze stirred the curtains at the open window. Courtney turned over in bed, stretching sleepily, and gasped as the hand clamped over her mouth. A weight fell on the bed, pressing on her, heavy, frightening, pinning her arms so she couldn't move at all. And this time she didn't have her gun under her pillow. She had thought she was safe.

"What in the goddamn hell are you doing here?"

His voice was rough and furious, but it was the sweetest sound Courtney had ever heard. She tried to speak, but he didn't move his hand.

"I nearly killed my horse getting here, only to find you're not where you're supposed to be! And I just about scared the life out of the old woman a few minutes ago, thinking you'd be bunking with her. But no, you're in the goddamn main house, the place I swore I'd never set foot in again. I must be loco! What the hell are you doing here?"

Courtney shook her head, trying to dislodge his hand. Why didn't he take his hand away? Surely he must know she wouldn't scream, that she was overjoyed to see him. But no, he didn't know that. She had run away from him. He'd tried to turn her against him, and he probably thought he'd succeeded. Then what was he doing here?

He put his forehead down against hers and sighed. He'd gotten the anger out of his system. What *was* he doing here? she asked herself again.

As if he'd read her mind, he said, "I couldn't let it rest. I had to see if you were all right, if everything turned out the way you wanted it to. Did it? No, of course it didn't, or you wouldn't be out here at the Bar M, instead of in town with your father. I know he's there. I saw him, the house, the wife. What happened, cateyes? You upset because he's got a wife? You can shake your head, you know, or nod."

She didn't. She wasn't going to let him get away with a one-sided conversation. She bared her teeth and bit him hard.

"Ow!" he growled, jerking his hand away.

"Serves you right, Chandos!" Courtney snapped. "Just what do you think you're doing, pinning me down and not letting me answer all these questions?" She sat up and said, "If the only reason you came here was to see if I'm all right, then you can just go." He got up from the bed. "Don't you dare leave!" she gasped, clutching his arm.

He didn't. A match flared and he located the lamp by her bed. In the seconds it took him to light the lamp, she feasted her eyes on him. He looked terrible, his dark clothes were dusty and there were tired lines around his eyes. He hadn't shaved. He was every inch a hard, dangerous, gunman, yet to her he was a splendid sight.

He looked down at her and Courtney felt a tension begin in her belly as those pale blue eyes moved over her. She was wearing a modest white cotton nightgown she had bought when Ella took her shopping. Her deep, golden tan glowed against it, and her eyes were only slightly darker than her skin. Her brown hair was loose and sun-streaked.

"How come you look . . . prettier?"

She tried not to let him see how flustered the question made her.

"Maybe because it's been so long since you've seen me?"

"Maybe."

Neither of them considered that ten days wasn't such a long time. He had been through hell, as she had. Ten days had been an eternity.

"I thought I would never see you again, Chandos," she said quietly.

"Yeah, that's what I thought." He sat down on the side of the bed, forcing her to move over and give him room. "I had every intention of heading down to Mexico after I left San Antonio," he told her. "And a day, one goddamn day's riding, that's as far as I got before I turned around."

She had been hoping for a declaration, but he was angry because he had returned, for whatever reason, against his will. Disappointment sparked her temper.

"Why?" she demanded. "And if you tell me again that it was just to see if I was all right, I swear I'll hit you!"

He almost but not quite smiled. "After the way we parted, I didn't think you'd accept any other reason."

"Try me."

"I couldn't leave it alone, cateyes," he said simply, looking her in the eye. "I thought I could. I thought if you hated me, that would be enough reason for me to stay away. But it didn't work. Where you're concerned, nothing has ever worked to keep me away."

Hope returned. "Is that so bad?" she asked softly.

"Isn't it? You can't have wanted to see me again."

She knew he was hoping for a denial, but after what he'd put her through, she wasn't letting him off that easy.

"If you believed that, I'm surprised you had the gall to come."

He scowled. "So am I. But I've already said I must be loco. Especially for coming to you here—*here!*" He gestured, taking in the whole Bar M.

"God sakes, you act as if this place is a prison," she retorted. "No one's going to force you to stay here, least of all your father."

He froze. Then his scowl darkened. "You know?"

"Yes. I don't see why you couldn't have told me. You must have known I'd hear about the rebellious Kane Straton."

"Don't presume to judge by what you've heard, cateyes. You've heard only the old man's side of it."

"Then tell me yours."

He shrugged. "He thought he had me, that I would want all this and would take anything he dished out just to stay. So he punished me for my mother's sins, punished me because she preferred life with the Comanche to living with him. He took all his hate and bitterness out on me, and then he wondered why he got back only contempt." He shook his head at the stupidity of it.

"Are you so sure that's the way it was, Chandos? Weren't you biased before you even got here? Your mother must have harbored resentment against Fletcher for giving her no choice but to leave here, and some of that had to rub off on you. After all, you were only a child. So maybe your father's behavior was just a reaction to the way you were behaving toward him."

"You don't know what you're talking about," he said, exasperated.

"I know he loves you," she stated flatly, "and he regrets all the mistakes he made with you. And I know he'd give anything for another chance with you."

"You mean another chance to turn me into what he wants me to be," he said, giving her a cynical look.

"No. He's learned his lesson. Oh, God sakes, Chandos, this is your *home*," she said in exasperation. "Doesn't that mean anything to you? It means something to me. It's why I'm here."

"Why? Because you thought this was the one place you could hide from me? That I wouldn't risk coming here?"

That stung. "No!" she cried. "Because this is where you left me, so I felt closer to you here."

He certainly wasn't expecting that. The declaration robbed him of the head of steam he'd been building, leaving him deflated. Strangely, it also left him feeling elated.

"Cateyes." His voice was rough.

His hand touched her cheek, his fingers gliding into the soft hair around her ear. He leaned closer. His lips touched hers, and it was like the breaking of a dam. Passion flooded them, drowning out everything else.

In mere moments their clothes were shed and their bodies were clinging as tightly as their mouths, each body suffering an agony of impatience. Chandos made love with a fierce possessiveness he had never shown before, and Courtney welcomed him with a savage intensity she had never equaled before.

They spoke with their bodies, saying all they couldn't say in words, each offering the other all the love and want and need that had always been there.

Tomorrow their lovemaking might be only another memory. But tonight, Courtney was Chandos's woman.

Chapter 43

Carefully, quietly, Courtney opened the door to her bedroom a few inches and peeked in. Chandos was still sleeping, and no wonder. Since he'd left her, he had gotten thirty hours of sleep, which wasn't enough for five days, let alone ten.

She closed the door quietly and stood there gazing at Chandos for a moment. She was going to let him sleep as long as he liked. She wasn't going to tell anyone he was here, either. Maggie knew, but she wasn't going to warn Fletcher. She'd said it would do the old coot good to be surprised. Maggie was sure Chandos wouldn't just take off.

Courtney hoped she was right, but she wasn't as confident as Maggie was. Oh, there was no denying Chandos still wanted her. For a long, long while last night he had proved that in every way possible. But that didn't mean he wanted her forever. And it didn't mean he wouldn't go off and leave her again.

Yet there was real hope now. He *had* come back. And he'd confessed that he couldn't stay away from her. Knowing that was enough to send Courtney's spirits soaring.

She put his saddlebags, which Maggie had brought in earlier, in the corner. Then she approached the mirror to check her appearance once more. She was still amazed at how radiant she looked this morning. Had love put that sparkle in her eyes? No, love had its ups and downs, as she could surely attest to by now! It was happiness that made her feel like laughing, singing, shouting even. And that happiness wasn't easy to contain.

For a while she sat by the window, watching Chandos sleep. That wasn't enough. She knew she should leave the room, go find something to do to keep her occupied. But she couldn't shake the fear that when she came back her Chandos would be gone. That was absurd, for he wouldn't disappear this time without at least telling her when she would see him again. He had to give her that much consideration. That was the *only* thing she was sure of, however, so she didn't want to let him out of her sight.

She approached the bed slowly, meaning

not to disturb him. She just wanted to be closer. After a few minutes standing by the bed, she lay down, very carefully. He didn't stir. He slept so soundly, which was unlike him, and just went to show how exhausted he was. He was so tired that he wouldn't wake even if . . .

She touched him, her fingers running lightly over the hard muscles on his chest. He lay with only the thin sheet covering his long limbs, and Courtney could envision all of him. He didn't make a sound when she touched him. He was still fast asleep, and Courtney got bolder, letting her fingers glide over the sheet, along his flanks, over his hard thighs.

And then she gasped as a particular area of him stirred, and he chuckled. "Don't stop now, kitten."

Hot color stained her neck and cheeks, vivid against her yellow lawn gown. "You weren't really asleep, were you?" she accused him.

"A drawback from the habits of the trail."

His eyes were sleepy as he gazed at her. He was so incredibly sexy, but Courtney was embarrassed now, and quickly vacated the bed. "Your gear is here, in case you want to shave. Unless you want to go back to sleep

. . . I didn't mean to disturb you. You can sleep some more if you like. No one knows you're here."

"Not yet." He sat up. "But it won't be long before someone spots Surefoot behind Maggie's house."

"Maggie took care of that." She grinned. "She dragged him into her parlor."

"What?"

Courtney giggled. "I couldn't believe it when I saw him there, but he's tolerating it just fine. Maggie's making up for telling Fletcher you brought me here. She said if anything happens this time, it should be up to you."

Chandos grunted, running a hand over his jaw. "I guess I could use a shave."

Courtney pointed to his saddlebags in the corner, then sat down on the bed to watch him. "Will you see your father?" she asked tentatively.

"No," he said flatly, putting on a pair of black pants. He glanced up, giving her a stern look. "And don't try to patch things up, woman. I want nothing to do with that man."

"He's gruff and hard, and he bellows a lot, but he's not so bad, Chandos."

He gave her a look and she sighed, lowering her eyes.

After a while she looked up to see him lathering his face by the washstand. She inquired hesitantly. "Did you find him, Chandos, the man in San Antonio?"

His back stiffened. "I found him. He'd had his trial, and he was set to hang."

"Then you didn't kill him?"

"I broke him out of jail," he said dispassionately. He slowly wiped his face clean, remembering. "It wasn't hard. Smith had no friends in San Antonio, so no one was expecting anything."

Chandos turned around then. She had never seen such a cold, hard look in his eyes, or heard such hate in anyone's voice. "I broke both of his arms, among other things, and then I hanged him. But the bastard was already dead. He must have suspected something. Maybe he recognized Trask's horse that I had waiting for him, I don't know. Maybe he just didn't trust my reasons for breaking him out. But he attacked me as soon as we stopped. He got hold of my knife and we fought over it. In the fight, he fell on it, and he died within seconds. It wasn't enough!" he said, anguished. "It wasn't *enough* for what he did to White Wing."

Courtney crossed the room and put her arms around him. It was some time before she felt his arms respond, but at last he drew her closer.

"Was White Wing your sister?"

"Yes."

In a distant voice, as though from far away, he told her about that day, about coming home to find his mother and sister raped and killed. Before he finished, Courtney was sobbing. It was he who ended up comforting her.

"Don't cry, cateyes. I never could stand to hear you cry. And it's over now. They aren't crying anymore, either. They can sleep in peace now."

He kissed her gently, and then he kissed her again. This was one way to draw solace from each other—and to forget.

Chapter 44

It was early afternoon when Courtney left the bed. Chandos was sleeping again, and this time she was determined to let him. It still upset her terribly to think of his mother and sister, but she told herself she wouldn't think about it. It had happened four years ago, and he had learned to live with it—though how, she couldn't begin to imagine.

Just as she finished dressing, there was a knock, and she glanced quickly at the bed. Chandos had heard it too, and his eyes were open. There was a warning in them, but he needn't have worried. She wasn't going to give his presence away to anyone.

She crossed quickly to the door, opening it a crack. "Yes?"

"You have a visitor, *señorita*," said one of the Mexican girls who helped Maggie. "A *Señor* Taylor. He is waiting on the porch with *Señor* Straton and—"

"Taylor?" Courtney interrupted sharply. "Did you say Taylor?"

"*Sí*."

"Thank you." Courtney closed the door with a bang, in the grip of a rage like nothing she had ever felt before. "Reed Taylor! I don't believe it!" she cried, furious. "How dare he show up after what he did? Having me kidnapped! That—that—oh!"

"Courtney! Goddammit, come back here!" Chandos shouted as she stormed out of the room. He swore savagely, because she'd kept right on going and he couldn't very well stop her without a stitch of clothes on.

In full steam, Courtney reached the front door and threw it open. There was Reed in his dark broadcloth suit and ruffled shirt, hat in hand, as immaculate as always. He was smiling at her. Smiling!

"You're crazy!" she hissed at him as she stepped out onto the porch, aware of no one but Taylor. "Do you know I could have you arrested for what you did?"

"Now, Courtney, honey, is that any way to greet me after I came all this way to find you?"

She blinked. God sakes, she should have remembered what a one-track mind he had. Everything she said had always bounced right off his thick head.

"Don't call me honey," she said savagely. "Don't even call me Courtney. Didn't you get the message when your men didn't come back? I didn't want to be found, Reed. You had no right to send those—those cutthroats after me!"

He took her arm forcibly and steered her away from the men standing around watching. But he didn't think to lower his voice, and he didn't realize he was igniting more tempers than just hers.

"One of those men did get back, Courtney—barely alive. That gunslinger you took off with had cut out his tongue and chopped off his hand! Good God, do you think I could leave you out there with that madman after I found out what he'd done?"

"I'm sure the story is a gross exaggeration," Courtney said smoothly.

"I'll say," Chandos said casually, having arrived in time to overhear. "I only slit the fellow's tongue, after he told me he'd left Courtney behind in camp to be raped by one of his cohorts. And I broke the first two fingers of his gunhand for good measure, before I staked him to a tree. He just had a low tolerance for pain, that's all. How's *your* tolerance, Taylor?"

Reed ignored that and demanded, "What's he doing here, Courtney?"

Courtney didn't answer. She was staring at Chandos, who stood in the doorway wearing only pants and gunbelt. She knew he was making a considerable effort to keep his hand away from his gun. And then she noticed the others for the first time—cowboys watching, and Fletcher, grinning from ear to ear as he gazed at Chandos, Sawtooth frowning at Reed, and behind Sawtooth . . . her father! God sakes, her *father!* He'd seen the whole thing!

"Reed, why don't you leave?" Courtney

suggested. He hadn't let go of her, and he was now wearing the bulldog expression she knew so well. It was useless, but she said anyway, "You've come down here for nothing, Reed. I'm not going to marry you, and I'm certainly not going back to Kansas with you. And if you try to force it, as you already did once, you'll have the law on your tail."

"You're upset," Reed replied tersely. "If you'll just give me a chance—"

"She already gave you a chance, Taylor—a chance to leave," Chandos growled, stepping forward. "Now you'll have to deal with me. Get your goddamn hands off my woman."

Reed faced him, but he still didn't let go of Courtney's arm. "You going to draw on me, fastgun?" he said, sneering. "You going to shoot me in front of all these witnesses?" He nodded to encompass their audience.

"Uh-uh." Smiling, Chandos drew his gun, twirled it, and handed it to Courtney. "This won't take long, cateyes," he muttered just as his fist came up and connected with Reed's jaw.

Reed flew backward, and Courtney was jerked forward. But Chandos caught her around the waist, keeping her from tumbling down the porch steps along with Reed.

Then he set her aside with an apologetic grin, and dived after the fallen man.

Courtney stood there at the top of the steps, watching two grown men try to kill each other with their fists. She didn't think to try and stop them. She was still in too much of a daze from hearing Chandos call her "my woman." He'd said it in front of his father. He'd said it in front of *her* father. God sakes, did he mean it?

An arm encircled her shoulders, and she glanced up. But her father wasn't looking at her. He was watching the fight.

"I don't suppose you objected to what that young man said?" he asked casually.

"No."

She heard a particularly grueling punch and turned to see Chandos hit the dust hard. She took an involuntary step forward, but he was already back on his feet, and throwing a hard right to Reed's midsection. Still, she began to worry. Chandos was taller, but Reed was built like a bull.

"Can I assume this is the man who brought you to Texas?" Edward's tone was still casual.

"Yes, yes." Her mind was on the fight.

"Courtney, honey, look at me."

She dragged her attention away from Chandos. "Yes, Daddy?"

"Do you love him?"

"Oh, yes! More than I thought possible." Then, she ventured, hesitantly, "Do you mind?"

"I'm not quite sure," Edward said. "Is he always this . . . impetuous?"

"No, but he's always protective of me."

"Well, at least there's that in his favor," her father said with a sigh.

"Oh, Daddy, don't judge him until you get to know him. Just because he's a gunfighter—"

"There are lots of good men who are gunfighters, honey. I know that."

"And he's been alone for so long that he's not used to being sociable or friendly, so don't mistake—"

"There are lots of good quiet men too, honey," he said.

She grinned sheepishly. "You really *are* going to be open-minded about it, aren't you?"

"Do I dare not be?" He chuckled. "I wouldn't care to have a taste of those fists myself."

"Oh, he wouldn't!" She started to reassure him, then realized he was only teasing her.

A cheer went up from the cowboys who'd been watching the fight. They'd quickly figured out who to cheer for, what with Fletcher hanging over the porch railing, shouting encouragement in his blustery voice. Right now Fletcher and Sawtooth were clapping each other on the back as if *they* had won the fight.

Courtney looked for Chandos in the group of well-wishers crowding around him. He was bent over, favoring his midsection. His face hadn't fared too well, either.

"It looks like my services might be needed," Edward called to her from the porch.

"Yes," Courtney agreed, intent on Chandos.

"I meant for the other fellow." Edward chuckled.

"What? Oh, don't waste your time," Courtney said without an iota of sympathy. Reed was knocked out cold on the ground. "If anyone deserved a beating, he did. Why, you wouldn't believe the gall of that man. He just won't take no for an answer."

"Well, let's hope he got the message this time, cateyes," Chandos said as he stumbled toward her. "I'd hate to have to shoot the bastard just because he's such a stubborn, pigheaded cuss."

"Oh, Chandos, sit down!" she gasped, leading him toward the porch.

"Don't start telling me what to do, woman."

She pushed him down to sit on the steps. "God sakes, look at you." She pushed the hair away from his brow, studying his face. "Daddy, you'd better get your bag."

"Daddy?" Chandos turned to look behind him, and grimaced. "You could have given me some warning."

She couldn't help grinning. "He enjoyed the fight."

Chandos grunted.

"So did your father."

He swore again, his eyes falling on Fletcher, who was giving his men orders to dump Taylor on his horse and send him back where he came from. "What is this, a goddamn family reunion?"

She knew he was being surly only because he felt cornered. "It could be if you let it," she ventured.

"I came here for you, woman, nothing else."

"Did you?"

"You know I did."

Suddenly, her tone matched his, "Then say so. I haven't heard you say it, Chandos."

He scowled. His father was standing only a few feet away now, leaning against the porch railing. Sawtooth was sitting on the railing next to him, trying not to grin. Neither of them tried in the least to hide their interest in the conversation between her and Chandos. Worse, her father was listening just as keenly.

Chandos felt all their eyes on him, but mostly he felt Courtney's, determined, fiery. And suddenly only hers mattered.

"You're my woman, cateyes. You've been my woman since I first laid eyes on you."

That didn't satisfy her. "Say it!"

He grinned and jerked her down onto his lap, where she sat stiffly, waiting, until at last he said, "I love you. Is that what you want to hear? I love you so much I've got no direction without you."

"Oh, Chandos." She melted against him, wrapping her arms around his neck. "I love—"

"Uh-uh." He stopped her. "You better think real carefully before you say anything, cateyes, because if you give me your love, I'm not going to let you take it back. I can't keep worrying about whether or not I can make you happy. I'll try my best but there isn't going to be any changing your mind later. Do you understand what I'm saying? If you're going to be my woman, there's no way in hell I'll *ever* let you go."

"Does that work both ways?" she asked indignantly, and Chandos laughed and said, "Damn right it does."

"Then let *me* lay down *my* law. You've already said you love me, and I'm not going to let you take it back, either. And I'll try my best to make you happy, too. But if you think about changing *your* mind later, let me warn you that there won't be anywhere in this whole land you can hide from me, because the first thing you're going to teach me is how to track. And the second thing you're going to teach me is how to shoot. Do you understand what *I'm* saying, Chandos?"

"Yes, ma'am," he drawled.

"Good." She smiled now, a bit of color stealing into her cheeks after being so bold. She leaned forward, her lips very close to his. "Because I love you. I love you so much I wanted to die when you left me. I don't ever want to feel like that again, Chandos."

"Neither do I," he said passionately, just before he leaned into her lips, kissing her

416

with exquisite tenderness. "You still know how to purr, kitten."

"Chandos!"

He chuckled. *Now* she was aware of their audience! He loved the way her eyes sparkled when she blushed. "You're sure, cat-eyes?" he said softly.

"Yes."

"And you can live the way I do?"

"I'll live any way you want, even if I have to carry my babies around in a backtote."

"Babies!"

"Not yet," she whispered furiously, mortified, her eyes darting toward her father.

He squeezed her, laughing. She had never seen him so carefree and happy. Oh, how she loved him.

"But we will have some babies, won't we?" he continued thoughtfully. "Maybe a house wouldn't be such a bad idea."

Courtney stiffened, amazed. "Do you mean it?"

"I could try ranching. The old man made sure I learned every aspect of it. He also dumped a fortune in the Waco bank in my name that I never got around to using. It ought to buy us a nice spread someplace around here. The old man could use the competition."

Courtney was the only one who could see the laughter in Chandos's eyes as they heard Fletcher spluttering. Sawtooth choked as he tried to hold back his guffaws. Edward was grinning too as he came down the steps to join them.

"I don't think I'll need my medical bag. Anyone with such a lively sense of humor can't be hurting that badly."

"You're right, doc. Mind if I call you doc?"

"Not at all, though 'Edward' wouldn't be out of line, seeing as how you'll be my son-in-law shortly."

"All I need is a bath right now, and—did I mention marriage, cateyes?"

"No, you didn't." She grinned at her father's expression. "Oh, Daddy, he's still teasing. Tell him, Chandos. Chandos?"

"Ouch!" He pulled her hand out of his hair. "Are you really going to put me through a white man's ceremony that's got nothing to do with feelings? I've declared myself—in front of witnesses. You've declared yourself. You're already my wife, cateyes."

"It would make my father happy, Chandos," Courtney said simply.

"And you?"

"Yes."

"Then I guess I was teasing," he said softly.

She hugged him, so overwhelmed with happiness that she could barely stand it. He might be ruthless and savage in some ways, but he was also her Chandos, gentle when it mattered. And he loved her! That he was willing to settle in one place for her proved that beyond any doubt.

Courtney leaned back, wanting everyone to be as happy as she was, including Fletcher. "Why don't you tell your father you were just pulling his leg, too?"

"Because I wasn't." Chandos swung around, meeting Fletcher's gaze. "Can you stand the competition, old man?"

"You're goddamn right I can!" Fletcher roared.

"That's what I thought." Chandos grinned.

It took a moment. Fletcher's eyes crinkled. He didn't quite allow himself to smile, though. That wouldn't have been at all in character.

He was, however, bursting with pleasure. He'd never seen his son like this, so warm and open and . . . approachable. It was a start. It was a goddamn good start.

The publishers hope that this
Large Print Book has brought
you pleasurable reading.
Each title is designed to make
the text as easy to see as possible.
G.K. Hall Large Print Books
are available from your library and
your local bookstore. Or, you can
receive information by mail on
upcoming and current Large Print Books
and order directly from the publishers.
Just send your name and address to:

G.K. Hall & Co.
70 Lincoln Street
Boston, Mass. 02111

or call, toll-free:

1-800-343-2806

A note on the text
Large print edition designed by
Bernadette Montalvo.
Composed in 18 pt Plantin
on a Xyvision /Linotron 202N
by Braun-Brumfield, Inc.